EX LIBRIS

_____

NAME

THE OMINOUS OMNIBUS

✳ A Series of Unfortunate Events ✳

THE OMINOUS OMNIBUS

BOOK *the First*
THE BAD BEGINNING

BOOK *the Second*
THE REPTILE ROOM

BOOK *the Third*
THE WIDE WINDOW

by LEMONY SNICKET

Illustrations by Brett Helquist

▬ HARPERCOLLINSPublishers

Library of Congress Cataloging-in-Publication Data
Snicket, Lemony.
    The ominous omnibus / by Lemony Snicket ; illustrations by Brett
Helquist.—1st ed.
        p.   cm. — (A series of unfortunate events ; bks. 1–3)
    Summary: Presents the first three books in the series which
chronicles the catastrophes and misfortunes of the resourceful
Baudelaire children, as they become wealthy orphans and must elude
a distant relative, the greedy and dastardly Count Olaf.
    ISBN 0-06-078252-8
    [1. Orphans—Fiction.   2. Brothers and sisters—Fiction.
3. Humorous stories.]   I. Helquist, Brett, ill.   II. Title: Bad
beginning.   III. Title: Reptile room.   IV. Title: Wide window.
V. Title.
PZ7.S6795Om 2005
[Fic]—dc22   2004027684

Typography by Margaret Wagner and Alison Donalty
3   5   7   10   9   8   6   4   2
❖
First Edition

CONTENTS

THE OMINOUS OMNIBUS

THE BAD BEGINNING

To Beatrice—
darling, dearest, dead.

CHAPTER
One

If you are interested in stories with happy endings, you would be better off reading some other book. In this book, not only is there no happy ending, there is no happy beginning and very few happy things in the middle. This is because not very many happy things happened in the lives of the three Baudelaire youngsters. Violet, Klaus, and Sunny Baudelaire were intelligent children, and they were charming, and resourceful, and had pleasant facial features, but they were extremely unlucky, and most everything that happened to them was rife with misfortune, misery, and despair. I'm sorry to tell you this, but that is how the story goes.

Their misfortune began one day at Briny Beach. The three Baudelaire children lived with their parents in an enormous mansion at the heart of a dirty and busy city, and occasionally their parents gave them permission to take a rickety trolley—the word "rickety," you probably know, here means "unsteady" or "likely to collapse"—alone to the seashore, where they would spend the day as a sort of vacation as long as they were home for dinner. This particular morning it was gray and cloudy, which didn't bother the Baudelaire youngsters one bit. When it was hot and sunny, Briny Beach was crowded with tourists and it was impossible to find a good place to lay one's blanket. On gray and cloudy days, the Baudelaires had the beach to themselves to do what they liked.

Violet Baudelaire, the eldest, liked to skip rocks. Like most fourteen-year-olds, she was right-handed, so the rocks skipped farther across the murky water when Violet used her right hand than when she used her left. As she skipped rocks, she was looking out at the horizon and thinking about an invention she wanted to build. Anyone who knew Violet well could tell she was thinking hard, because her long hair was tied up in a ribbon to keep it out of her eyes. Violet had a real knack for inventing and building strange devices, so her brain was often filled with images of pulleys, levers, and gears, and she never wanted to be distracted by something as trivial as her hair. This morning she was thinking about how to construct a device that could retrieve a rock after you had skipped it into the ocean.

Klaus Baudelaire, the middle child, and the only boy, liked to examine creatures in tidepools. Klaus was a little older than twelve and wore glasses, which made him look intelligent. He *was* intelligent. The Baudelaire parents had an enormous library in their mansion, a room filled with thousands of books on nearly every subject. Being only twelve, Klaus of course had not read all of the books in the Baudelaire library, but he had read a great many of them and had retained a lot of the information from his readings. He knew how to tell an alligator from a crocodile. He knew who killed Julius Caesar. And he knew much about the tiny, slimy animals found at Briny Beach, which he was examining now.

Sunny Baudelaire, the youngest, liked to bite things. She was an infant, and very small for her age, scarcely larger than a boot. What she lacked in size, however, she made up for with the size and sharpness of her four teeth. Sunny was at an age where one mostly speaks in a series of unintelligible shrieks. Except when she used the few actual words in her vocabulary, like "bottle," "mommy," and "bite," most people had trouble understanding what it was that Sunny was saying. For instance, this morning she was saying "Gack!" over and over, which probably meant, "Look at that mysterious figure emerging from the fog!"

Sure enough, in the distance along the misty

shore of Briny Beach there could be seen a tall figure striding toward the Baudelaire children. Sunny had already been staring and shrieking at the figure for some time when Klaus looked up from the spiny crab he was examining, and saw it too. He reached over and touched Violet's arm, bringing her out of her inventing thoughts.

"Look at that," Klaus said, and pointed toward the figure. It was drawing closer, and the children could see a few details. It was about the size of an adult, except its head was tall, and rather square.

"What do you think it is?" Violet asked.

"I don't know," Klaus said, squinting at it, "but it seems to be moving right toward us."

"We're alone on the beach," Violet said, a little nervously. "There's nobody else it could be moving toward." She felt the slender, smooth stone in her left hand, which she had been about to try to skip as far as she could. She had a sudden thought to throw it at the figure, because it seemed so frightening.

"It only seems scary," Klaus said, as if reading his sister's thoughts, "because of all the mist."

This was true. As the figure reached them, the children saw with relief that it was not anybody frightening at all, but somebody they knew: Mr. Poe. Mr. Poe was a friend of Mr. and Mrs. Baudelaire's whom the children had met many times at dinner parties. One of the things Violet, Klaus, and Sunny really liked about their parents was that they didn't send their children away when they had company over, but allowed them to join the adults at the dinner table and participate in the conversation as long as they helped clear the table. The children remembered Mr. Poe because he always had a cold and was constantly excusing himself from the table to have a fit of coughing in the next room.

Mr. Poe took off his top hat, which had made his head look large and square in the fog, and stood for a moment, coughing loudly into a white handkerchief. Violet and Klaus moved forward to shake his hand and say how do you do.

"How do you do?" said Violet.

"How do you do?" said Klaus.

"Odo yow!" said Sunny.

"Fine, thank you," said Mr. Poe, but he looked very sad. For a few seconds nobody said anything, and the children wondered what Mr. Poe was doing there at Briny Beach, when he should have been at the bank in the city, where he worked. He was not dressed for the beach.

"It's a nice day," Violet said finally, making conversation. Sunny made a noise that sounded like an angry bird, and Klaus picked her up and held her.

"Yes, it is a nice day," Mr. Poe said absently, staring out at the empty beach. "I'm afraid I have some very bad news for you children."

The three Baudelaire siblings looked at him. Violet, with some embarrassment, felt the stone in her left hand and was glad she had not thrown it at Mr. Poe.

"Your parents," Mr. Poe said, "have perished in a terrible fire."

The children didn't say anything.

"They perished," Mr. Poe said, "in a fire that destroyed the entire house. I'm very, very sorry to tell you this, my dears."

Violet took her eyes off Mr. Poe and stared out at the ocean. Mr. Poe had never called the Baudelaire children "my dears" before. She understood the words he was saying but thought he must be joking, playing a terrible joke on her and her brother and sister.

"'Perished,'" Mr. Poe said, "means 'killed.'"

"We *know* what the word 'perished' means," Klaus said, crossly. He did know what the word "perished" meant, but he was still having trouble understanding exactly what it was that Mr. Poe had said. It seemed to him that Mr. Poe must somehow have misspoken.

"The fire department arrived, of course," Mr. Poe said, "but they were too late. The entire house was engulfed in fire. It burned to the ground."

Klaus pictured all the books in the library, going up in flames. Now he'd never read all of them.

Mr. Poe coughed several times into his handkerchief before continuing. "I was sent to retrieve you here, and to take you to my home, where you'll stay for some time while we figure things out. I am the executor of your parents' estate. That means I will be handling their enormous fortune and figuring out where you children will go. When Violet comes of age, the fortune will be yours, but the bank will take charge of it until you are old enough."

Although he said he was the executor, Violet felt like Mr. Poe was the executioner. He had simply walked down the beach to them and changed their lives forever.

"Come with me," Mr. Poe said, and held out his hand. In order to take it, Violet had to drop the stone she was holding. Klaus took Violet's other hand, and Sunny took Klaus's other hand, and in that manner the three Baudelaire children—the Baudelaire orphans, now—were led away from the beach and from their previous lives.

It is useless for me to describe to you how terrible Violet, Klaus, and even Sunny felt in the time that followed. If you have ever lost someone very important to you, then you already know how it feels, and if you haven't, you cannot possibly imagine it. For the Baudelaire children, it was of course especially terrible because they had lost both their parents at the same time, and for several days they felt so miserable they could scarcely get out of bed. Klaus found he had little interest in books. The gears in Violet's inventive brain seemed to stop. And even Sunny, who of course was too young to really understand what was going on, bit things with less enthusiasm.

Of course, it didn't make things any easier that they had lost their home as well, and all their possessions. As I'm sure you know, to be in one's own room, in one's own bed, can often make a bleak situation a little better, but the beds of the Baudelaire orphans had been reduced to charred rubble. Mr. Poe had taken them to the remains of the Baudelaire mansion to see if anything had been unharmed, and it was terrible: Violet's microscope had fused together in the heat of the fire, Klaus's favorite pen had turned to ash, and all of Sunny's teething rings had melted. Here and there, the children could see traces of the enormous home they had loved: fragments of their grand piano, an elegant bottle in which Mr. Baudelaire kept brandy, the scorched cushion of the windowseat where their mother liked to sit and read.

Their home destroyed, the Baudelaires had to recuperate from their terrible loss in the Poe household, which was not at all agreeable. Mr. Poe was scarcely at home, because he was very busy attending to the Baudelaire affairs, and when he was home he was often coughing so much he could barely have a conversation. Mrs. Poe purchased clothing for the orphans that was in grotesque colors, and itched. And the two Poe children—Edgar and Albert—were loud and obnoxious boys with whom the Baudelaires had to share a tiny room that smelled of some sort of ghastly flower.

But even given the surroundings, the children had mixed feelings when, over a dull dinner of boiled chicken, boiled potatoes and blanched—the word "blanched" here means "boiled"—string beans, Mr. Poe announced that they were to leave his household the next morning.

"Good," said Albert, who had a piece of potato stuck between his teeth. "Now we can get our room back. I'm tired of sharing it. Violet and Klaus are always moping around, and are never any fun."

"And the baby bites," Edgar said, tossing a chicken bone to the floor as if he were an animal in a zoo and not the son of a well-respected member of the banking community.

"Where will we go?" Violet asked nervously.

Mr. Poe opened his mouth to say something, but erupted into a brief fit of coughing. "I have made arrangements," he said finally, "for you to be raised by a distant relative of yours who lives on the other side of town. His name is Count Olaf."

Violet, Klaus, and Sunny looked at one another, unsure of what to think. On one hand, they didn't want to live with the Poes any longer. On the other hand, they had never heard of Count Olaf and didn't know what he would be like.

"Your parents' will," Mr. Poe said, "instructs that you be raised in the most convenient way possible. Here in the city, you'll be used to your surroundings, and this Count Olaf is the only relative who lives within the urban limits."

Klaus thought this over for a minute as he swallowed a chewy bit of bean. "But our parents never mentioned Count Olaf to us. Just how is he related to us, exactly?"

Mr. Poe sighed and looked down at Sunny, who was biting a fork and listening closely. "He is either a third cousin four times removed, or a fourth cousin three times removed. He is not your closest relative on the family tree, but he is the closest geographically. That's why—"

"If he lives in the city," Violet said, "why didn't our parents ever invite him over?"

"Possibly because he was very busy," Mr. Poe

said. "He's an actor by trade, and often travels around the world with various theater companies."

"I thought he was a count," Klaus said.

"He is both a count and an actor," Mr. Poe said. "Now, I don't mean to cut short our dinner, but you children have to pack up your things, and I have to return to the bank to do some more work. Like your new legal guardian, I am very busy myself."

The three Baudelaire children had many more questions for Mr. Poe, but he had already stood up from the table, and with a slight wave of his hand departed from the room. They heard him coughing into his handkerchief and then the front door creaked shut as he left the house.

"Well," Mrs. Poe said, "you three had better start packing. Edgar, Albert, please help me clear the table."

The Baudelaire orphans went to the bedroom and glumly packed their few belongings. Klaus

looked distastefully at each ugly shirt Mrs. Poe
had bought for him as he folded them and put
them into a small suitcase. Violet looked around
the cramped, smelly room in which they had
been living. And Sunny crawled around solemnly
biting each of Edgar and Albert's shoes, leaving
small teeth marks in each one so she would not
be forgotten. From time to time, the Baudelaire
children looked at one another, but with their
future such a mystery they could think of nothing to say. At bedtime, they tossed and turned all
night, scarcely getting any sleep between the
loud snoring of Edgar and Albert and their own
worried thoughts. Finally, Mr. Poe knocked on
the door and stuck his head into the bedroom.

"Rise and shine, Baudelaires," he said. "It's
time for you to go to Count Olaf's."

Violet looked around the crowded bedroom,
and even though she didn't like it, she felt very
nervous about leaving. "Do we have to go right
this minute?" she asked.

Mr. Poe opened his mouth to speak, but had to cough a few times before he began. "Yes you do. I'm dropping you off on my way to the bank, so we need to leave as soon as possible. Please get out of bed and get dressed," he said briskly. The word "briskly" here means "quickly, so as to get the Baudelaire children to leave the house."

The Baudelaire children left the house. Mr. Poe's automobile rumbled along the cobblestone streets of the city toward the neighborhood where Count Olaf lived. They passed horse-drawn carriages and motorcycles along Doldrum Drive. They passed the Fickle Fountain, an elaborately carved monument that occasionally spat out water in which young children played. They passed an enormous pile of dirt where the Royal Gardens once stood. Before too long, Mr. Poe drove his car down a narrow alley lined with houses made of pale brick and stopped halfway down the block.

"Here we are," Mr. Poe said, in a voice

undoubtedly meant to be cheerful. "Your new home."

The Baudelaire children looked out and saw the prettiest house on the block. The bricks had been cleaned very well, and through the wide and open windows one could see an assortment of well-groomed plants. Standing in the doorway, with her hand on the shiny brass doorknob, was an older woman, smartly dressed, who was smiling at the children. In one hand she carried a flowerpot.

"Hello there!" she called out. "You must be the children Count Olaf is adopting."

Violet opened the door of the automobile and got out to shake the woman's hand. It felt firm and warm, and for the first time in a long while Violet felt as if her life and the lives of her siblings might turn out well after all. "Yes," she said. "Yes, we are. I am Violet Baudelaire, and this is my brother Klaus and my sister Sunny. And this is Mr. Poe, who has been arranging things for us since the death of our parents."

"Yes, I heard about the accident," the woman said, as everyone said how do you do. "I am Justice Strauss."

"That's an unusual first name," Klaus remarked.

"It is my title," she explained, "not my first name. I serve as a judge on the High Court."

"How fascinating," Violet said. "And are you married to Count Olaf?"

"Goodness me no," Justice Strauss said. "I don't actually know him that well. He is my next-door neighbor."

The children looked from the well-scrubbed house of Justice Strauss to the dilapidated one next door. The bricks were stained with soot and grime. There were only two small windows, which were closed with the shades drawn even though it was a nice day. Rising above the windows was a tall and dirty tower that tilted slightly to the left. The front door needed to be repainted, and carved in the middle of it was an image of an eye. The entire building sagged to the side, like a crooked tooth.

"Oh!" said Sunny, and everyone knew what she meant. She meant, "What a terrible place! I don't want to live there at all!"

"Well, it was nice to meet you," Violet said to Justice Strauss.

"Yes," said Justice Strauss, gesturing to her flowerpot. "Perhaps one day you could come over and help me with my gardening."

"That would be very pleasant," Violet said, very sadly. It would, of course, be very pleasant to help Justice Strauss with her gardening, but Violet could not help thinking that it would be far more pleasant to live in Justice Strauss's house, instead of Count Olaf's. What kind of a man, Violet wondered, would carve an image of an eye into his front door?

Mr. Poe tipped his hat to Justice Strauss, who smiled at the children and disappeared into her lovely house. Klaus stepped forward and knocked on Count Olaf's door, his knuckles rapping right in the middle of the carved eye. There was a pause, and then the door creaked open and the children saw Count Olaf for the first time.

"Hello hello hello," Count Olaf said in a wheezy whisper. He was very tall and very thin, dressed in a gray suit that had many dark stains on it. His face was unshaven, and rather than two eyebrows, like most human beings have, he had just one long one. His eyes were very, very shiny, which made him look both hungry and angry. "Hello, my children. Please step into your new home, and wipe your feet outside so no mud gets indoors."

As they stepped into the house, Mr. Poe behind them, the Baudelaire orphans realized what a ridiculous thing Count Olaf had just said. The room in which they found themselves was the dirtiest they had ever seen, and a little bit of mud from outdoors wouldn't have made a bit of difference. Even by the dim light of the one bare lightbulb that hung from the ceiling, the three children could see that everything in this room was filthy, from the stuffed head of a lion which was nailed to the wall to the bowl of apple cores which sat on a small wooden table. Klaus willed himself not to cry as he looked around.

"This room looks like it needs a little work," Mr. Poe said, peering around in the gloom.

"I realize that my humble home isn't as fancy as the Baudelaire mansion," Count Olaf said, "but perhaps with a bit of your money we could fix it up a little nicer."

Mr. Poe's eyes widened in surprise, and his coughs echoed in the dark room before he spoke. "The Baudelaire fortune," he said sternly, "will not be used for such matters. In fact, it will not be used at all, until Violet is of age."

Count Olaf turned to Mr. Poe with a glint in his eye like an angry dog. For a moment Violet thought he was going to strike Mr. Poe across the face. But then he swallowed—the children could see his Adam's apple bob in his skinny throat—and shrugged his patchy shoulders.

"All right then," he said. "It's the same to me. Thank you very much, Mr. Poe, for bringing them here. Children, I will now show you to your room."

"Good-bye, Violet, Klaus, and Sunny," Mr. Poe said, stepping back through the front door. "I hope you will be very happy here. I will continue to see you occasionally, and you can always contact me at the bank if you have any questions."

"But we don't even know where the bank is," Klaus said.

"I have a map of the city," Count Olaf said. "Good-bye, Mr. Poe."

He leaned forward to shut the door, and the Baudelaire orphans were too overcome with despair to get a last glimpse of Mr. Poe. They now wished they could all stay at the Poe household, even though it smelled. Rather than looking at the door, then, the orphans looked down, and saw that although Count Olaf was wearing shoes, he wasn't wearing any socks. They could see, in the space of pale skin between his tattered trouser cuff and his black shoe, that Count Olaf had an image of an eye tattooed on his ankle, matching the eye on his front door. They wondered how many other eyes were in Count Olaf's house, and whether, for the rest of their lives, they would always feel as though Count Olaf were watching them even when he wasn't nearby.

CHAPTER Three

I don't know if you've ever noticed this, but first impressions are often entirely wrong. You can look at a painting for the first time, for example, and not like it at all, but after looking at it a little longer you may find it very pleasing. The first time you try Gorgonzola cheese you may find it too strong, but when you are older you may want to eat nothing but Gorgonzola cheese. Klaus, when Sunny was born, did not like her at all, but by the time she was six weeks old the two of them were thick as thieves. Your initial opinion on just about anything may change over time.

I wish I could tell you that the Baudelaires' first impressions of Count Olaf and his house were incorrect, as first impressions so often are. But these impressions—that Count Olaf was a horrible person, and his house a depressing pigsty—were absolutely correct. During the first few days after the orphans' arrival at Count Olaf's, Violet, Klaus, and Sunny attempted to make themselves feel at home, but it was really no use. Even though Count Olaf's house was quite large, the three children were placed together in one filthy bedroom that had only one small bed in it. Violet and Klaus took turns sleeping in it, so that every other night one of them was in the bed and the other was sleeping on the hard wooden floor, and the bed's mattress was so lumpy it was difficult to say who was more uncomfortable. To make a bed for Sunny, Violet removed the dusty curtains from the curtain rod that hung over the bedroom's one window and bunched them together to form a sort of cushion, just big enough for her sister. However, without curtains over the cracked glass, the sun streamed through the window every morning, so the children woke up early and sore each day. Instead of a closet, there was a large cardboard box that had once held a refrigerator and would now hold the three children's clothes, all piled in a heap. Instead of toys, books, or other things to amuse the youngsters, Count Olaf had provided a small pile of rocks. And the only decoration on the peeling walls was a large and ugly painting of an eye, matching the one on Count Olaf's ankle and all over the house.

But the children knew, as I'm sure you know, that the worst surroundings in the world can be tolerated if the people in them are interesting and kind. Count Olaf was neither interesting nor kind; he was demanding, short-tempered, and bad-smelling. The only good thing to be said for Count Olaf is that he wasn't around very often. When the children woke up and chose their clothing out of the refrigerator box, they would walk into the kitchen and find a list of instructions left for them by Count Olaf, who would often not appear until nighttime. Most of the day he spent out of the house, or up in the high tower, where the children were forbidden to go. The instructions he left for them were usually difficult chores, such as repainting the back porch or repairing the windows, and instead of a signature Count Olaf would draw an eye at the bottom of the note.

One morning his note read, "My theater troupe will be coming for dinner before tonight's performance. Have dinner ready for all ten of them by the time they arrive at seven o'clock. Buy the food, prepare it, set the table, serve dinner, clean up afterwards, and stay out of our way." Below that there was the usual eye, and underneath the note was a small sum of money for the groceries.

Violet and Klaus read the note as they ate their breakfast, which was a gray and lumpy oatmeal Count Olaf left for them each morning in a large pot on the stove. Then they looked at each other in dismay.

"None of us knows how to cook," Klaus said.

"That's true," Violet said. "I knew how to repair those windows, and how to clean the chimney, because those sorts of things interest me. But I don't know how to cook anything except toast."

"And sometimes you burn the toast," Klaus said, and they smiled. They were both remembering a time when the two of them got up early to make a special breakfast for their parents. Violet had burned the toast, and their parents, smelling smoke, had run downstairs to see what the matter was. When they saw Violet and Klaus, looking forlornly at pieces of pitch-black toast, they laughed and laughed, and then made pancakes for the whole family.

"I wish they were here," Violet said. She did

not have to explain she was talking about their parents. "They would never let us stay in this dreadful place."

"If they were here," Klaus said, his voice rising as he got more and more upset, "we would not be with Count Olaf in the first place. I *hate* it here, Violet! I *hate* this house! I *hate* our room! I *hate* having to do all these chores, and I *hate* Count Olaf!"

"I hate it too," Violet said, and Klaus looked at his older sister with relief. Sometimes, just saying that you hate something, and having someone agree with you, can make you feel better about a terrible situation. "I hate everything about our lives right now, Klaus," she said, "but we have to keep our chin up." This was an expression the children's father had used, and it meant "try to stay cheerful."

"You're right," Klaus said. "But it is very difficult to keep one's chin up when Count Olaf keeps shoving it down."

"Jook!" Sunny shrieked, banging on the table

with her oatmeal spoon. Violet and Klaus were jerked out of their conversation and looked once again at Count Olaf's note.

"Perhaps we could find a cookbook, and read about how to cook," Klaus said. "It shouldn't be that difficult to make a simple meal."

Violet and Klaus spent several minutes opening and shutting Count Olaf's kitchen cupboards, but there weren't any cookbooks to be found.

"I can't say I'm surprised," Violet said. "We haven't found any books in this house at all."

"I know, " Klaus said miserably. "I miss reading very much. We must go out and look for a library sometime soon."

"But not today," Violet said. "Today we have to cook for ten people."

At that moment there was a knock on the front door. Violet and Klaus looked at one another nervously.

"Who in the world would want to visit Count Olaf?" Violet wondered out loud.

"Maybe somebody wants to visit *us*," Klaus said, without much hope. In the time since the Baudelaire parents' death, most of the Baudelaire orphans' friends had fallen by the wayside, an expression which here means "they stopped calling, writing, and stopping by to see any of the Baudelaires, making them very lonely." You and I, of course, would never do this to any of our grieving acquaintances, but it is a sad truth in life that when someone has lost a loved one, friends sometimes avoid the person, just when the presence of friends is most needed.

Violet, Klaus, and Sunny walked slowly to the front door and peered through the peephole, which was in the shape of an eye. They were delighted to see Justice Strauss peering back at them, and opened the door.

"Justice Strauss!" Violet cried. "How lovely to see you." She was about to add, "Do come in," but then she realized that Justice Strauss would probably not want to venture into the dim and dirty room.

"Please forgive me for not stopping by sooner," Justice Strauss said, as the Baudelaires stood awkwardly in the doorway. "I wanted to see how you children were settling in, but I had a very difficult case in the High Court and it was taking up much of my time."

"What sort of case was it?" Klaus asked. Having been deprived of reading, he was hungry for new information.

"I can't really discuss it," Justice Strauss said, "because it's official business. But I can tell you it concerns a poisonous plant and illegal use of someone's credit card."

"Yeeka!" Sunny shrieked, which appeared to mean "How interesting!" although of course there is no way that Sunny could understand what was being said.

Justice Strauss looked down at Sunny and laughed. "Yeeka indeed," she said, and reached down to pat the child on the head. Sunny took Justice Strauss's hand and bit it, gently.

"That means she likes you," Violet explained.

"She bites very, very hard if she doesn't like you, or if you want to give her a bath."

"I see," Justice Strauss said. "Now then, how are you children getting on? Is there anything you desire?"

The children looked at one another, thinking of all the things they desired. Another bed, for example. A proper crib for Sunny. Curtains for the window in their room. A closet instead of a cardboard box. But what they desired most of all, of course, was not to be associated with Count Olaf in any way whatsoever. What they desired most was to be with their parents again, in their true home, but that, of course, was impossible. Violet, Klaus, and Sunny all looked down at the floor unhappily as they considered the question. Finally, Klaus spoke.

"Could we perhaps borrow a cookbook?" he said. "Count Olaf has instructed us to make dinner for his theater troupe tonight, and we can't find a cookbook in the house."

"Goodness," Justice Strauss said. "Cooking

dinner for an entire theater troupe seems like a lot to ask of children."

"Count Olaf gives us a lot of responsibility," Violet said. What she wanted to say was, "Count Olaf is an evil man," but she was well mannered.

"Well, why don't you come next door to my house," Justice Strauss said, "and find a cookbook that pleases you?"

The youngsters agreed, and followed Justice Strauss out the door and over to her well-kept house. She led them through an elegant hallway smelling of flowers into an enormous room, and when they saw what was inside, they nearly fainted from delight, Klaus especially.

The room was a library. Not a public library, but a private library; that is, a large collection of books belonging to Justice Strauss. There were shelves and shelves of them, on every wall from the floor to the ceiling, and separate shelves and shelves of them in the middle of the room. The only place there weren't books was in one corner, where there were some large, comfortable-looking chairs and a wooden table with lamps hanging over them, perfect for reading. Although it was not as big as their parents' library, it was as cozy, and the Baudelaire children were thrilled.

"My word!" Violet said. "This is a wonderful library!"

"Thank you very much," Justice Strauss said. "I've been collecting books for years, and I'm very proud of my collection. As long as you keep them in good condition, you are welcome to use any of my books, at any time. Now, the cookbooks are over here on the eastern wall. Shall we have a look at them?"

"Yes," Violet said, "and then, if you don't mind, I should love to look at any of your books concerning mechanical engineering. Inventing things is a great interest of mine."

"And I would like to look at books on wolves," Klaus said. "Recently I have been fascinated by the subject of wild animals of North America."

"Book!" Sunny shrieked, which meant "Please don't forget to pick out a picture book for me."

Justice Strauss smiled. "It is a pleasure to see young people interested in books," she said. "But first I think we'd better find a good recipe, don't you?"

The children agreed, and for thirty minutes or so they perused several cookbooks that Justice Strauss recommended. To tell you the truth, the three orphans were so excited to be out of Count Olaf's house, and in this pleasant library, that they were a little distracted and unable to concentrate on cooking. But finally Klaus found a dish that sounded delicious, and easy to make.

"Listen to this," he said. "'Puttanesca.' It's an Italian sauce for pasta. All we need to do is sauté olives, capers, anchovies, garlic, chopped parsley, and tomatoes together in a pot, and prepare spaghetti to go with it."

"That sounds easy," Violet agreed, and the

Baudelaire orphans looked at one another. Perhaps, with the kind Justice Strauss and her library right next door, the children could prepare pleasant lives for themselves as easily as making puttanesca sauce for Count Olaf.

Four

The Baudelaire orphans copied the puttanesca
recipe from the cookbook onto a piece of scrap
paper, and Justice Strauss was
kind enough to escort them to
the market to buy the necessary ingredients. Count Olaf
had not left them very
much money, but the chil-
dren were able to buy
everything they needed.
From a street vendor,
they purchased olives
after tasting several

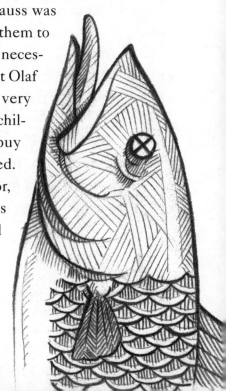

varieties and choosing their favorites. At a pasta store they selected interestingly shaped noodles and asked the woman running the store the proper amount for thirteen people—the ten people Count Olaf mentioned, and the three of them. Then, at the supermarket, they purchased garlic, which is a sharp-tasting bulbous plant; anchovies, which are small salty fish; capers, which are flower buds of a small shrub and taste marvelous; and tomatoes, which are actually fruits and not vegetables as most people believe. They thought it would be proper to serve dessert, and bought several envelopes of pudding mix. Perhaps, the orphans thought, if they made a delicious meal, Count Olaf might be a bit kinder to them.

"Thank you so much for helping us out today," Violet said, as she and her siblings walked home with Justice Strauss. "I don't know what we would have done without you."

"You seem like very intelligent people," Justice Strauss said. "I daresay you would have thought of something. But it continues to strike me as odd that Count Olaf has asked you to prepare such an enormous meal. Well, here we are. I must go inside and put my own groceries away. I hope you children will come over soon and borrow books from my library."

"Tomorrow?" Klaus said quickly. "Could we come over tomorrow?"

"I don't see why not," Justice Strauss said, smiling.

"I can't tell you how much we appreciate this," Violet said, carefully. With their kind parents dead and Count Olaf treating them so abominably, the three children were not used to kindness from adults, and weren't sure if they were expected to do anything back. "Tomorrow, before we use your library again, Klaus and I would be more than happy to do household chores for you. Sunny isn't really old enough to work, but I'm sure we could find some way she could help you."

Justice Strauss smiled at the three children,

but her eyes were sad. She reached out a hand and put it on Violet's hair, and Violet felt more comforted than she had in some time. "That won't be necessary," Justice Strauss said. "You are always welcome in my home." Then she turned and went into her home, and after a moment of staring after her, the Baudelaire orphans went into theirs.

For most of the afternoon, Violet, Klaus, and Sunny cooked the puttanesca sauce according to the recipe. Violet roasted the garlic and washed and chopped the anchovies. Klaus peeled the tomatoes and pitted the olives. Sunny banged on a pot with a wooden spoon, singing a rather repetitive song she had written herself. And all three of the children felt less miserable than they had since their arrival at Count Olaf's. The smell of cooking food is often a calming one, and the kitchen grew cozy as the sauce simmered, a culinary term which means "cooked over low heat." The three orphans spoke of pleasant

memories of their parents and about Justice
Strauss, who they agreed was a wonderful neighbor and in whose library they planned to spend
a great deal of time. As they talked, they mixed
and tasted the chocolate pudding.

Just as they were placing the pudding in the
refrigerator to cool, Violet, Klaus, and Sunny
heard a loud, booming sound as the front door
was flung open, and I'm sure I don't have to tell
you who was home.

"Orphans?" Count Olaf called out in his
scratchy voice. "Where are you, orphans?"

"In the kitchen, Count Olaf," Klaus called.
"We're just finishing dinner."

"You'd better be," Count Olaf said, and
strode into the kitchen. He gazed at all three
Baudelaire children with his shiny, shiny eyes.
"My troupe is right behind me and they are very
hungry. Where is the roast beef?"

"We didn't make roast beef," Violet said.
"We made puttanesca sauce."

"What?" Count Olaf asked. "No roast beef?"

"You didn't tell us you wanted roast beef," Klaus said.

Count Olaf slid toward the children so that he looked even taller than he was. His eyes grew even brighter, and his one eyebrow raised in anger. "In agreeing to adopt you," he said, "I have become your father, and as your father I am not someone to be trifled with. I demand that you serve roast beef to myself and my guests."

"We don't have any!" Violet cried. "We made puttanesca sauce!"

"*No! No! No!*" Sunny shouted.

Count Olaf looked down at Sunny, who had spoken so suddenly. With an inhuman roar he picked her up in one scraggly hand and raised her so she was staring at him in the eye. Needless to say, Sunny was very frightened and began crying immediately, too scared to even try to bite the hand that held her.

"Put her down immediately, you beast!"

Klaus shouted. He jumped up, trying to rescue Sunny from the grasp of the Count, but he was holding her too high to reach. Count Olaf looked down at Klaus and smiled a terrible, toothy grin, raising the wailing Sunny up even higher in the air. He seemed about to drop her to the floor when there was a large burst of laughter in the next room.

"Olaf! Where's Olaf?" voices called out. Count Olaf paused, still holding the wailing Sunny up in the air, as members of his theater troupe walked into the kitchen. Soon they were crowding the room—an assortment of strange-looking characters of all shapes and sizes. There was a bald man with a very long nose, dressed in a long black robe. There were two women who had bright white powder all over their faces, making them look like ghosts. Behind the women was a man with very long and skinny arms, at the end of which were two hooks instead of hands. There was a person who was extremely fat, and who looked like neither a man nor a woman. And behind this person, standing in the doorway, were an assortment of people the children could not see but who promised to be just as frightening.

"Here you are, Olaf," said one of the white-faced women. "What in the world are you doing?"

"I'm just disciplining these orphans," Count Olaf said. "I asked them to make dinner, and all they have made is some disgusting sauce."

"You can't go easy on children," the man with the hook-hands said. "They must be taught to obey their elders."

The tall, bald man peered at the youngsters. "Are these," he said to Count Olaf, "those wealthy children you were telling me about?"

"Yes," Count Olaf said. "They are so awful I can scarcely stand to touch them." With that, he lowered Sunny, who was still wailing, to the floor. Violet and Klaus breathed a sigh of relief that he had not dropped her from that great height.

"I don't blame you," said someone in the doorway.

Count Olaf rubbed his hands together as if he had been holding something revolting instead of an infant. "Well, enough talk," he said. "I suppose we will eat their dinner, even though it is all wrong. Everyone, follow me to the dining room and I will pour us some wine. Perhaps by the time these brats serve us, we will be too drunk to care if it is roast beef or not."

"Hurrah!" cried several members of the troupe, and they marched through the kitchen, following Count Olaf into the dining room. Nobody paid a bit of attention to the children, except for the bald man, who stopped and stared Violet in the eye.

"You're a pretty one," he said, taking her face in his rough hands. "If I were you I would try not to anger Count Olaf, or he might wreck that pretty little face of yours." Violet shuddered, and the bald man gave a high-pitched giggle and left the room.

The Baudelaire children, alone in the kitchen, found themselves breathing heavily, as if they had just run a long distance. Sunny continued to wail, and Klaus found that his eyes were wet with tears as well. Only Violet didn't cry, but merely trembled with fear and revulsion, a word which here means "an unpleasant mixture of horror and disgust." For several moments none of them could speak.

"This is terrible, terrible," Klaus said finally. "Violet, what can we do?"

"I don't know," she said. "I'm afraid."

"Me too," Klaus said.

"Hux!" Sunny said, as she stopped crying.

"Let's have some dinner!" someone shouted from the dining room, and the theater troupe began pounding on the table in strict rhythm, which is an exceedingly rude thing to do.

"We'd better serve the puttanesca," Klaus said, "or who knows what Count Olaf will do to us."

Violet thought of what the bald man had said, about wrecking her face, and nodded. The two of them looked at the pot of bubbling sauce, which had seemed so cozy while they were making it and now looked like a vat of blood. Then, leaving Sunny behind in the kitchen, they walked into the dining room, Klaus carrying a bowl of the interestingly shaped noodles and Violet carrying the pot of puttanesca sauce and a large ladle with which to serve it. The theater troupe was talking and cackling, drinking again and again from their wine cups and paying no attention to the Baudelaire orphans as they circled the table serving everyone dinner. Violet's right hand ached from holding the heavy ladle. She thought of switching to her left hand, but because she was right-handed she was afraid she might spill the sauce with her left hand, which could enrage Count Olaf again. She stared miserably at Olaf's plate of food and found herself wishing she had bought poison at the market and put it in the puttanesca sauce. Finally, they were through serving, and Klaus and Violet slipped back into the kitchen. They listened to the wild, rough laughter of Count

Olaf and his theater troupe, and they picked at
their own portions of food, too miserable to eat.
Before long, Olaf's friends were pounding on
the table in strict rhythm again, and the orphans
went out to the dining room to clear the table,
and then again to serve the chocolate pudding.
By now it was obvious that Count Olaf and his
associates had drunk a great deal of wine, and
they slouched at the table and spoke much less.
Finally, they roused themselves, and trooped
back through the kitchen, scarcely glancing at
the children on their way out of the house.
Count Olaf looked around the room, which was
filled with dirty dishes.

"Because you haven't cleaned up yet," he
said to the orphans, "I suppose you can be
excused from attending tonight's performance.
But after cleaning up, you are to go straight to
your beds."

Klaus had been glaring at the floor, trying to
hide how upset he was. But at this he could not
remain silent. "You mean our *bed*!" he shouted.

"You have only provided us with one bed!"

Members of the theater troupe stopped in their tracks at this outburst, and glanced from Klaus to Count Olaf to see what would happen next. Count Olaf raised his one eyebrow, and his eyes shone bright, but he spoke calmly.

"If you would like another bed," he said, "tomorrow you may go into town and purchase one."

"You know perfectly well we haven't any money," Klaus said.

"Of course you do," Count Olaf said, and his voice began to get a little louder. "You are the inheritors of an enormous fortune."

"That money," Klaus said, remembering what Mr. Poe said, "is not to be used until Violet is of age."

Count Olaf's face grew very red. For a moment he said nothing. Then, in one sudden movement, he reached down and struck Klaus across the face. Klaus fell to the floor, his face inches from the eye tattooed on Olaf's ankle. His glasses leaped from his face and skittered into a corner. His left cheek, where Olaf had struck him, felt as if it were on fire. The theater troupe laughed, and a few of them applauded as if Count Olaf had done something very brave instead of something despicable.

"Come on, friends," Count Olaf said to his comrades. "We'll be late for our own performance."

"If I know you, Olaf," said the man with the hook-hands, "you'll figure out a way to get at that Baudelaire money."

"We'll see," Count Olaf said, but his eyes were shining bright as if he already had an idea. There was another loud boom as the front door shut behind Count Olaf and his terrible friends, and the Baudelaire children were alone in the kitchen. Violet knelt at Klaus's side, giving him a hug to try to make him feel better. Sunny crawled over to his glasses, picked them up, and brought them to him. Klaus began to sob, not so much from the pain but from rage at the terrible situation they were in. Violet and Sunny cried with him, and they continued weeping as they washed the dishes, and as they blew out the candles in the dining room, and as they changed out of their clothes and lay down to go to sleep, Klaus in the bed, Violet on the floor, Sunny on her little cushion of curtains. The moonlight shone through the window, and if anyone had looked into the Baudelaire orphans' bedroom, they would have seen three children crying quietly all night long.

CHAPTER Five

Unless you have been very, very lucky, you have undoubtedly experienced events in your life that have made you cry. So unless you have been very, very lucky, you know that a good, long session of weeping can often make you feel better, even if your circumstances have not changed one bit. So it was with the Baudelaire orphans. Having cried all night, they rose the next morning feeling as if a weight were off their shoulders. The three children knew, of course, that they were still in a terrible situation, but they thought they might do something to make it better.

The morning's note from Count Olaf ordered them to chop firewood in the backyard, and as Violet and Klaus swung the axe down over each log to break it into smaller pieces, they discussed possible plans of action, while Sunny chewed meditatively on a small piece of wood.

"Clearly," Klaus said, fingering the ugly bruise on his face where Olaf had struck him, "we cannot stay here any longer. I would rather take my chances on the streets than live in this terrible place."

"But who knows what misfortunes would befall us on the streets?" Violet pointed out. "At least here we have a roof over our heads."

"I wish our parents' money *could* be used now, instead of when you come of age," Klaus said. "Then we could buy a castle and live in it, with armed guards patrolling the outside to keep out Count Olaf and his troupe."

"And I could have a large inventing studio," Violet said wistfully. She swung the axe down and split a log neatly in two. "Filled with gears and pulleys and wires and an elaborate computer system."

"And I could have a large library," Klaus said, "as comfortable as Justice Strauss's, but more enormous."

"Gibbo!" Sunny shrieked, which appeared to mean "And I could have lots of things to bite."

"But in the meantime," Violet said, "we have to do something about our predicament."

"Perhaps Justice Strauss could adopt us," Klaus said. "She said we were always welcome in her home."

"But she meant for a visit, or to use her library," Violet pointed out. "She didn't mean to *live*."

"Perhaps if we explained our situation to her,

she would agree to adopt us," Klaus said hopefully, but when Violet looked at him she saw that he knew it was of no use. Adoption is an enormous decision, and not likely to happen impulsively. I'm sure you, in your life, have occasionally wished to be raised by different people than the ones who are raising you, but knew in your heart that the chances of this were very slim.

"I think we should go see Mr. Poe," Violet said. "He told us when he dropped us here that we could contact him at the bank if we had any questions."

"We don't really have a question," Klaus said. "We have a complaint." He was thinking of Mr. Poe walking toward them at Briny Beach, with his terrible message. Even though the fire was of course not Mr. Poe's fault, Klaus was reluctant to see Mr. Poe because he was afraid of getting more bad news.

"I can't think of anyone else to contact,"

Violet said. "Mr. Poe is in charge of our affairs, and I'm sure if he knew how horrid Count Olaf is, he would take us right out of here."

Klaus pictured Mr. Poe arriving in his car and putting the Baudelaire orphans inside, to go somewhere else, and felt a stirring of hope. Anywhere would be better than here. "Okay," he said. "Let's get this firewood all chopped and we'll go to the bank."

Invigorated by their plan, the Baudelaire orphans swung their axes at an amazing speed, and soon enough they were done chopping firewood and ready to go to the bank. They remembered Count Olaf saying he had a map of the city, and they looked thoroughly for it, but they couldn't find any trace of a map, and decided it must be in the tower, where they were forbidden to go. So, without directions of any sort, the Baudelaire children set off for the city's banking district in hopes of finding Mr. Poe.

After walking through the meat district, the flower district, and the sculpture district, the three children arrived at the banking district, pausing to take a refreshing sip of water at the Fountain of Victorious Finance. The banking district consisted of several wide streets with large marble buildings on each side of them, all banks. They went first to Trustworthy Bank, and then to Faithful Savings and Loan, and then to Subservient Financial Services, each time inquiring for Mr. Poe. Finally, a receptionist at Subservient said she knew that Mr. Poe worked down the street, at Mulctuary Money Management. The building was square and rather plain-looking, though once inside, the three orphans were intimidated by the hustle and bustle of the people as they raced around the large, echoey room. Finally, they asked a uniformed guard whether they had arrived at the right place to speak to Mr. Poe, and he led them into a large office with many file cabinets and no windows.

"Why, hello," said Mr. Poe, in a puzzled tone

of voice. He was sitting at a desk covered in typed papers that looked important and boring. Surrounding a small framed photograph of his wife and his two beastly sons were three telephones with flashing lights. "Please come in."

"Thank you," said Klaus, shaking Mr. Poe's hand. The Baudelaire youngsters sat down in three large and comfortable chairs.

Mr. Poe opened his mouth to speak, but had to cough into a handkerchief before he could begin. "I'm very busy today," he said, finally. "So I don't have too much time to chat. Next time you should call ahead of time when you plan on being in the neighborhood, and I will put some time aside to take you to lunch."

"That would be very pleasant," Violet said, "and we're sorry we didn't contact you before we stopped by, but we find ourselves in an urgent situation."

"Count Olaf is a madman," Klaus said, getting right to the point. "We cannot stay with him."

"He struck Klaus across the face. See his bruise?" Violet said, but just as she said it, one of the telephones rang, in a loud, unpleasant wail. "Excuse me," Mr. Poe said, and picked up the phone. "Poe here," he said into the receiver. "What? Yes. Yes. Yes. Yes. No. Yes. Thank you." He hung up the phone and looked at the Baudelaires as if he had forgotten they were there.

"I'm sorry," Mr. Poe said, "what were we talking about? Oh, yes, Count Olaf. I'm sorry you don't have a good first impression of him."

"He has only provided us with one bed," Klaus said.

"He makes us do a great many difficult chores."

"He drinks too much wine."

"Excuse me," Mr. Poe said, as another telephone rang. "Poe here," he said. "Seven. Seven. Seven. Seven. Six and a half. Seven. You're welcome." He hung up and quickly wrote something down on one of his papers, then looked at the children. "I'm sorry," he said, "what were you saying about Count Olaf? Making you do chores doesn't sound too bad."

"He calls us orphans."

"He has terrible friends."

"He is always asking about our money."

"Poko!" (This was from Sunny.)

Mr. Poe put up his hands to indicate he had heard enough. "Children, children," he said. "You must give yourselves time to adjust to your new home. You've only been there a few days."

"We have been there long enough to know Count Olaf is a bad man," Klaus said.

Mr. Poe sighed, and looked at each of the three children. His face was kind, but it didn't look like he really believed what the Baudelaire orphans were saying. "Are you familiar with the Latin term 'in loco parentis'?" he asked.

Violet and Sunny looked at Klaus. The biggest reader of the three, he was the most likely to know vocabulary words and foreign phrases. "Something about trains?" he asked. Maybe Mr. Poe was going to take them by train to another relative.

Mr. Poe shook his head. "'In loco parentis' means 'acting in the role of parent,'" he said. "It is a legal term and it applies to Count Olaf. Now that you are in his care, the Count may raise you using any methods he sees fit. I'm sorry if your parents did not make you do any household chores, or if you never saw them drink any wine, or if you like their friends better than Count Olaf's friends, but these are things that you must get used to, as Count Olaf is acting in loco parentis. Understand?"

"But he *struck* my brother!" Violet said. "Look at his face!"

As Violet spoke, Mr. Poe reached into his pocket for his handkerchief and, covering his mouth, coughed many, many times into it. He coughed so loudly that Violet could not be certain he had heard her.

"Whatever Count Olaf has done," Mr. Poe said, glancing down at one of his papers and circling a number, "he has acted in loco parentis, and there's nothing I can do about it. Your money will be well protected by myself and by the bank, but Count Olaf's parenting techniques are his own business. Now, I hate to usher you out posthaste, but I have very much work to do."

The children just sat there, stunned. Mr. Poe looked up, and cleared his throat. "'Posthaste,'" he said, "means—"

"—means you'll do nothing to help us," Violet finished for him. She was shaking with anger and frustration. As one of the phones began ringing, she stood up and walked out of the room, followed by Klaus, who was carrying Sunny. They stalked out of the bank and stood on the street, not knowing what to do next.

"What shall we do next?" Klaus asked sadly.

Violet stared up at the sky. She wished she could invent something that could take them out of there. "It's getting a bit late," she said. "We might as well just go back and think of something else tomorrow. Perhaps we can stop and see Justice Strauss."

"But you said she wouldn't help us," Klaus said.

"Not for help," Violet said, "for books."

It is very useful, when one is young, to learn the difference between "literally" and "figuratively." If something happens literally, it actually happens; if something happens figuratively, it *feels like* it's happening. If you are literally jumping for joy, for instance, it means you are leaping in the air because you are very happy. If you are figuratively jumping for joy, it means you are so happy that you *could* jump for joy, but are saving your energy for other matters. The Baudelaire orphans walked back to Count Olaf's neighborhood and stopped at the home of Justice Strauss, who welcomed them inside and let them choose books from the library. Violet chose several about mechanical inventions,

Klaus chose several about wolves, and Sunny found a book with many pictures of teeth inside. They then went to their room and crowded together on the one bed, reading intently and happily. *Figuratively*, they escaped from Count Olaf and their miserable existence. They did not *literally* escape, because they were still in his house and vulnerable to Olaf's evil in loco parentis ways. But by immersing themselves in their favorite reading topics, they felt far away from their predicament, as if they had escaped. In the situation of the orphans, figuratively escaping was not enough, of course, but at the end of a tiring and hopeless day, it would have to do. Violet, Klaus, and Sunny read their books and, in the back of their minds, hoped that soon their figurative escape would eventually turn into a literal one.

The next morning, when the children stumbled sleepily from their bedroom into the kitchen, rather than a note from Count Olaf they found Count Olaf himself.

"Good morning, orphans," he said. "I have your oatmeal all ready in bowls for you."

The children took seats at the kitchen table and stared nervously into their oatmeal. If you knew Count Olaf, and he suddenly served you a meal, wouldn't you be afraid there was something terrible in it, like poison or ground glass? But instead, Violet, Klaus, and Sunny found that fresh raspberries had been sprinkled on top of each of their portions. The Baudelaire orphans hadn't had raspberries since their parents died, although they were extremely fond of them.

"Thank you," Klaus said, carefully, picking up one of the raspberries and examining it. Perhaps these were poison berries that just looked like delicious ones. Count Olaf, seeing how suspiciously Klaus was looking at the berries, smiled and plucked a berry out of Sunny's bowl. Looking at each of the three youngsters, he popped it into his mouth and ate it.

"Aren't raspberries delicious?" he asked. "They were my favorite berries when I was your age."

Violet tried to picture Count Olaf as a youngster, but couldn't. His shiny eyes, bony hands, and shadowy smile all seemed to be things only adults possess. Despite her fear of him, however, she took her spoon in her right hand and began to eat her oatmeal. Count Olaf had eaten some, so it probably wasn't poisonous, and anyway she was very hungry. Klaus began to eat, too, as did Sunny, who got oatmeal and raspberries all over her face.

"I received a phone call yesterday," Count Olaf said, "from Mr. Poe. He told me you children had been to see him."

The children exchanged glances. They had hoped their visit would be taken in confidence, a phrase which here means "kept a secret between Mr. Poe and themselves and not blabbed to Count Olaf."

"Mr. Poe told me," Count Olaf said, "that you appeared to be having some difficulty adjusting to the life I have so graciously provided for you. I'm very sorry to hear that."

The children looked at Count Olaf. His face was very serious, as if he *were* very sorry to hear that, but his eyes were shiny and bright, the way they are when someone is telling a joke.

"Is that so?" Violet said. "I'm sorry Mr. Poe bothered you."

"I'm glad he did," Count Olaf said, "because

I want the three of you to feel at home here, now that I am your father."

The children shuddered a little at that, remembering their own kind father and gazing sadly at the poor substitute now sitting across the table from them.

"Lately," Count Olaf said, "I have been very nervous about my performances with the theater troupe, and I'm afraid I may have acted a bit standoffish."

The word "standoffish" is a wonderful one, but it does not describe Count Olaf's behavior toward the children. It means "reluctant to associate with others," and it might describe somebody who, during a party, would stand in a corner and not talk to anyone. It would *not* describe somebody who provides one bed for three people to sleep in, forces them to do horrible chores, and strikes them across the face. There are many words for people like that, but "standoffish" is not one of them. Klaus knew the word "standoffish" and almost laughed out loud at Olaf's incorrect use of it. But his face still had a bruise on it, so Klaus remained silent.

"Therefore, to make you feel a little more at home here, I would like to have you participate in my next play. Perhaps if you took part in the work I do, you would be less likely to run off complaining to Mr. Poe."

"In what way would we participate?" Violet asked. She was thinking of all the chores they already did for Count Olaf, and was not in the mood to do more.

"Well," Count Olaf said, his eyes shining brightly, "the play is called *The Marvelous Marriage*, and it is written by the great playwright Al Funcoot. We will give only one performance, on this Friday night. It is about a man who is very brave and intelligent, played by me. In the finale, he marries the young, beautiful woman he loves, in front of a crowd of cheering people. *You*, Klaus, and *you*, Sunny, will play some of the cheering people in the crowd."

"But we're shorter than most adults," Klaus said. "Won't that look strange to the audience?"

"You will be playing two midgets who attend the wedding," Olaf said patiently.

"And what will I do?" Violet asked. "I am very handy with tools, so perhaps I could help you build the set."

"Build the set? Heavens, no," Count Olaf said. "A pretty girl like you shouldn't be working backstage."

"But I'd *like* to," Violet said.

Count Olaf's one eyebrow raised slightly, and the Baudelaire orphans recognized this sign of his anger. But then the eyebrow went down again as he forced himself to remain calm. "But I have such an important role for you onstage," he said. "You are going to play the young woman I marry."

Violet felt her oatmeal and raspberries shift around in her stomach as if she had just caught the flu. It was bad enough having Count Olaf acting in loco parentis and announcing himself as their father, but to consider this man her husband, even for the purposes of a play, was even more dreadful.

"It's a *very* important role," he continued, his mouth curling up into an unconvincing smile, "although you have no lines other than 'I do,' which you will say when Justice Strauss asks you if you will have me."

"Justice Strauss?" Violet said. "What does she have to do with it?"

"She has agreed to play the part of the judge," Count Olaf said. Behind him, one of the eyes painted on the kitchen walls closely watched over each of the Baudelaire children. "I asked Justice Strauss to participate because I wanted to be neighborly, as well as fatherly."

"Count Olaf," Violet said, and then stopped herself. She wanted to argue her way out of playing his bride, but she didn't want to make him angry. *"Father,"* she said, "I'm not sure I'm talented enough to perform professionally. I would hate to disgrace your good name and the name of Al Funcoot. Plus I'll be very busy in the next few weeks working on my inventions—and learning how to prepare roast beef," she added quickly, remembering how he had behaved about dinner.

Count Olaf reached out one of his spidery hands and stroked Violet on the chin, looking deep into her eyes. *"You will,"* he said, "participate in this theatrical performance. I would prefer it if you would participate voluntarily, but as I believe Mr. Poe explained to you, I can order you to participate and *you must obey."* Olaf's sharp and dirty fingernails gently scratched on Violet's chin, and she shivered. The room was very, very quiet as Olaf finally let go, and stood up and left without a word. The Baudelaire children listened to his heavy footsteps go up the stairs to the tower they were forbidden to enter.

"Well," Klaus said hesitantly, "I guess it won't hurt to be in the play. It seems to be very important to him, and we want to keep on his good side."

"But he must be up to something," Violet said.

"You don't think those berries were poisoned, do you?" Klaus asked worriedly.

"No," Violet said. "Olaf is after the fortune we will inherit. Killing us would do him no good."

"But what good does it do him to have us be in his stupid play?"

"I don't know," Violet admitted miserably. She stood up and started washing out the oatmeal bowls.

"I wish we knew something more about inheritance law," Klaus said. "I'll bet Count Olaf has cooked up some plan to get our money, but I don't know what it could be."

"I guess we could ask Mr. Poe about it," Violet said doubtfully, as Klaus stood beside her and dried the dishes. "He knows all those Latin legal phrases."

"But Mr. Poe would probably call Count Olaf

again, and then he'd know we were on to him,"
Klaus pointed out. "Maybe we should try to talk
to Justice Strauss. She's a judge, so she must
know all about the law."

"But she's also Olaf's neighbor," Violet
replied, "and she might tell him that we had
asked."

Klaus took his glasses off, which he often did
when he was thinking hard. "How could we find
out about the law without Olaf's knowledge?"

"Book!" Sunny shouted suddenly. She probably meant something like "Would somebody
please wipe my face?" but it made Violet and
Klaus look at each other. *Book.* They were both
thinking the same thing: Surely Justice Strauss
would have a book on inheritance law.

"Count Olaf didn't leave us any chores to do,"
Violet said, "so I suppose we are free to visit
Justice Strauss and her library."

Klaus smiled. "Yes indeed," he said. "And
you know, today I don't think I'll choose a book
on wolves."

"Nor I," Violet said, "on mechanical engineering. I think I'd like to read about inheritance law."

"Well, let's go," Klaus said. "Justice Strauss said we could come over soon, and we don't want to be *standoffish*."

At the mention of the word that Count Olaf had used so ridiculously, the Baudelaire orphans all laughed, even Sunny, who of course did not have a very big vocabulary. Swiftly they put away the clean oatmeal bowls in the kitchen cupboards, which watched them with painted eyes. Then the three young people ran next door. Friday, the day of the performance, was only a few days off, and the children wanted to figure out Count Olaf's plan as quickly as possible.

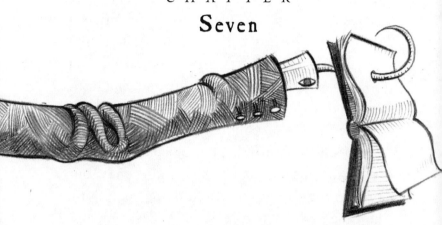

There are many, many types of books in the
world, which makes good sense, because there
are many, many types of people, and everybody
wants to read something different. For instance,
people who hate stories in which terrible things
happen to small children should put this book
down immediately. But one type of book that
practically no one likes to read is a book about
the law. Books about the law are notorious for
being very long, very dull, and very difficult to

read. This is one reason many lawyers make heaps of money. The money is an incentive—the word "incentive" here means "an offered reward to persuade you to do something you don't want to do"—to read long, dull, and difficult books.

The Baudelaire children had a slightly different incentive for reading these books, of course. Their incentive was not heaps of money, but preventing Count Olaf from doing something horrible to them in order to get heaps of money. But even with this incentive, getting through the law books in Justice Strauss's private library was a very, very, very hard task.

"Goodness," Justice Strauss said, when she came into the library and saw what they were reading. She had let them in the house but immediately went into the backyard to do her gardening, leaving the Baudelaire orphans alone in her glorious library. "I thought you were interested in mechanical engineering, animals of North America, and teeth. Are you sure you want to read those enormous law books? Even *I* don't like reading them, and I work in law."

"Yes," Violet lied, "I find them very interesting, Justice Strauss."

"So do I," Klaus said. "Violet and I are considering a career in law, so we are fascinated by these books."

"Well," Justice Strauss said, "Sunny can't possibly be interested. Maybe she'd like to come help me with the gardening."

"Wipi!" Sunny shrieked, which meant "I'd much prefer gardening to sitting around watching my siblings struggle through law books."

"Well, make sure she doesn't eat any dirt," Klaus said, bringing Sunny over to the judge.

"Of course," said Justice Strauss. "We wouldn't want her to be sick for the big performance."

Violet and Klaus exchanged a look. "Are you excited about the play?" Violet asked hesitantly.

Justice Strauss's face lit up. "Oh yes," she said. "I've always wanted to perform onstage, ever since I was a little girl. And now Count Olaf has given me the opportunity to live my lifelong dream. Aren't you thrilled to be a part of the theater?"

"I guess so," Violet said.

"Of course you are," Judge Strauss said, stars in her eyes and Sunny in her hands. She left the library and Klaus and Violet looked at each other and sighed.

"She's stagestruck," Klaus said. "She won't believe that Count Olaf is up to something, no matter what."

"She wouldn't help us anyway," Violet pointed out glumly. "She's a judge, and she'd just start babbling about in loco parentis like Mr. Poe."

"That's why we've got to find a legal reason to stop the performance," Klaus said firmly. "Have you found anything in your book yet?"

"Nothing helpful," Violet said, glancing down at a piece of scrap paper on which she had been taking notes. "Fifty years ago there was a woman who left an enormous sum of money to her pet weasel, and none to her three sons. The three sons tried to prove that the woman was insane so the money would go to them."

"What happened?" Klaus asked.

"I think the weasel died," Violet replied, "but I'm not sure. I have to look up some of the words."

"I don't think it's going to help us anyway," Klaus said.

"Maybe Count Olaf is trying to prove that *we're* insane, so he'd get the money," Violet said.

"But why would making us be in *The Marvelous Marriage* prove we were insane?" Klaus asked.

"I don't know," Violet admitted. "I'm stuck. Have you found anything?"

"Around the time of your weasel lady," Klaus said, flipping through the enormous book he had been reading, "a group of actors put on a production of Shakespeare's *Macbeth*, and none of them wore any clothing."

Violet blushed. "You mean they were all naked, onstage?"

"Only briefly," Klaus said, smiling. "The police came and shut down the production. I don't think that's very helpful, either. It was just pretty interesting to read about."

Violet sighed. "Maybe Count Olaf isn't up to anything," she said. "I'm not interested in performing in his play, but perhaps we're all worked up about nothing. Maybe Count Olaf really *is* just trying to welcome us into the family."

"How can you say that?" Klaus cried. "He struck me across the face."

"But there's no way he can get hold of our fortune just by putting us in a play," Violet said. "My eyes are tired from reading these books, Klaus, and they aren't helping us. I'm going to go out and help Justice Strauss in the garden."

Klaus watched his sister leave the library and felt a wave of hopelessness wash over him. The day of the performance was not far off, and he hadn't even figured out what Count Olaf was up to, let alone how to stop him. All his life, Klaus had believed that if you read enough books you could solve any problem, but now he wasn't so sure.

"You there!" A voice coming from the doorway startled Klaus out of his thoughts. "Count Olaf sent me to look for you. You are to return to the house immediately."

Klaus turned and saw one of the members of Count Olaf's theater troupe, the one with hooks for hands, standing in the doorway. "What are you doing in this musty old room, anyway?" he asked in his croak of a voice, walking over to where Klaus was sitting. Narrowing his beady eyes, he read the title of one of the books. *"Inheritance Law and Its Implications?"* he said sharply. "Why are you reading that?"

"Why do you think I'm reading it?" Klaus said.

"I'll tell you what I think." The man put one of his terrible hooks on Klaus's shoulder. "I think you should never be allowed inside this library again, at least until Friday. We don't want a little boy getting big ideas. Now, where is your sister and that hideous baby?"

"In the garden," Klaus said, shrugging the hook off of his shoulder. "Why don't you go and get them?"

The man leaned over until his face was just inches from Klaus's, so close that the man's features flickered into a blur. "Listen to me very carefully, little boy," he said, breathing out foul steam with every word. "The only reason Count Olaf hasn't torn you limb from limb is that he hasn't gotten hold of your money. He allows you to live while he works out his plans. But ask yourself this, you little bookworm: What reason will he have to keep you alive after he has your money? What do you think will happen to you then?"

Klaus felt an icy chill go through him as the horrible man spoke. He had never been so terrified in all his life. He found that his arms and legs were shaking uncontrollably, as if he were having some sort of fit. His mouth was making strange sounds, like Sunny always did, as he struggled to find something to say. "Ah—" Klaus heard himself choke out. "Ah—"

"When the time comes," the hook-handed man said smoothly, ignoring Klaus's noises, "I believe Count Olaf just might leave you to me. So if I were you, I'd start acting a little nicer." The man stood up again and put both his hooks in front of Klaus's face, letting the light from the reading lamps reflect off the wicked-looking devices. "Now, if you will excuse me, I have to fetch your poor orphan siblings."

Klaus felt his body go limp as the hook-handed man left the room, and he wanted to sit there for a moment and catch his breath. But his mind wouldn't let him. This was his last moment in the library, and perhaps his last opportunity to foil Count Olaf's plan. But what to do? Hearing the faint sounds of the hook-handed man talking to Justice Strauss in the garden, Klaus looked frantically around the library for something that could be helpful.

Then, just as he heard the man's footsteps heading back his way, Klaus spied one book, and quickly grabbed it. He untucked his shirt and put the book inside, hastily retucking it just as the hook-handed man reentered the library, escorting Violet and carrying Sunny, who was trying without success to bite the man's hooks.

"I'm ready to go," Klaus said quickly, and walked out the door before the man could get a good look at him. He walked quickly ahead of his siblings, hoping that nobody would notice the book-shaped lump in his shirt. Maybe, just maybe, the book Klaus was smuggling could save their lives.

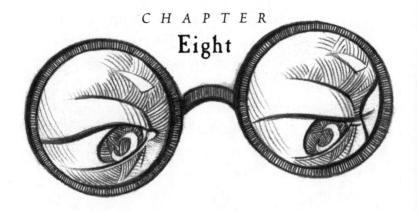

CHAPTER
Eight

Klaus stayed up all night reading, which was normally something he loved to do. Back when his parents were alive, Klaus used to take a flashlight to bed with him and hide under the covers, reading until he couldn't keep his eyes open. Some mornings, his father would come into Klaus's room to wake him up and find him asleep, still clutching his flashlight in one hand and his book in the other. But on this particular night, of course, the circumstances were much different.

Klaus stood by the window, squinting as he read his smuggled book by the moonlight that trickled into the room. He occasionally glanced at his sisters. Violet was sleeping fitfully—a word which here means "with much tossing and turning"—on the lumpy bed, and Sunny had wormed her way into the pile of curtains so that she just looked like a small heap of cloth. Klaus had not told his siblings about the book, because he didn't want to give them false hope. He wasn't sure the book would help them out of their dilemma.

The book was long, and difficult to read, and Klaus became more and more tired as the night wore on. Occasionally his eyes would close. He found himself reading the same sentence over and over. He found himself reading the same sentence over and over. He found himself reading the same sentence over and over. But then he would remember the way the hook-hands of Count Olaf's associate had glinted in the library, and would imagine them tearing into his flesh, and he would wake right up and continue reading. He found a small scrap of paper and tore it into strips, which he used to mark significant parts of the book.

By the time the light outside grew gray with the approaching dawn, Klaus had found out all he needed to know. His hopes rose along with the sun. Finally, when the first few birds began to sing, Klaus tiptoed to the door of the bedroom and eased it open quietly, careful not to wake the restless Violet or Sunny, who was still hidden in the pile of curtains. Then he went to the kitchen and sat and waited for Count Olaf.

He didn't have to wait long before he heard Olaf tromping down the tower stairs. When Count Olaf walked into the kitchen, he saw Klaus sitting at the table and smirked, a word which here means "smiled in an unfriendly, phony way."

"Hello, orphan," he said. "You're up early."

Klaus's heart was beating fast, but he felt calm on the outside, as if he had on a layer of invisible armor. "I've been up all night," he said, "reading this book." He put the book out on the table so Olaf could see it. "It's called *Nuptial Law,*" Klaus said, "and I learned many interesting things while reading it."

Count Olaf had taken out a bottle of wine to pour himself some breakfast, but when he saw the book he stopped, and sat down.

"The word 'nuptial,'" Klaus said, "means 'relating to marriage.'"

"I *know* what the word means," Count Olaf growled. "Where did you get that book?"

"From Justice Strauss's library," Klaus said. "But that's not important. What's important is that I have found out your plan."

"Is that so?" Count Olaf said, his one eyebrow raising. "And what is my plan, you little runt?"

Klaus ignored the insult and opened the book to where one of the scraps of paper was marking his place. "'The laws of marriage in this community are very simple,'" he read out loud.

"'The requirements are as follows: the presence of a judge, a statement of "I do" by both the bride and the groom, and the signing of an explanatory document in the bride's own hand.'" Klaus put down the book and pointed at Count Olaf. "If my sister says 'I do' and signs a piece of paper, while Justice Strauss is in the room, then she is legally married. This play you're putting on shouldn't be called *The Marvelous Marriage*. It should be called *The Menacing Marriage*. You're not going to marry Violet figuratively—you're going to marry her literally! This play won't be pretend; it will be real and legally binding."

Count Olaf laughed a rough, hoarse laugh. "Your sister isn't old enough to get married."

"She can get married if she has the permission of her legal guardian, acting in loco parentis," Klaus said. "I read that, too. You can't fool me."

"Why in the world would I want to actually marry your sister?" Count Olaf asked. "It is true she is very pretty, but a man like myself can acquire any number of beautiful women."

Klaus turned to a different section of *Nuptial Law*. "'A legal husband,'" he read out loud, "'has the right to control any money in the possession of his legal wife.'" Klaus gazed at Count Olaf in triumph. "You're going to marry my sister to gain control of the Baudelaire fortune! Or at least, that's what you *planned* to do. But when I show this information to Mr. Poe, your play will *not* be performed, and you will go to jail!"

Count Olaf's eyes grew very shiny, but he continued to smirk at Klaus. This was surprising. Klaus had guessed that once he announced what he knew, this dreadful man would have been very angry, even violent. After all, he'd had a furious outburst just because he'd wanted roast beef instead of puttanesca sauce. Surely he'd be even more enraged to have his plan discovered. But Count Olaf just sat there as calmly as if they were discussing the weather.

"I guess you've found me out," Olaf said

simply. "I suppose you're right: I'll go to prison, and you and the other orphans will go free. Now, why don't you run up to your room and wake your sisters? I'm sure they'll want to know all about your grand victory over my evil ways."

Klaus looked closely at Count Olaf, who was continuing to smile as if he had just told a clever joke. Why wasn't he threatening Klaus in anger, or tearing his hair out in frustration, or running to pack his clothes and escape? This wasn't happening at all the way Klaus had pictured it.

"Well, I *will* go tell my sisters," he said, and walked back into his bedroom. Violet was still dozing on the bed and Sunny was still hidden beneath the curtains. Klaus woke Violet up first.

"I stayed up all night reading," Klaus said breathlessly, as his sister opened her eyes, "and I discovered what Count Olaf is up to. He plans to marry you for real, when you and Justice Strauss and everyone all think it's just a play, and once he's your husband he'll have control of our parents' money and he can dispose of us."

"How can he marry me for real?" Violet asked. "It's only a play."

"The only legal requirements of marriage in this community," Klaus explained, holding up *Nuptial Law* to show his sister where he'd learned the information, "are your saying 'I do,' and signing a document in your own hand in the presence of a judge—like Justice Strauss!"

"But surely I'm not old enough to get married," Violet said. "I'm only fourteen."

"Girls under the age of eighteen," Klaus said, flipping to another part of the book, "can marry if they have the permission of their legal guardian. That's Count Olaf."

"Oh no!" Violet cried. "What can we do?"

"We can show this to Mr. Poe," Klaus said, pointing to the book, "and he will finally believe us that Count Olaf is up to no good. Quick, get dressed while I wake up Sunny, and we can be at the bank by the time it opens."

Violet, who usually moved slowly in the mornings, nodded and immediately got out of bed and went to the cardboard box to find some proper clothing. Klaus walked over to the lump of curtains to wake up his younger sister.

"Sunny," he called out kindly, putting his hand on where he thought his sister's head was. "Sunny."

There was no answer. Klaus called out "Sunny" again, and pulled away the top fold of the curtains to wake up the youngest Baudelaire child. "Sunny," he said, but then he stopped. For underneath the curtain was nothing but another curtain. He moved aside all the layers, but his little sister was nowhere to be found. "*Sunny!*" he yelled, looking around the room. Violet dropped the dress she was holding and began to help him search. They looked in every corner, under the bed, and even inside the cardboard box. But Sunny was gone.

"Where can she be?" Violet asked worriedly. "She's not the type to run off."

"Where can she be indeed?" said a voice behind them, and the two children turned around. Count Olaf was standing in the doorway, watching Violet and Klaus as they searched the room. His eyes were shining brighter than they ever had, and he was still smiling like he'd just uttered a joke.

"*Yes,*" Count Olaf continued, "it certainly is strange to find a child missing. And one so small, and helpless."

"Where's Sunny?" Violet cried. "What have you done with her?"

Count Olaf continued to speak as if he had not heard Violet. "But then again, one sees strange things every day. In fact, if you two orphans follow me out to the backyard, I think we will all see something rather unusual."

The Baudelaire children didn't say anything, but followed Count Olaf through the house and out the back door. Violet looked around the small, scraggly yard, in which she had not been since she and Klaus had been forced to chop wood. The pile of logs they had made was still lying there untouched, as if Count Olaf had merely made them chop logs for his own amusement, rather than for any purpose. Violet shivered, still in her nightgown, but as she gazed here and there she saw nothing unusual.

"You're not looking in the right place," Count Olaf said. "For children who read so much, you two are remarkably unintelligent."

Violet looked over in the direction of Count Olaf, but could not meet his eyes. The eyes on his face, that is. She was staring at his feet, and could see the tattooed eye that had been watching the Baudelaire orphans since their troubles had begun. Then her eyes traveled up Count Olaf's lean, shabbily dressed body, and she saw that he was pointing up with one scrawny hand. She followed his gesture and found herself looking at the forbidden tower. It was made of dirty stone, with only one lone window, and just barely visible in the window was what looked like a birdcage.

"Oh no," Klaus said in a small, scared voice, and Violet looked again. It *was* a birdcage, dangling from the tower window like a flag in the wind, but inside the birdcage she could see a small and frightened Sunny. When Violet looked closely, she could see there was a large piece of tape across her sister's mouth, and ropes around her body. She was utterly trapped.

"Let her go!" Violet said to Count Olaf. "She has done nothing to you! She is an *infant*!"

"Well, now," Count Olaf said, sitting on a stump. "If you really want me to let her go, I will. But surely even a stupid brat like you might realize that if I let her go—or, more accurately, if I ask my comrade to let her go—poor little Sunny might not survive the fall down to

the ground. That's a thirty-foot tower, which is a very long way for a very little person to fall, even when she's inside a cage. But if you insist—"

"*No!*" Klaus cried. "*Don't!*"

Violet looked into Count Olaf's eyes, and then at the small parcel that was her sister, hanging from the top of the tower and moving slowly in the breeze. She pictured Sunny toppling from the tower and onto the ground, pictured her sister's last thoughts being ones of sheer terror. "*Please,*" she said to Olaf, feeling tears in her eyes. "She's just a baby. We'll do *anything, anything.* Just don't harm her."

"*Anything?*" Count Olaf asked, his eyebrow rising. He leaned in toward Violet and gazed into her eyes. "*Anything?* Would you, for instance, consider marrying me during tomorrow night's performance?"

Violet stared at him. She had an odd feeling in her stomach, as if *she* were the one being thrown from a great height. The really frightening thing about Olaf, she realized, was that he was very smart after all. He wasn't merely an unsavory drunken brute, but an unsavory, *clever* drunken brute.

"While you were busy reading books and making accusations," Count Olaf said, "I had one of my quietest, sneakiest assistants skulk into your bedroom and steal little Sunny away. She is perfectly safe, for now. But I consider her to be a stick behind a stubborn mule."

"Our sister is not a stick," Klaus said.

"A stubborn mule," Count Olaf explained, "does not move in the direction its owner wants it to. In that way, it is like you children, who insist on mucking up my plans. Any animal owner will tell you that a stubborn mule will move in the proper direction if there is a carrot in front of it, and a stick behind it. It will move toward the carrot, because it wants the reward of food, and away from the stick, because it does not want the punishment of pain. Likewise, you will do what I say, to avoid the punishment of the loss of your sister, and because you want the reward of surviving this experience. Now, Violet, let me ask you again: *will* you marry me?"

Violet swallowed, and looked down at Count Olaf's tattoo. She could not bring herself to answer.

"Come now," Count Olaf said, his voice faking—a word which here means "feigning"— kindness. He reached out a hand and stroked Violet's hair. "Would it be so terrible to be my bride, to live in my house for the rest of your life? You're such a lovely girl, after the marriage I wouldn't dispose of you like your brother and sister."

Violet imagined sleeping beside Count Olaf, and waking up each morning to look at this terrible man. She pictured wandering around the house, trying to avoid him all day, and cooking for his terrible friends at night, perhaps every night, for the rest of her life. But then she looked up at her helpless sister and knew what her answer must be. "If you let Sunny go," she said finally, "I will marry you."

"I will let Sunny go," Count Olaf answered, "after tomorrow night's performance. In the meantime, she will remain in the tower for safe-keeping. And, as a warning, I will tell you that my assistants will stand guard at the door to the tower staircase, in case you were getting any ideas."

"You're a terrible man," Klaus spat out, but Count Olaf merely smiled again.

"I may be a terrible man," Count Olaf said, "but I have been able to concoct a foolproof way of getting your fortune, which is more than you've been able to do." With that, he began to stride toward the house. "Remember that, orphans," he said. "You may have read more books than I have, but it didn't help you gain the upper hand in this situation. Now, give me that book which gave you such grand ideas, and do the chores assigned to you."

Klaus sighed, and relinquished—a word which here means "gave to Count Olaf even though he didn't want to"—the book on nuptial law. He began to follow Count Olaf into the house, but Violet stayed still as a statue. She hadn't been listening to that last speech of Count Olaf's, knowing it would be full of the usual self-congratulatory nonsense and despicable insults. She was staring at the tower, not at the top, where her sister was dangling, but the whole length of it. Klaus looked back at her and saw something he hadn't seen in quite some time. To those who hadn't been around Violet long, nothing would have seemed unusual, but those who knew her well knew that when she tied her hair up in a ribbon to keep it out of her eyes, it meant that the gears and levers of her inventing brain were whirring at top speed.

That night, Klaus was the Baudelaire orphan sleeping fitfully in the bed, and Violet was the Baudelaire orphan staying up, working by the light of the moon. All day, the two siblings had wandered around the house, doing the assigned chores and scarcely speaking to each other. Klaus was too tired and despondent to speak, and Violet was holed up in the inventing area of her mind, too busy planning to talk.

When night approached, Violet gathered up the curtains that had been Sunny's bed and brought them to the door to the tower stairs, where the enormous assistant of Count Olaf's, the one who looked like neither a man nor a woman, was standing guard. Violet asked whether she could bring the blankets to her sister, to make her more comfortable during the night. The enormous creature merely looked at Violet with its blank white eyes and shook its head, then dismissed her with a silent gesture.

Violet knew, of course, that Sunny was too terrified to be comforted by a handful of draperies, but she hoped that she would be allowed a few moments to hold her and tell her that everything would turn out all right. Also, she wanted to do something known in the crime industry as "casing the joint." "Casing the joint" means observing a particular location in order to formulate a plan. For instance, if you are a bank robber—although I hope you aren't—you might go to the bank a few days before you planned to rob it. Perhaps wearing a disguise, you would look around the bank and observe security guards, cameras, and other obstacles, so you could plan how to avoid capture or death during your burglary.

Violet, a law-abiding citizen, was not planning to rob a bank, but she was planning to rescue Sunny, and was hoping to catch a glimpse of the tower room in which her sister was being held prisoner, so as to make her plan more easily. But it appeared that she wasn't going to be able to case the joint after all. This made Violet nervous as she sat on the floor by the window, working on her invention as quietly as she could.

Violet had very few materials with which to invent something, and she didn't want to wander around the house looking for more for fear of arousing the suspicions of Count Olaf and his troupe. But she had enough to build a rescuing device. Above the window was a sturdy metal rod from which the curtains had hung, and

Violet took it down. Using one of the rocks Olaf had left in a pile in the corner, she broke the curtain rod into two pieces. She then bent each piece of the rod into several sharp angles, leaving tiny cuts on her hands as she did so. Then Violet took down the painting of the eye. On the back of the painting, as on the back of many paintings, was a small piece of wire to hang on the hook. She removed the wire and used it to connect the two pieces together. Violet had now made what looked like a large metal spider.

She then went over to the cardboard box and took out the ugliest of the clothes that Mrs. Poe had purchased, the outfits the Baudelaire orphans would never wear no matter how desperate they were. Working quickly and quietly, she began to tear these into long, narrow strips, and to tie these strips together. Among Violet's many useful skills was a vast knowledge of different types of knots. The particular knot she was using was called the Devil's Tongue. A group of female Finnish pirates invented it back in the fifteenth century, and named it the Devil's Tongue because it twisted this way and that, in a most complicated and eerie way. The Devil's Tongue was a very useful knot, and when Violet tied the cloth strips together, end to end, it formed a sort of rope. As she worked, she re-membered something her parents had said to her when Klaus was born, and again when they brought Sunny home from the hospital. "You are the eldest Baudelaire child," they had said, kindly but firmly. "And as the eldest, it will always be your responsibility to look after your younger siblings. Promise us that you will always watch out for them and make sure they don't get into trouble." Violet remembered her promise, and thought of Klaus, whose bruised face still looked sore, and Sunny, dangling from the top of the tower like a flag, and began working faster. Even though Count Olaf was of course the cause of all this misery, Violet felt as if she had broken her promise to her parents, and vowed to make it right.

Eventually, using enough of the ugly clothing, Violet had a rope that was, she hoped, just over thirty feet long. She tied one end of it to the metal spider, and looked at her handiwork. What she had made was called a grappling hook, which is something used for climbing up the sides of buildings, usually for a nefarious purpose. Using the metal end to hook onto something at the top of the tower, and the rope to aid her climb, Violet hoped to reach the top of the tower, untie Sunny's cage, and climb back down. This was, of course, a very risky plan, both because it was dangerous, and because she had made the grappling hook herself, instead of purchasing it at a store that sold such things. But a grappling hook was all Violet could think of to make without a proper inventing laboratory, and time was running short. She hadn't told Klaus about her plan, because she didn't want to give him false hope, so without waking him, she gathered up her grappling hook and tiptoed out of the room.

Once outside, Violet realized her plan was even more difficult than she had thought. The night was quiet, which would mean she would have to make practically no noise at all. The night also had a slight breeze, and when she pictured herself swinging in the breeze, clinging to a rope made of ugly clothing, she almost gave up entirely. And the night was dark, so it was hard to see where she could toss the grappling hook and have the metal arms hook onto something. But, standing there shivering in her nightgown, Violet knew she had to try. Using her right hand, she threw the grappling hook as high and as hard as she could, and waited to see if it would catch onto something.

Clang! The hook made a loud noise as it hit the tower, but it didn't stick to anything, and came crashing back down. Her heart pounding, Violet stood stock-still, wondering if Count Olaf or one of his accomplices would come and investigate. But nobody arrived after a few moments, and Violet, swinging the hook over her head like a lasso, tried again.

Clang! Clang! The grappling hook hit the tower twice as it bounced back down to the ground. Violet waited again, listening for footsteps, but all she heard was her own terrified pulse. She decided to try one more time.

Clang! The grappling hook hit the tower, and fell down again, hitting Violet hard in the shoulder. One of the arms tore her nightgown and cut through her skin. Biting down on her hand to keep from crying out in pain, Violet felt the place in her shoulder where she had been struck, and it was wet with blood. Her arm throbbed in pain.

At this point in the proceedings, if I were Violet, I would have given up, but just as she was about to turn around and go inside the house, she pictured how scared Sunny must be, and, ignoring the pain in her shoulder, Violet used her right hand to throw the hook again.

Cla— The usual *clang!* sound stopped halfway through, and Violet saw in the dim light of the moon that the hook wasn't falling. Nervously, she gave the rope a good yank, and it stayed put. The grappling hook had worked!

Her feet touching the side of the stone tower and her hands grasping the rope, Violet closed her eyes and began to climb. Never daring to look around, she pulled herself up the tower, hand over hand, all the time keeping in mind her promise to her parents and the horrible things Count Olaf would do if his villainous plan worked. The evening wind blew harder and harder as she climbed higher and higher, and several times Violet had to stop climbing as the rope moved in the wind. She was certain that at any moment the cloth would tear, or the hook would slip, and Violet would be sent tumbling to her death. But thanks to her adroit inventing skills—the word "adroit" here means "skillful"— everything worked the way it was supposed to work, and suddenly Violet found herself feeling a piece of metal instead of a cloth rope. She opened her eyes and saw her sister Sunny, who was looking at her frantically and trying to say something past the strip of tape. Violet had arrived at the top of the tower, right at the window where Sunny was tied.

The eldest Baudelaire orphan was about to grab her sister's cage and begin her descent when she saw something that made her stop. It was the spidery end of the grappling hook, which after several attempts had finally stuck onto something on the tower. Violet had guessed, during her climb, that it had found some notch in the stone, or part of the window, or perhaps a piece of furniture inside the tower room, and stuck there. But that wasn't what the hook had stuck on. Violet's grappling hook had stuck on another hook. It was one of the hooks on the hook-handed man. And his other hook, Violet saw, was glinting in the moonlight as it reached right toward her.

Eleven

"*How* pleasant that you could join us," the hook-handed man said in a sickly sweet voice. Violet immediately tried to scurry back down the rope, but Count Olaf's assistant was too quick for her. In one movement he hoisted her into the tower room and, with a flick of his hook, sent her rescue device clanging to the ground. Now Violet was as trapped as her sister. "I'm so glad you're here," the hook-handed man

said. "I was just thinking how much I wanted to see your pretty face. Have a seat."

"What are you going to do with me?" Violet asked.

"I said *have a seat!*" the hook-handed man snarled, and pushed her into a chair.

Violet looked around the dim and messy room. I am certain that over the course of your own life, you have noticed that people's rooms reflect their personalities. In my room, for instance, I have gathered a collection of objects that are important to me, including a dusty accordion on which I can play a few sad songs, a large bundle of notes on the activities of the Baudelaire orphans, and a blurry photograph, taken a very long time ago, of a woman whose name is Beatrice. These are items that are very precious and dear to me. The tower room held objects that were very dear and precious to Count Olaf, and they were terrible things. There were scraps of paper on which he had written his evil ideas in an illegible scrawl, lying

in messy piles on top of the copy of *Nuptial Law*
he had taken away from Klaus. There were a
few chairs and a handful of candles which were
giving off flickering shadows. Littered all over
the floor were empty wine bottles and dirty
dishes. But most of all were the drawings and
paintings and carvings of eyes, big and small, all
over the room. There were eyes painted on the
ceilings, and scratched into the grimy wooden
floors. There were eyes scrawled along the win-
dowsill, and one big eye painted on the knob of
the door that led to the stairs. It was a terrible
place.

The hook-handed man reached into a pocket
of his greasy overcoat and pulled out a walkie-
talkie. With some difficulty, he pressed a button
and waited a moment. "Boss, it's me," he said.
"Your blushing bride just climbed up here to try
and rescue the biting brat." He paused as Count
Olaf said something. "I don't know. With some
sort of rope."

"It was a grappling hook," Violet said, and

tore off a sleeve of her nightgown to make a bandage for her shoulder. "I made it myself."

"She says it was a grappling hook," the hook-handed man said into the walkie-talkie. "I don't know, boss. Yes, boss. Yes, boss, of course I understand she's *yours*. Yes, boss." He pressed a button to disconnect the line, and then turned to face Violet. "Count Olaf is very displeased with his bride."

"I'm not his bride," Violet said bitterly.

"Very soon you will be," the hook-handed man said, wagging his hook the way most people would wag a finger. "In the meantime, however, I have to go and fetch your brother. The three of you will be locked in this room until night falls. That way, Count Olaf can be sure you will all stay out of mischief." With that, the hook-handed man stomped out of the room. Violet heard the door lock behind him, and then listened to his footsteps fading away down the stairs. She immediately went over to Sunny, and put a hand on her little head. Afraid to untie or untape her sister for fear of incurring—a word which here means "bringing about"—Count Olaf's wrath, Violet stroked Sunny's hair and murmured that everything was all right.

But of course, everything was *not* all right. Everything was all wrong. As the first light of morning trickled into the tower room, Violet reflected on all the awful things she and her siblings had experienced recently. Their parents had died, suddenly and horribly. Mrs. Poe had bought them ugly clothing. They had moved into Count Olaf's house and were treated terribly. Mr. Poe had refused to help them. They had discovered a fiendish plot involving marrying Violet and stealing the Baudelaire fortune. Klaus had tried to confront Olaf with knowledge he'd learned in Justice Strauss's library and failed. Poor Sunny had been captured. And now, Violet had tried to rescue Sunny and found herself captured as well. All in all, the Baudelaire orphans had encountered catastrophe after catastrophe, and Violet found their situation lamentably deplorable, a phrase which here means "it was not at all enjoyable."

The sound of footsteps coming up the stairs brought Violet out of her thoughts, and soon the hook-handed man opened the door and thrust a very tired, confused, and scared Klaus into the room.

"Here's the last orphan," the hook-handed man said. "And now, I must go help Count Olaf with final preparations for tonight's performance. No monkey business, you two, or I will have to tie you up and let you dangle out of the window as well." Glaring at them, he locked the door again and tromped downstairs.

Klaus blinked and looked around the filthy room. He was still in his pajamas. "What has happened?" he asked Violet. "Why are we up here?"

"I tried to rescue Sunny," Violet said, "using an invention of mine to climb up the tower."

Klaus went over to the window and looked down at the ground. "It's so high up," he said.

"You must have been terrified."

"It was very scary," she admitted, "but not as scary as the thought of marrying Count Olaf."

"I'm sorry your invention didn't work," Klaus said sadly.

"The invention worked fine," Violet said, rubbing her sore shoulder. "I just got caught. And now we're doomed. The hook-handed man said he'd keep us here until tonight, and then it's *The Marvelous Marriage.*"

"Do you think you could invent something that would help us escape?" Klaus asked, looking around the room.

"Maybe," Violet said. "And why don't you go through those books and papers? Perhaps there's some information that could be of use."

For the next few hours, Violet and Klaus searched the room and their own minds for anything that might help them. Violet looked for objects with which she could invent something. Klaus read through Count Olaf's papers and books. From time to time, they would go over to Sunny and smile at her, and pat her head, to reassure her. Occasionally, Violet and Klaus would speak to each other, but mostly they were silent, lost in their own thoughts.

"If we had any kerosene," Violet said, around noon, "I could make Molotov cocktails with these bottles."

"What are Molotov cocktails?" Klaus asked.

"They're small bombs made inside bottles," Violet explained. "We could throw them out the window and attract the attention of passersby."

"But we don't have any kerosene," Klaus said mournfully.

They were silent for several hours.

"If we were polygamists," Klaus said, "Count Olaf's marriage plan wouldn't work."

"What are polygamists?" Violet asked.

"Polygamists are people who marry more than one person,'" Klaus explained. "In this community, polygamists are breaking the law, even if they have married in the presence of a judge, with the statement of 'I do' and the signed document in their own hand. I read it here in *Nuptial Law*."

"But we're not polygamists," Violet said mournfully.

They were silent for several *more* hours.

"We could break these bottles in half," Violet said, "and use them as knives, but I'm afraid that Count Olaf's troupe would overpower us."

"You could say 'I don't' instead of 'I do,'" Klaus said, "but I'm afraid Count Olaf would order Sunny dropped off the tower."

"I certainly would," Count Olaf said, and the children jumped. They had been so involved in their conversation that they hadn't heard him come up the stairs and open the door. He was wearing a fancy suit and his eyebrow had been waxed so it looked as shiny as his eyes. Behind him stood the hook-handed man, who smiled and waved a hook at the youngsters. "Come, orphans," Count Olaf said. "It is time for the big event. My associate here will stay behind in this room, and we will keep in constant contact through our walkie-talkies. If *anything* goes wrong during tonight's performance, your sister will be dropped to her death. Come along now."

Violet and Klaus looked at each other, and then at Sunny, still dangling in her cage, and followed Count Olaf out the door. As Klaus walked down the tower stairs, he felt a heavy sinking in his heart as all hope left him. There truly seemed to be no way out of their predicament. Violet was feeling the same way, until she reached out with her right hand to grasp the banister, for balance. She looked at her right hand for a second, and began to think. All the way down the stairs, and out the door, and the short walk down the block to the theater, Violet thought and thought and thought, harder than she had in her entire life.

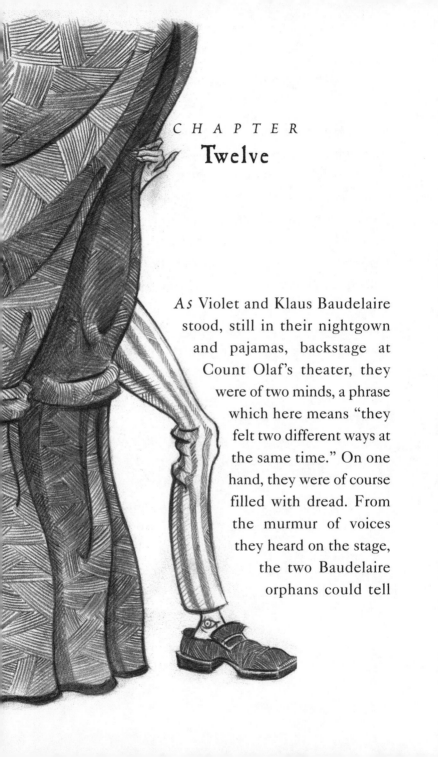

CHAPTER

Twelve

As Violet and Klaus Baudelaire stood, still in their nightgown and pajamas, backstage at Count Olaf's theater, they were of two minds, a phrase which here means "they felt two different ways at the same time." On one hand, they were of course filled with dread. From the murmur of voices they heard on the stage, the two Baudelaire orphans could tell that the performance of *The Marvelous Marriage* had begun, and it seemed too late to do anything to foil Count Olaf's plan. On the other hand, however, they were fascinated, as they had never been backstage at a theatrical production and there was so much to see. Members of Count Olaf's theater troupe hurried this way and that, too busy to even glance at the children. Three very short men were carrying a large flat piece of wood, painted to look like a living room. The two white-faced women were arranging flowers in a vase that from far away appeared to be marble, but close up looked more like cardboard. An important-looking man with warts all over his face was adjusting enormous light fixtures. As the children peeked onstage, they could see Count Olaf, in his fancy suit, declaiming some lines from the play, just as the curtain came down, controlled by a woman with very short hair who was pulling on a long rope, attached to a pulley. Despite their fear, you see, the two older Baudelaires were very interested in what was going on, and only wished that they were not involved in any way.

As the curtain fell, Count Olaf strode offstage and looked at the children. "It's the end of Act Two! Why aren't the orphans in their costumes?" he hissed to the two white-faced women. Then, as the audience broke into applause, his angry expression turned to one of joy, and he walked back onstage. Gesturing to the short-haired woman to raise the curtain, he strode to the exact center of the stage and took elaborate bows as the curtain came up. He waved and blew kisses to the audience as the curtain came down again, and then his face once again filled with anger. "Intermission is only ten minutes," he said, "and then the children must perform. Get them into costumes, quickly!"

Without a word the two white-faced women grabbed Violet and Klaus by the wrists and led them into a dressing room. The room was dusty but shiny, covered in mirrors and tiny lights so the actors could see better to put on their

makeup and wigs, and there were people calling out to one another and laughing as they
changed their clothes. One white-faced woman
yanked Violet's arms up and pulled her nightgown off over her head, and thrust a dirty, lacy
white dress at her to put on. Klaus, meanwhile,
had his pajamas removed by the other white-
faced woman, and was hurriedly stuffed into a
blue sailor suit that itched and made him look
like a toddler.

"Isn't this exciting?" said a voice, and the
children turned to see Justice Strauss, all
dressed up in her judge's robes and powdered
wig. She was clutching a small book. "You children look wonderful!"

"So do you," Klaus said. "What's that book?"

"Why, those are my lines," Justice Strauss
said. "Count Olaf told me to bring a law book
and read the real wedding ceremony, in order to
make the play as realistic as possible. All *you*
have to say, Violet, is 'I do,' but I have to make

quite a speech. This is going to be such fun."

"You know what would be fun," Violet said carefully, "is if you changed your lines around, just a little."

Klaus's face lit up. "Yes, Justice Strauss. Be creative. There's no reason to stick to the legal ceremony. It's not as if it's a real wedding."

Justice Strauss frowned. "I don't know about that, children," she said. "I think it would be best to follow Count Olaf's instructions. After all, he's in charge."

"Justice Strauss!" a voice called. "Justice Strauss! Please report to the makeup artist!"

"Oh my word! I get to wear makeup." Justice Strauss had on a dreamy expression, as if she were about to be crowned queen, instead of just having some powders and creams smeared on her face. "Children, I must go. See you onstage, my dears!"

Justice Strauss ran off, leaving the children to finish changing into their costumes. One of the white-faced women put a flowered headdress on Violet, who realized in horror that the dress she had changed into was a bridal gown. The other woman put a sailor cap on Klaus, who gazed in one of the mirrors, astonished at how ugly he looked. His eyes met those of Violet, who was looking in the mirror as well.

"What can we do?" Klaus said quietly. "Pretend to be sick? Maybe they'd call off the performance."

"Count Olaf would know what we were up to," Violet replied glumly.

"Act Three of *The Marvelous Marriage* by Al Funcoot is about to begin!" a man with a clipboard shouted. "Everyone, please, get in your places for Act Three!"

The actors rushed out of the room, and the white-faced women grabbed the children and hustled them out after them. The backstage area was in complete pandemonium—a word which here means "actors and stagehands running around attending to last-minute details." The bald man with the long nose hurried by the children, then stopped himself, looked at Violet in her wedding dress, and smirked.

"No funny stuff," he said to them, waggling a bony finger. "Remember, when you go out there, just do exactly what you're supposed to do. Count Olaf will be holding his walkie-talkie during the entire act, and if you do even *one thing* wrong, he'll be giving Sunny a call up there in the tower."

"Yes, yes," Klaus said bitterly. He was tired of being threatened in the same way, over and over.

"You'd better do exactly as planned," the man said again.

"I'm sure they will," said a voice suddenly, and the children turned to see Mr. Poe, dressed very formally and accompanied by his wife. He smiled at the children and came over to shake their hands. "Polly and I just wanted to tell you to break a leg."

"What?" Klaus said, alarmed.

"That's a theater term," Mr. Poe explained, "meaning 'good luck on tonight's performance.' I'm glad that you children have adjusted to life with your new father and are participating in family activities."

"Mr. Poe," Klaus said quickly, "Violet and I have something to tell you. It's very important."

"What is it?" Mr. Poe said.

"Yes," said Count Olaf, "what is it you have to tell Mr. Poe, children?"

Count Olaf had appeared, seemingly out of nowhere, and his shiny eyes glared at the children meaningfully. In one hand, Violet and Klaus could see, he held a walkie-talkie.

"Just that we appreciate all you've done for us, Mr. Poe," Klaus said weakly. "That's all we wanted to say."

"Of course, of course," Mr. Poe said, patting him on the back. "Well, Polly and I had better take our seats. Break a leg, Baudelaires!"

"I wish we *could* break a leg," Klaus whispered to Violet, and Mr. Poe left.

"You will, soon enough," Count Olaf said, pushing the two children toward the stage. Other actors were milling about, finding their places for Act Three, and Justice Strauss was off in a corner, practicing her lines from her law book. Klaus took a look around the stage, wondering if anyone there could help. The bald man with the long nose took Klaus's hand and led him to one side.

"You and I will stand *here* for the duration of the act. That means the whole thing."

"I *know* what the word 'duration' means," Klaus said.

"No nonsense," the bald man said. Klaus watched his sister in her wedding gown take her place next to Count Olaf as the curtain rose. Klaus heard applause from the audience as Act Three of *The Marvelous Marriage* began.

It will be of no interest to you if I describe the action of this insipid—the word "insipid" here means "dull and foolish"—play by Al Funcoot, because it was a dreadful play and of no real importance to our story. Various actors and actresses performed very dull dialogue and moved around the set, as Klaus tried to make eye contact with them and see if they would help. He soon realized that this play must have been chosen merely as an excuse for Olaf's evil plan, and not for its entertainment value, as he sensed the audience losing interest and moving around in their seats. Klaus turned his attention to the audience to see whether any of them would notice that something was afoot, but the way the wart-faced man had arranged the lights prevented Klaus from seeing the faces in the auditorium, and he could only make out the dim outlines of the people in the audience. Count Olaf had a great number of very long speeches, which he performed with elaborate gestures and facial expressions. No one seemed to notice that he held a walkie-talkie the entire time.

Finally, Justice Strauss began speaking, and Klaus saw that she was reading directly from the legal book. Her eyes were sparkling and her face flushed as she performed onstage for the first time, too stagestruck to realize she was a part of Olaf's plan. She spoke on and on about Olaf and Violet caring for each other in sickness and in health, in good times and bad, and all of those things that are said to many people who decide, for one reason or another, to get married.

When she finished her speech, Justice Strauss turned to Count Olaf and asked, "Do you take this woman to be your lawfully wedded wife?"

"I do," Count Olaf said, smiling. Klaus saw Violet shudder.

"Do *you*," Justice Strauss said, turning to Violet, "take this man to be your lawfully wedded husband?"

"I do," Violet said. Klaus clenched his fists. His sister had said "I do" in the presence of a judge. Once she signed the official document, the wedding was legally valid. And now, Klaus could see that Justice Strauss was taking the document from one of the other actors and holding it out to Violet to sign.

"Don't move an inch," the bald man muttered to Klaus, and Klaus thought of poor Sunny, dangling at the top of the tower, and stood still as he watched Violet take a long quill pen from Count Olaf. Violet's eyes were wide as she looked down at the document, and her face was pale, and her left hand was trembling as she signed her name.

Thirteen

"*And* now, ladies and gentlemen," Count Olaf said, stepping forward to address the audience, "I have an announcement. There is no reason to continue tonight's performance, for its purpose has been served. This has not been a scene of fiction. My marriage to Violet Baudelaire is perfectly legal, and now I am in control of her entire fortune."

There were gasps from the audience, and some of the actors looked at one another in shock. Not everyone, apparently, had known about Olaf's plan. "That can't be!" Justice Strauss cried.

"The marriage laws in this community are quite simple," Count Olaf said. "The bride must say 'I do' in the presence of a judge like yourself, and sign an explanatory document. And all of you"—here Count Olaf gestured out to the audience—"are witnesses."

"But Violet is only a child!" one of the actors said. "She's not old enough to marry."

"She is if her legal guardian agrees," Count Olaf said, "and in addition to being her husband, I am her legal guardian."

"But that piece of paper is not an official document!" Justice Strauss said. "That's just a stage prop!"

Count Olaf took the paper from Violet's hand and gave it to Justice Strauss. "I think if you look at it closely you will see it is an official document from City Hall."

Justice Strauss took the document in her hand and read it quickly. Then, closing her eyes, she sighed deeply and furrowed her brow, thinking hard. Klaus watched her and wondered if this were the expression Justice Strauss had on her face whenever she was serving on the High Court. "You're right," she said finally, to Count Olaf, "this marriage, unfortunately, is completely legal. Violet said 'I do,' and signed her name here on this paper. Count Olaf, you are Violet's husband, and therefore in complete control of her estate."

"That can't be!" said a voice from the audience, and Klaus recognized it as the voice of Mr. Poe. He ran up the stairs to the stage and took the document from Justice Strauss. "This is dreadful nonsense."

"I'm afraid this dreadful nonsense is the law," Justice Strauss said. Her eyes were filling up with tears. "I can't believe how easily I was tricked," she said. "I would never do anything to harm you children. *Never.*"

"You *were* easily tricked," Count Olaf said, grinning, and the judge began to cry. "It was child's play, winning this fortune. Now, if all of you will excuse me, my bride and I need to go home for our wedding night."

"First let Sunny go!" Klaus burst out. "You promised to let her go!"

"Where is Sunny?" Mr. Poe asked.

"She's all tied up at the moment," Count Olaf said, "if you will pardon a little joke." His eyes shone as he pressed buttons on the walkie-talkie, and waited while the hook-handed man answered. "Hello? Yes, of course it's me, you idiot. Everything has gone according to plan. Please remove Sunny from her cage and bring her directly to the theater. Klaus and Sunny have some chores to do before they go to bed." Count Olaf gave Klaus a sharp look. "Are you satisfied now?" he asked.

"Yes," Klaus said quietly. He wasn't satisfied at all, of course, but at least his baby sister was no longer dangling from a tower.

"Don't think you're so safe," the bald man whispered to Klaus. "Count Olaf will take care of you and your sisters later. He doesn't want to do it in front of all these people." He did not have to explain to Klaus what he meant by the phrase "take care of."

"Well, I'm not satisfied *at all*," Mr. Poe said. "This is absolutely horrendous. This is completely monstrous. This is financially dreadful."

"I'm afraid, however," Count Olaf said, "that it is legally binding. Tomorrow, Mr. Poe, I shall come down to the bank and withdraw the complete Baudelaire fortune."

Mr. Poe opened his mouth as if to say something, but began to cough instead. For several seconds he coughed into a handkerchief while everyone waited for him to speak. "I won't allow it," Mr. Poe finally gasped, wiping his mouth. "I absolutely will not allow it."

"I'm afraid you have to," Count Olaf replied.

"I'm—I'm afraid Olaf is right," Justice Strauss said, through her tears. "This marriage is legally binding."

"Begging your pardon," Violet said suddenly, "but I think you may be wrong."

Everyone turned to look at the eldest Baudelaire orphan.

"What did you say, Countess?" Olaf said.

"I'm *not* your countess," Violet said testily, a word which here means "in an extremely annoyed tone." "At least, I don't *think* I am."

"And why is that?" Count Olaf said.

"I did not sign the document in my own hand, as the law states," Violet said.

"What do you mean? We all saw you!" Count Olaf's eyebrow was beginning to rise in anger.

"I'm afraid your husband is right, dear," Justice Strauss said sadly. "There's no use denying it. There are too many witnesses."

"Like most people," Violet said, "I am right-handed. But I signed the document with my left hand."

"*What?*" Count Olaf cried. He snatched the paper from Justice Strauss and looked down at it. His eyes were shining very bright. "You are a *liar*!" he hissed at Violet.

"No she's not," Klaus said excitedly. "I remember, because I watched her left hand trembling as she signed her name."

"It is impossible to prove," Count Olaf said.

"If you like," Violet said, "I shall be happy to sign my name again, on a separate sheet of paper, with my right hand and then with my left. Then we can see which signature the one on the document most resembles."

"A small detail, like which hand you used to sign," Count Olaf said, "doesn't matter in the least."

"If you don't mind, sir," Mr. Poe said, "I'd like Justice Strauss to make that decision."

Everyone looked at Justice Strauss, who was

wiping away the last of her tears. "Let me see," she said quietly, and closed her eyes again. She sighed deeply, and the Baudelaire orphans, and all who liked them, held their breath as Justice Strauss furrowed her brow, thinking hard on the situation. Finally, she smiled. "If Violet is indeed right-handed," she said carefully, "and she signed the document with her left hand, then it follows that the signature does not fulfill the requirements of the nuptial laws. The law clearly states the document must be signed in the bride's *own hand*. Therefore, we can conclude that this marriage is invalid. Violet, you are *not* a countess, and Count Olaf, you are *not* in control of the Baudelaire fortune."

"Hooray!" cried a voice from the audience, and several people applauded. Unless you are a lawyer, it will probably strike you as odd that Count Olaf's plan was defeated by Violet signing with her left hand instead of her right. But the law is an odd thing. For instance, one country in Europe has a law that requires all its bakers to sell bread at the exact same price. A certain island has a law that forbids anyone from removing its fruit. And a town not too far from where you live has a law that bars me from coming within five miles of its borders. Had Violet signed the marriage contract with her right hand, the law would have made her a miserable contessa, but because she signed it with her left, she remained, to her relief, a miserable orphan.

What was good news to Violet and her siblings, of course, was bad news to Count Olaf. Nevertheless, he gave everyone a grim smile. "In that case," he said to Violet, pushing a button on the walkie-talkie, "you will either marry me again, and correctly this time, or I will—"

"Neepo!" Sunny's unmistakable voice rang out over Count Olaf's as she tottered onstage toward her siblings. The hook-handed man followed behind her, his walkie-talkie buzzing and crackling. Count Olaf was too late.

"Sunny! You're safe!" Klaus cried, and

embraced her. Violet rushed over and the two older Baudelaires fussed over the youngest one.

"Somebody bring her something to eat," Violet said. "She must be very hungry after hanging in a tower window all that time."

"Cake!" Sunny shrieked.

"Argh!" Count Olaf roared. He began to pace back and forth like an animal in a cage, pausing only to point a finger at Violet. "You may not be my wife," he said, "but you are still my daughter, and—"

"Do you honestly think," Mr. Poe said in an exasperated voice, "that I will allow you to continue to care for these three children, after the treachery I have seen here tonight?"

"The orphans are mine," Count Olaf insisted, "and with me they shall stay. There is nothing illegal about trying to marry someone."

"But there *is* something illegal about dangling an infant out of a tower window," Justice Strauss said indignantly. "You, Count Olaf, will go to jail, and the three children will live with me."

"Arrest him!" a voice said from the audience, and other people took up the cry.

"Send him to jail!"

"He's an evil man!"

"And give us our money back! It was a lousy play!"

Mr. Poe took Count Olaf's arm and, after a brief eruption of coughs, announced in a harsh voice, "I hereby arrest you in the name of the law."

"Oh, Justice Strauss!" Violet said. "Did you really mean what you said? Can we really live with you?"

"Of course I mean it," Justice Strauss said. "I am very fond of you children, and I feel responsible for your welfare."

"Can we use your library every day?" Klaus asked.

"Can we work in the garden?" Violet asked.

"Cake!" Sunny shrieked again, and everyone laughed.

At this point in the story, I feel obliged to interrupt and give you one last warning. As I said at the very beginning, the book you are holding in your hands does not have a happy ending. It may appear now that Count Olaf will go to jail and that the three Baudelaire youngsters will live happily ever after with Justice Strauss, but it is not so. If you like, you may shut the book this instant and not read the unhappy ending that is to follow. You may spend the rest of your life believing that the Baudelaires triumphed over Count Olaf and lived the rest of their lives in the house and library of Justice Strauss, but that is not how the story goes. For as everyone was laughing at Sunny's cry for cake, the important-looking man with all the warts on his face was sneaking toward the controls for the lighting of the theater.

Quick as a wink, the man flicked the main switch so that all the lights went off and every-

one was standing in darkness. Instantly, pandemonium ensued as everyone ran this way and
that, shouting at one another. Actors tripped
over members of the audience. Members of the
audience tripped over theatrical props. Mr. Poe
grabbed his wife, thinking it was Count Olaf.
Klaus grabbed Sunny and held her up as high
as he could, so she wouldn't get hurt. But Violet
knew at once what had happened, and made her
way carefully to where she remembered the
lights had been. When the play was being performed, Violet had watched the light controls
carefully, taking mental notes in case these
devices came in handy for an invention. She was
certain if she could find the switch she could
turn it back on. Her arms stretched in front of
her as if she were blind, Violet made her way
across the stage, stepping carefully around
pieces of furniture and startled actors. In the
darkness, Violet looked like a ghost, her white
wedding gown moving slowly across the stage.
Then, just as she had reached the switch, Violet

felt a hand on her shoulder. A figure leaned in to whisper into her ear.

"I'll get my hands on your fortune if it's the last thing I do," the voice hissed. "And when I have it, I'll kill you and your siblings with my own two hands."

Violet gave a little cry of terror, but flicked the switch on. The entire theater was flooded with light. Everyone blinked and looked around. Mr. Poe let go of his wife. Klaus put Sunny down. But nobody was touching Violet's shoulder. Count Olaf was gone.

"Where did he go?" Mr. Poe shouted. "Where did they *all* go?"

The Baudelaire youngsters looked around and saw that not only had Count Olaf vanished, but his accomplices—the wart-faced man, the hook-handed man, the bald man with the long nose, the enormous person who looked like neither a man nor a woman, and the two white-faced women—had vanished along with him.

"They must have run outside," Klaus said, "while it was still dark."

Mr. Poe led the way outside, and Justice Strauss and the children followed. Way, way down the block, they could see a long black car driving away into the night. Maybe it contained Count Olaf and his associates. Maybe it didn't. But in any case, it turned a corner and disappeared into the dark city as the children watched without a word.

"Blast it," Mr. Poe said. "They're gone. But don't worry, children, we'll catch them. I'm going to go call the police immediately."

Violet, Klaus, and Sunny looked at one another and knew that it wasn't as simple as Mr. Poe said. Count Olaf would take care to stay out of sight as he planned his next move. He was far too clever to be captured by the likes of Mr. Poe.

"Well, let's go home, children," Justice Strauss said. "We can worry about this in the morning, when I've fixed you a good breakfast."

Mr. Poe coughed. "Wait a minute," he said,

looking down at the floor. "I'm sorry to tell you this, children, but I cannot allow you to be raised by someone who is not a relative."

"What?" Violet cried. "After all Justice Strauss has done for us?"

"We never would have figured out Count Olaf's plan without her and her library," Klaus said. "Without Justice Strauss, we would have lost our lives."

"That may be so," Mr. Poe said, "and I thank Justice Strauss for her generosity, but your parents' will is very specific. You must be adopted by a relative. Tonight you will stay with me in my home, and tomorrow I shall go to the bank and figure out what to do with you. I'm sorry, but that is the way it is."

The children looked at Justice Strauss, who sighed heavily and hugged each of the Baudelaire youngsters in turn. "Mr. Poe is right," she said sadly. "He must respect your parents' wishes. Don't you want to do what your parents wanted, children?"

Violet, Klaus, and Sunny pictured their loving parents, and wished more than ever that the fire had not occurred. Never, never had they felt so alone. They wanted very badly to live with this kind and generous woman, but they knew that it simply could not be done. "I guess you're right, Justice Strauss," Violet said finally. "We will miss you very much."

"I will miss you, too," she said, and her eyes filled with tears once more. Then they each gave Justice Strauss one last embrace, and followed Mr. and Mrs. Poe to their car. The Baudelaire orphans piled into the backseat, and peered out the back window at Justice Strauss, who was crying and waving to them. Ahead of them were the darkened streets, where Count Olaf had escaped to plan more treachery. Behind them was the kind judge, who had taken such an interest in the three children. To Violet, Klaus, and Sunny, it seemed that Mr. Poe and the law had made the incorrect decision to take them away from the possibility of a happy life with Justice Strauss and toward an unknown fate with some unknown relative. They didn't understand it, but like so many unfortunate events in life, just because you don't understand it doesn't mean it isn't so. The Baudelaires bunched up together against the cold night air, and kept waving out the back window. The car drove farther and farther away, until Justice Strauss was merely a speck in the darkness, and it seemed to the children that they were moving in an aberrant—the word "aberrant" here means "very, very wrong, and causing much grief"—direction.

To My Kind Editor,

I am writing to you from the London branch of the Herpetological Society, where I am trying to find out what happened to the reptile collection of Dr. Montgomery Montgomery following the tragic events that occurred while the Baudelaire orphans were in his care.

An associate of mine will place a small waterproof box in the phone booth of the Elektra Hotel at 11 P.M. next Tuesday. Please retrieve it before midnight to avoid it falling into the wrong hands. In the box you will find my description of these terrible events, entitled THE REPTILE ROOM, as well as a map of Lousy Lane, a copy of the film *Zombies in the Snow*, and Dr. Montgomery's recipe for coconut cream cake. I have also managed to track down one of the few photographs of Dr. Lucafont, in order to help Mr. Helquist with his illustrations.

Remember, you are my last hope that the tales of the Baudelaire orphans can finally be told to the general public.

With all due respect,

Lemony Snicket

Lemony Snicket

THE REPTILE ROOM

For Beatrice—
My love for you shall live forever.
You, however, did not.

The stretch of road that leads out of the city, past Hazy Harbor and into the town of Tedia, is perhaps the most unpleasant in the world. It is called Lousy Lane. Lousy Lane runs through fields that are a sickly gray color, in which a handful of scraggly trees produce apples so sour that one only has to look at them to feel ill. Lousy Lane traverses the Grim River, a body of water that is nine-tenths mud and that contains extremely unnerving fish, and it encircles a horseradish factory, so the entire area smells bitter and strong.

I am sorry to tell you that this story begins with the Baudelaire orphans traveling along this most displeasing road, and that from this moment on, the story only gets worse. Of all the people in the world who have miserable lives—and, as I'm sure you know, there are quite a few—the Baudelaire youngsters take the cake, a phrase which here means that more horrible things have happened to them than just about anybody. Their misfortune began with an enormous fire that destroyed their home and killed both their loving parents, which is enough sadness to last anyone a lifetime, but in the case of these three children it was only the bad beginning. After the fire, the siblings were sent to live with a distant relative named Count Olaf, a terrible and greedy man. The Baudelaire parents had left behind an enormous fortune, which would go to the children when Violet came of age, and Count Olaf was so obsessed with getting his filthy hands on the money that he hatched a devious plan that gives me nightmares to this day. He was caught just in time, but he escaped and vowed to get ahold of the Baudelaire fortune sometime in the future. Violet, Klaus, and Sunny still had nightmares about Count Olaf's shiny, shiny eyes, and about his one scraggly eyebrow, and most of all about the tattoo of an eye he had on his ankle. It seemed like that eye was watching the Baudelaire orphans wherever they went.

So I must tell you that if you have opened this book in the hope of finding out that the children lived happily ever after, you might as well shut it and read something else. Because Violet, Klaus, and Sunny, sitting in a small, cramped car and staring out the windows at Lousy Lane, were heading toward even more misery and woe. The Grim River and the horseradish factory were only the first of a sequence of tragic and unpleasant episodes that bring a frown to my face and a tear to my eye whenever I think about them.

The driver of the car was Mr. Poe, a family friend who worked at a bank and always had a cough. He was in charge of overseeing the orphans' affairs, so it was he who decided that the children would be placed in the care of a distant relative in the country after all the unpleasantness with Count Olaf.

"I'm sorry if you're uncomfortable," Mr. Poe said, coughing into a white handkerchief, "but this new car of mine doesn't fit too many people. We couldn't even fit any of your suitcases. In a week or so I'll drive back here and bring them to you."

"Thank you," said Violet, who at fourteen was the oldest of the Baudelaire children. Anyone who knew Violet well could see that her mind was not really on what Mr. Poe was saying, because her long hair was tied up in a ribbon to keep it out of her eyes. Violet was an inventor, and when she was thinking up inventions she liked to tie her hair up this way. It helped her think clearly about the various gears, wires, and ropes involved in most of her creations.

"After living so long in the city," Mr. Poe continued, "I think you will find the countryside to be a pleasant change. Oh, here is the turn. We're almost there."

"Good," Klaus said quietly. Klaus, like many people on car rides, was very bored, and he was sad not to have a book with him. Klaus loved to read, and at approximately twelve years of age had read more books than many people read in their whole lives. Sometimes he read well into the night, and in the morning could be found fast asleep, with a book in his hand and his glasses still on.

"I think you'll like Dr. Montgomery, too," Mr. Poe said. "He has traveled a great deal, so he has plenty of stories to tell. I've heard his house is filled with things he's brought from all the places he's been."

"Bax!" Sunny shrieked. Sunny, the youngest of the Baudelaire orphans, often talked like this, as infants tend to do. In fact, besides biting things with her four very sharp teeth, speaking in fragments was how Sunny spent most of her time. It was often difficult to tell what she meant to say. At this moment she probably meant something along the lines of "I'm nervous about meeting a new relative." All three children were.

"How exactly is Dr. Montgomery related to us?" Klaus asked.

"Dr. Montgomery is—let me see—your late father's cousin's wife's brother. I think that's right. He's a scientist of some sort, and receives a great deal of money from the government." As a banker, Mr. Poe was always interested in money.

"What should we call him?" Klaus asked.

"You should call him Dr. Montgomery," Mr. Poe replied, "unless he tells you to call him Montgomery. Both his first and last names are Montgomery, so it doesn't really make much difference."

"His name is Montgomery Montgomery?" Klaus said, smiling.

"Yes, and I'm sure he's very sensitive about that, so don't ridicule him," Mr. Poe said, coughing again into his handkerchief. "'Ridicule' means 'tease.'"

Klaus sighed. "I *know* what 'ridicule' means," he said. He did not add that of course he also knew not to make fun of someone's name. Occasionally, people thought that because the orphans were unforunate, they were also dim-witted.

Violet sighed too, and took the ribbon out of her hair. She had been trying to think up an invention that would block the smell of horseradish from reaching one's nose, but she was too nervous about meeting Dr. Montgomery to focus on it. "Do you know what sort of scientist he is?" she asked. She was thinking Dr. Montgomery might have a laboratory that would be of use to her.

"I'm afraid not," Mr. Poe admitted. "I've been very busy making the arrangements for you three, and I didn't have much time for chit-chat. Oh, here's the driveway. We've arrived."

Mr. Poe pulled the car up a steep gravel driveway and toward an enormous stone house. The house had a square front door made of dark wood, with several columns marking the front porch. To each side of the door were lights in the shapes of torches, which were brightly lit even though it was morning. Above the front door, the house had rows and rows of square windows, most of which were open to let in the breeze. But in front of the house was what was truly unusual: a vast, well-kept lawn, dotted with long, thin shrubs in remarkable shapes. As Mr. Poe's car came to a halt, the Baudelaires could see that the shrubs had been trimmed so as to look like snakes. Each hedge was a different kind of serpent, some long, some short, some with their tongues out and some with their mouths open, showing green, fearsome teeth. They were quite eerie, and Violet, Klaus, and Sunny were a bit hesitant about walking beside them on their way up to the house.

Mr. Poe, who led the way, didn't seem to notice the hedges at all, possibly because he was busy coaching the children on how to behave.

"Now, Klaus, don't ask too many questions right away. Violet, what happened to the ribbon in your hair? I thought you looked very distinguished in it. And somebody please make sure Sunny doesn't bite Dr. Montgomery. That wouldn't be a good first impression."

Mr. Poe stepped up to the door and rang a doorbell that was one of the loudest the children had ever heard. After a moment's pause, they could hear approaching footsteps, and Violet, Klaus, and Sunny all looked at one another. They had no way of knowing, of course, that very soon there would be more misfortune within their unlucky family, but they nevertheless felt uneasy. *Would Dr. Montgomery be a kind person?* they wondered. *Would he at least be better than Count Olaf? Could he possibly be worse?*

The door creaked open slowly, and the Baudelaire orphans held their breath as they peered into the dark entryway. They saw a dark burgundy carpet that lay on the floor. They saw a stained-glass light fixture that dangled from the ceiling. They saw a large oil painting of two snakes entwined together that hung on the wall. But where was Dr. Montgomery?

"Hello?" Mr. Poe called out. "Hello?"

"Hello hello hello!" a loud voice boomed out, and from behind the door stepped a short, chubby man with a round red face. "I am your Uncle Monty, and this is really perfect timing! I just finished making a coconut cream cake!"

CHAPTER
Two

"*Doesn't* Sunny like coconut?" Uncle Monty asked. He, Mr. Poe, and the Baudelaire orphans were all sitting around a bright green table, each with a slice of Uncle Monty's cake. Both the kitchen and the cake were still warm from baking. The cake was a magnificent thing, rich and creamy with the perfect amount of coconut. Violet, Klaus, and Uncle Monty were almost finished with their pieces, but Mr. Poe and Sunny had taken only one small bite each.

"To tell you the truth," Violet said, "Sunny doesn't really like anything soft to eat. She prefers very hard food."

"How unusual for a baby," Uncle Monty said, "but not at all unusual for many snakes. The Barbary Chewer, for example, is a snake that must have something in its mouth at all times, otherwise it begins to eat its own mouth. Very difficult to keep in captivity. Would Sunny perhaps like a raw carrot? That's plenty hard."

"A raw carrot would be perfect, Dr. Montgomery," Klaus replied.

The children's new legal guardian got up and walked toward the refrigerator, but then turned around and wagged a finger at Klaus. "None of that 'Dr. Montgomery' stuff," he said. "That's way too stuffy for me. Call me Uncle Monty! Why, my fellow herpetologists don't even call me Dr. Montgomery."

"What are herpetologists?" Violet asked.

"What do they call you?" Klaus asked.

"Children, children," Mr. Poe said sternly. "Not so many questions."

Uncle Monty smiled at the orphans. "That's quite all right," he said. "Questions show an inquisitive mind. The word 'inquisitive' means—"

"We know what it means," Klaus said. "'Full of questions.'"

"Well, if you know what that means," Uncle Monty said, handing a large carrot to Sunny, "then you should know what herpetology is."

"It's the study of something," Klaus said. "Whenever a word has *ology*, it's the study of something."

"Snakes!" Uncle Monty cried. "Snakes, snakes, snakes! That's what I study! I love snakes, all kinds, and I circle the globe looking for different kinds to study here in my laboratory! Isn't that interesting?"

"That *is* interesting," Violet said, "*very* interesting. But isn't it dangerous?"

"Not if you know the facts," Uncle Monty said. "Mr. Poe, would you like a raw carrot as well? You've scarcely touched your cake."

Mr. Poe turned red, and coughed into his handkerchief for quite some time before replying, "No, thank you, Dr. Montgomery."

Uncle Monty winked at the children. "If you like, you may call me Uncle Monty as well, Mr. Poe."

"Thank you, Uncle Monty," Mr. Poe said stiffly. "Now, *I* have a question, if you don't mind. You mentioned that you circle the globe. Is there someone who will come and take care of the children while you are out collecting specimens?"

"We're old enough to stay by ourselves," Violet said quickly, but inside she was not so sure. Uncle Monty's line of work did sound interesting, but she wasn't sure if she was ready to stay alone with her siblings, in a house full of snakes.

"I wouldn't hear of it," Uncle Monty said. "You three must come with me. In ten days we leave for Peru, and I want you children right there in the jungle with me."

"Really?" Klaus said. Behind his glasses, his eyes were shining with excitement. "You'd really take us to Peru with you?"

"I will be glad to have your help," Uncle Monty said, reaching over to take a bite of Sunny's piece of cake. "Gustav, my top assistant, left an unexpected letter of resignation for me just yesterday. There's a man named Stephano whom I have hired to take his place, but he won't arrive for a week or so, so I am way behind on preparations for the expedition. Somebody has to make sure all the snake traps are working, so I don't hurt any of our specimens. Somebody has to read up on the terrain of Peru so we can navigate through the jungle without any trouble. And somebody has to slice an enormous length of rope into small, workable pieces."

"I'm interested in mechanics," Violet said, licking her fork, "so I would be happy to learn about snake traps."

"I find guidebooks fascinating," Klaus said, wiping his mouth with a napkin, "so I would love to read up on Peruvian terrain."

"Eojip!" Sunny shrieked, taking a bite of carrot. She probably meant something along the lines of "I would be thrilled to bite an enormous length of rope into small, workable pieces!"

"Wonderful!" Uncle Monty cried. "I'm glad you have such enthusiasm. It will make it easier to do without Gustav. It was very strange, his leaving like that. I was unlucky to lose him." Uncle Monty's face clouded over, a phrase which here means "took on a slightly gloomy look as Uncle Monty thought about his bad luck," although if Uncle Monty had known what bad luck was soon to come, he wouldn't have wasted a moment thinking about Gustav. I wish—and I'm sure you wish as well—that we could go back in time and warn him, but we can't, and that is that. Uncle Monty seemed to think that was that as well, as he shook his head and smiled, clearing his brain of troubling thoughts.

"Well, we'd better get started. No time like the present, I always say. Why don't you show Mr. Poe to his car, and then I'll show you to the Reptile Room."

The three Baudelaire children, who had been so anxious when they had walked through the snake-shaped hedges the first time, raced confidently through them now as they escorted Mr. Poe to his automobile.

"Now, children," Mr. Poe said, coughing into his handkerchief, "I will be back here in about a week with your luggage and to make sure everything is all right. I know that Dr. Montgomery might seem a bit intimidating to you, but I'm sure in time you will get used to—"

"He doesn't seem intimidating at all," Klaus interrupted. "He seems very easy to get along with."

"I can't wait to see the Reptile Room," Violet said excitedly.

"Meeka!" Sunny said, which probably meant "Good-bye, Mr. Poe. Thank you for driving us."

"Well, good-bye," Mr. Poe said. "Remember, it is just a short drive here from the city, so please contact me or anyone else at Mulctuary Money Management if you have any trouble. See you soon." He gave the orphans an awkward little wave with his handkerchief, got into his small car, and drove back down the steep gravel driveway onto Lousy Lane. Violet, Klaus, and Sunny waved back, hoping that Mr. Poe would remember to roll up the car windows so the stench of horseradish would not be too unbearable.

"*Bambini!*" Uncle Monty cried out from the front door. "Come along, bambini!"

The Baudelaire orphans raced back through the hedges to where their new guardian was waiting for them. "*Violet*, Uncle Monty," Violet said. "My name is Violet, my brother's is Klaus, and Sunny is our baby sister. None of us is named Bambini."

"'Bambini' is the Italian word for 'children,'" Uncle Monty explained. "I had a sudden urge to speak a little Italian. I'm so excited to have you three here with me, you're lucky I'm not speaking gibberish."

"Have you never had any children of your own?" Violet asked.

"I'm afraid not," Uncle Monty said. "I always meant to find a wife and start a family, but it just kept slipping my mind. Shall I show you the Reptile Room?"

"Yes, please," Klaus said.

Uncle Monty led them past the painting of snakes in the entryway into a large room with a grand staircase and very, very high ceilings. "Your rooms will be up there," Uncle Monty said, gesturing up the stairs. "You can each choose whatever room you like and move the furniture around to suit your taste. I understand that Mr. Poe has to bring your luggage later in that puny car of his, so please make a list of anything you might need and we'll go into town tomorrow and buy it so you don't have to spend the next few days in the same underwear."

"Do we really each get our own room?" Violet asked.

"Of course," Uncle Monty said. "You don't think I'd coop you all up in one room when I have this enormous house, do you? What sort of person would do that?"

"Count Olaf did," Klaus said.

"Oh, that's right, Mr. Poe told me," Uncle Monty said, grimacing as if he had just tasted something terrible. "Count Olaf sounds like an awful person. I hope he is torn apart by wild animals someday. Wouldn't that be satisfying? Oh, well, here we are: the Reptile Room."

Uncle Monty had reached a very tall wooden door with a large doorknob right in the middle of it. It was so high up that he had to stand on his tiptoes to open it. When it swung open on its creaky hinges, the Baudelaire orphans all gasped in astonishment and delight at the room they saw.

The Reptile Room was made entirely out of glass, with bright, clear glass walls and a high glass ceiling that rose up to a point like the inside of a cathedral. Outside the walls was a bright green field of grasses and shrubs which was of course perfectly visible through the transparent walls, so standing in the Reptile Room was like being inside and outside at the same time. But as remarkable as the room itself was, what was inside the Reptile Room was much more exciting. Reptiles, of course, were lined up in locked metal cages that sat on wooden tables in four neat rows all the way down the room. There were all sorts of snakes, naturally, but there were also lizards, toads, and assorted other animals that the children had never seen before, not even in pictures, or at the zoo. There was a very fat toad with two wings coming out of its back, and a two-headed lizard that had bright yellow stripes on its belly. There was a snake that had three mouths, one on top of the other, and another that seemed to have no mouth at all. There was a lizard that looked like an owl, with wide eyes that gazed at them from the log on which it was perched in its cage, and a toad that looked just like a church, complete with stained-glass eyes. And there was a cage with a white cloth on top of it, so you couldn't see what was inside at all. The children walked down the aisles of cages, peering into each one in amazed silence. Some of the creatures looked friendly, and some of them looked scary, but all of them looked fascinating, and the Baudelaires took a long, careful look at each one, with Klaus holding Sunny up so she could see.

The orphans were so interested in the cages that they didn't even notice what was at the far end of the Reptile Room until they had walked the length of each aisle, but once they reached the far end they gasped in astonishment and delight once more. For here, at the end of the rows and rows of cages, were rows and rows of bookshelves, each one stuffed with books of different sizes and shapes, with a cluster of tables, chairs, and reading lamps in one corner. I'm sure you remember that the Baudelaire children's parents had an enormous collection of books, which the orphans remembered fondly and missed dreadfully, and since the terrible fire, the children were always delighted to meet someone who loved books as much as they did. Violet, Klaus, and Sunny examined the books as carefully as they had the reptile cages, and realized immediately that most of the books were about snakes and other reptiles. It seemed as if every book written on reptiles, from *An Introduction to Large Lizards* to *The Care and Feeding of the Androgynous Cobra*, were lined up on the shelves, and all three children, Klaus especially, looked forward to reading up on the creatures in the Reptile Room.

"This is an amazing place," Violet said finally, breaking the long silence.

"Thank you," Uncle Monty said. "It's taken me a lifetime to put together."

"And are we really allowed to come inside here?" Klaus asked.

"*Allowed?*" Uncle Monty repeated. "Of course

not! You are *implored* to come inside here, my boy. Starting first thing tomorrow morning, all of us must be here every day in preparation for the expedition to Peru. I will clear off one of those tables for you, Violet, to work on the traps. Klaus, I expect you to read all of the books about Peru that I have, and make careful notes. And Sunny can sit on the floor and bite rope. We will work all day until suppertime, and after supper we will go to the movies. Are there any objections?"

Violet, Klaus, and Sunny looked at one another and grinned. Any *objections*? The Baudelaire orphans had just been living with Count Olaf, who had made them chop wood and clean up after his drunken guests, while plotting to steal their fortune. Uncle Monty had just described a delightful way to spend one's time, and the children smiled at him eagerly. Of course there would be no objections. Violet, Klaus, and Sunny gazed at the Reptile Room and envisioned an end to their troubles as they lived their lives under Uncle Monty's care. They were wrong, of course, about their misery being over, but for the moment the three siblings were hopeful, excited, and happy.

"No, no, no," Sunny cried out, in apparent answer to Uncle Monty's question.

"Good, good, good," Uncle Monty said, smiling. "Now, let's go figure out whose room is whose."

"Uncle Monty?" Klaus asked shyly. "I just have one question."

"What is that?" Uncle Monty said.

"What's in that cage with the cloth on top of it?"

Uncle Monty looked at the cage, and then at the children. His face lit up with a smile of pure joy. "That, my dears, is a new snake which I brought over from my last journey. Gustav and myself are the only people to have seen it. Next month I will present it to the Herpetological Society as a new discovery, but in the meantime I will allow you to look at it. Gather 'round."

The Baudelaire orphans followed Uncle Monty to the cloth-covered cage, and with a flourish—the word "flourish" here means "a sweeping gesture, often used to show off"—he swooped the cloth off the cage. Inside was a large black snake, as dark as a coal mine and as thick as a sewer pipe, looking right at the orphans with shiny green eyes. With the cloth off its cage, the snake began to uncoil itself and slither around its home.

"Because I discovered it," Uncle Monty said, "I got to name it."

"What is it called?" Violet asked.

"The Incredibly Deadly Viper," Uncle Monty replied, and at that moment something happened which I'm sure will interest you. With one flick of its tail, the snake unlatched the door of its cage and slithered out onto the table, and before Uncle Monty or any of the Baudelaire orphans could say anything, it opened its mouth and bit Sunny right on the chin.

I *am* very, very sorry to leave you hanging
like that, but as I was writing the tale of the
Baudelaire orphans, I happened to look at the
clock and realized I was running late for a formal
dinner party given by a friend of mine, Madame
diLustro. Madame diLustro is a good friend, an
excellent detective, and a fine cook, but she flies
into a rage if you arrive even five minutes later
than her invitation states, so you understand
that I had to dash off. You must have thought,
at the end of the previous chapter, that Sunny
was dead and that this was the terrible thing that
happened to the Baudelaires at Uncle Monty's
house, but I promise you Sunny survives this

particular episode. It is Uncle Monty, unfortunately, who will be dead, but not yet.

As the fangs of the Incredibly Deadly Viper closed on Sunny's chin, Violet and Klaus watched in horror as Sunny's little eyes closed and her face grew quiet. Then, moving as suddenly as the snake, Sunny smiled brightly, opened her mouth, and bit the Incredibly Deadly Viper right on its tiny, scaled nose. The snake let go of her chin, and Violet and Klaus could see that it had left barely a mark. The two older Baudelaire siblings looked at Uncle Monty, and Uncle Monty looked back at them and laughed. His loud laughter bounced off the glass walls of the Reptile Room.

"Uncle Monty, what can we do?" Klaus said in despair.

"Oh, I'm sorry, my dears," Uncle Monty said, wiping his eyes with his hands. "You must be very frightened. But the Incredibly Deadly Viper is one of the *least* dangerous and most friendly creatures in the animal kingdom. Sunny has nothing to worry about, and neither do you."

Klaus looked at his baby sister, who was still in his arms, as she playfully gave the Incredibly Deadly Viper a big hug around its thick body, and he realized Uncle Monty must be telling the truth. "But then why is it called the Incredibly Deadly Viper?"

Uncle Monty laughed again. "It's a misnomer," he said, using a word which here means "a very wrong name." "Because I discovered it, I got to name it, remember? Don't tell anyone about the Incredibly Deadly Viper, because I'm going to present it to the Herpetological Society and give them a good scare before explaining that the snake is completely harmless! Lord knows they've teased me many times, because of my name. 'Hello hello, Montgomery Montgomery,' they say. 'How are you how are you, Montgomery Montgomery?' But at this year's conference I'm going to get back at them with this prank." Uncle Monty drew himself up to his full height and began talking in a silly, scientific voice. "'Colleagues,' I'll say, 'I would like to introduce to you a new species, the Incredibly Deadly Viper, which I found in the southwest forest of—my God! It's escaped!' And then, when all my fellow herpetologists have jumped up on chairs and tables and are shrieking in fear, I'll tell them that the snake wouldn't hurt a fly! Won't that be hysterical?"

Violet and Klaus looked at each other, and then began laughing, half in relief that their sister was unharmed, and half with amusement, because they thought Uncle Monty's prank was a good one.

Klaus put Sunny down on the floor, and the Incredibly Deadly Viper followed, wriggling its tail affectionately around Sunny, the way you might put your arm around someone of whom you were fond.

"Are there any snakes in this room that *are* dangerous?" Violet asked.

"Of course," Uncle Monty said. "You can't study snakes for forty years without encountering some dangerous ones. I have a whole cabinet of venom samples from every poisonous snake known to people, so I can study the ways in which these dangerous snakes work. There is a snake in this room whose venom is so deadly that your heart would stop before you even knew he'd bitten you. There is a snake who can open her mouth so wide she could swallow all of us, together, in one gulp. There is a pair of snakes who have learned to drive a car so recklessly that they would run you over in the street and never stop to apologize. But all of these snakes are in cages with much sturdier locks, and all of them can be handled safely when one has studied them enough. I promise that if you take time to learn the facts, no harm will come to you here in the Reptile Room."

There is a type of situation, which occurs all too often and which is occurring at this point in the story of the Baudelaire orphans, called "dramatic irony." Simply put, dramatic irony is when a person makes a harmless remark, and someone else who hears it knows something that makes the remark have a different, and usually unpleasant, meaning. For instance, if you were in a restaurant and said out loud, "I can't wait to eat the veal marsala I ordered," and there were people around who knew that the veal marsala was poisoned and that you would die as soon as you took a bite, your situation would be one of dramatic irony. Dramatic irony is a cruel occurrence, one that is almost always upsetting, and I'm sorry to have it appear in this story, but Violet, Klaus, and Sunny have such unfortunate lives that it was only a matter of time before dramatic irony would rear its ugly head.

As you and I listen to Uncle Monty tell the three Baudelaire orphans that no harm will ever come to them in the Reptile Room, we should be experiencing the strange feeling that accompanies the arrival of dramatic irony. This feeling is not unlike the sinking in one's stomach when one is in an elevator that suddenly goes down, or when you are snug in bed and your closet door suddenly creaks open to reveal the person who has been hiding there. For no matter how safe and happy the three children felt, no matter how comforting Uncle Monty's words were, you and I know that soon Uncle Monty will be dead and the Baudelaires will be miserable once again.

During the week that followed, however, the Baudelaires had a wonderful time in their new home. Each morning, they woke up and dressed in the privacy of their very own rooms, which they had chosen and decorated to their liking. Violet had chosen a room that had an enormous window looking out onto the snake-shaped hedges on the front lawn. She thought such a view might inspire her when she was inventing things. Uncle Monty had allowed her to tack up large pieces of white paper on each wall, so she could sketch out her ideas, even if they came to her in the middle of the night. Klaus had chosen a room with a cozy alcove in it—the word "alcove" here means "a very, very small nook just perfect for sitting and reading." With Uncle Monty's permission, he had carried up a large cushioned chair from the living room and placed it right in the alcove, under a heavy brass reading lamp. Each night, rather than reading in bed, he would curl himself in the chair with a book from Uncle Monty's library, sometimes until morning. Sunny had chosen a room right between Violet's and Klaus's, and filled it with small, hard objects from all over the house, so she could bite them when she felt like it. There were also assorted toys for the Incredibly Deadly Viper so the two of them could play together whenever they wanted, within reason.

But where the Baudelaire orphans most liked to be was the Reptile Room. Each morning, after breakfast, they would join Uncle Monty, who would have already started work on the upcoming expedition. Violet sat at a table with the ropes, gears, and cages that made up the different snake traps, learning how they worked, repairing them if they were broken, and occasionally making improvements to make the traps more comfortable for the snakes on their long journey from Peru to Uncle Monty's house. Klaus sat nearby, reading the books on Peru Uncle Monty had and taking notes on a pad of paper so they could refer to them later. And Sunny sat on the floor, biting a long rope into shorter pieces with great enthusiasm. But what the Baudelaire youngsters liked best was learning all about the reptiles from Uncle Monty. As they worked, he would show them the Alaskan Cow Lizard, a long green creature that produced delicious milk. They met the Dissonant Toad, which could imitate human speech in a gravelly voice. Uncle Monty taught them how to handle the Inky Newt without getting its black dye all over their fingers, and how to tell when the Irascible Python was grumpy and best left alone. He taught them not to give the Green Gimlet Toad too much water, and to never, under any circumstances, let the Virginian Wolfsnake near a typewriter.

While he was telling them about the different reptiles, Uncle Monty would often segue— a word which here means "let the conversation veer off"—to stories from his travels, describing the men, snakes, women, toads, children, and lizards he'd met on his journeys. And before too long, the Baudelaire orphans were telling Uncle Monty all about their own lives, eventually talking about their parents and how much they missed them. Uncle Monty was as interested in the Baudelaires' stories as they were in his, and sometimes they got to talking so long they scarcely had time to gobble down dinner before cramming themselves into Uncle Monty's tiny jeep and heading to the movies.

One morning, however, when the three children finished their breakfast and went into the Reptile Room, they found not Uncle Monty, but a note from him. The note read as follows:

Dear Bambini,

I have gone into town to buy a few last things we
need for the expedition: Peruvian wasp repellent,
toothbrushes, canned peaches, and a fireproof
canoe. It will take a while to find the peaches, so
don't expect me back until dinnertime.

 Stephano, Gustav's replacement, will arrive
today by taxi. Please make him feel welcome. As
you know, it is only two days until the expedition,
so please work very hard today.

Your giddy uncle,
Monty

"What does 'giddy' mean?" Violet asked,
when they had finished reading the note.

"'Dizzy and excited,'" Klaus said, having
learned the word from a collection of poetry
he'd read in first grade. "I guess he means excited about Peru. Or maybe he's excited about
having a new assistant."

"Or maybe he's excited about us," Violet said.

"Kindal!" Sunny shrieked, which probably meant "Or maybe he's excited about all these things."

"I'm a little giddy myself," Klaus said. "It's really fun to live with Uncle Monty."

"It certainly is," Violet agreed. "After the fire, I thought I would never be happy again. But our time here has been wonderful."

"I still miss our parents, though," Klaus said. "No matter how nice Uncle Monty is, I wish we still lived in our real home."

"Of course," Violet said quickly. She paused, and slowly said out loud something she had been thinking about for the past few days. "I think we'll always miss our parents. But I think we can miss them without being miserable all the time. After all, they wouldn't want us to be miserable."

"Remember that time," Klaus said wistfully, "when we were bored one rainy afternoon, and all of us painted our toenails bright red?"

"Yes," Violet said, grinning, "and I spilled some on the yellow chair."

"Archo!" Sunny said quietly, which probably meant something like "And the stain never really came out." The Baudelaire orphans smiled at each other and, without a word, began to do the day's work. For the rest of the morning they worked quietly and steadily, realizing that their contentment here at Uncle Monty's house did not erase their parents' death, not at all, but at least it made them feel better after feeling so sad, for so long.

It is unfortunate, of course, that this quiet happy moment was the last one the children would have for quite some time, but there is nothing anyone can do about it now. Just when the Baudelaires were beginning to think about lunch, they heard a car pull up in front of the house and toot its horn. To the children it signaled the arrival of Stephano. To us it should signal the beginning of more misery.

"I expect that's the new assistant," Klaus said, looking up from *The Big Peruvian Book of Small Peruvian Snakes*. "I hope he's as nice as Monty."

"Me too," Violet said, opening and shutting a toad trap to make sure it worked smoothly. "It would be unpleasant to travel to Peru with somebody who was boring or mean."

"Gerja!" Sunny shrieked, which probably meant something like "Well, let's go find out what Stephano is like!"

The Baudelaires left the Reptile Room and walked out the front door to find a taxi parked next to the snake-shaped hedges. A very tall, thin man with a long beard and no eyebrows over his eyes was getting out of the backseat, carrying a black suitcase with a shiny silver padlock.

"I'm not going to give you a tip," the bearded man was saying to the driver of the taxi, "because you talk too much. Not everybody wants to hear about your new baby, you know. Oh, hello there. I am Stephano, Dr. Montgomery's new assistant. How do you do?"

"How do you do?" Violet said, and as she approached him, there was something about his wheezy voice that seemed vaguely familiar.

"How do you do?" Klaus said, and as he looked up at Stephano, there was something about his shiny eyes that seemed quite familiar.

"Hooda!" Sunny shrieked. Stephano wasn't wearing any socks, and Sunny, crawling on the ground, could see his bare ankle between his pant cuff and his shoe. There on his ankle was something that was most familiar of all.

The Baudelaire orphans all realized the same thing at the same time, and took a step back as you might from a growling dog. This man wasn't Stephano, no matter what he called himself. The three children looked at Uncle Monty's new assistant from head to toe and saw that he was none other than Count Olaf. He may have shaved off his one long eyebrow, and grown a beard over his scraggly chin, but there was no way he could hide the tattoo of an eye on his ankle.

One of the most difficult things to think about in life is one's regrets. Something will happen to you, and you will do the wrong thing, and for years afterward you will wish you had done something different. For instance, sometimes when I am walking along the seashore, or visiting the grave of a friend, I will remember a day, a long time ago, when I didn't bring a flashlight with me to a place where I should have brought a flashlight, and the results were disastrous. *Why didn't I bring a flashlight?* I think to myself, even though it is too late to do anything about it. *I should have brought a flashlight.*

For years after this moment in the lives of the Baudelaire orphans, Klaus thought of the time when he and his siblings realized that Stephano was actually Count Olaf, and was filled with regret that he didn't call out to the driver of the taxicab who was beginning to drive back down the driveway. *Stop!* Klaus would think to himself, even though it was too late to do anything about it. *Stop! Take this man away!* Of course, it is perfectly understandable that Klaus and his sisters were too surprised to act so quickly, but Klaus would lie awake in bed, years later, thinking that maybe, just maybe, if he had acted in time, he could have saved Uncle Monty's life.

But he didn't. As the Baudelaire orphans stared at Count Olaf, the taxi drove back down the driveway and the children were alone with their nemesis, a word which here means "the worst enemy you could imagine." Olaf smiled at them the way Uncle Monty's Mongolian Meansnake would smile when a white mouse was placed in its cage each day for dinner. "Perhaps one of you might carry my suitcase into my room," he suggested in his wheezy voice. "The ride along that smelly road was dull and unpleasant and I am very tired."

"If anyone ever deserved to travel along Lousy Lane," Violet said, glaring at him, "it is you, Count Olaf. We will certainly not help you with your luggage, because we will not let you in this house."

Olaf frowned at the orphans, and then looked this way and that as if he expected to see someone hiding behind the snake-shaped hedges. "Who is Count Olaf?" he asked quizzically. "My name is Stephano. I am here to assist Montgomery Montgomery with his upcoming expedition to Peru. I assume you three are midgets who work as servants in the Montgomery home."

"We are not midgets," Klaus said sternly. "We are children. And you are not Stephano. You are Count Olaf. You may have grown a beard and shaved your eyebrow, but you are still the same despicable person and we will not let you in this house."

"Futa!" Sunny shrieked, which probably meant something like "I agree!"

Count Olaf looked at each of the Baudelaire orphans, his eyes shining brightly as if he were telling a joke. "I don't know what you're talking about," he said, "but if I did, and I were this Count Olaf you speak of, I would think that you were being very rude. And if I thought you were rude, I might get angry. And if I got angry, who knows what I would do?"

The children watched as Count Olaf raised his scrawny arms in a sort of shrug. It probably isn't necessary to remind you just how violent he could be, but it certainly wasn't necessary at all to remind the Baudelaires. Klaus could still feel the bruise on his face from the time Count Olaf had struck him, when they were living in his house. Sunny still ached from being stuffed into a birdcage and dangled from the tower where he made his evil plans. And while Violet had not been the victim of any physical violence from this terrible man, she had almost been forced to marry him, and that was enough to make her pick up his suitcase and drag it slowly toward the door to the house.

"Higher," Olaf said. "Lift it higher. I don't want it dragged along the ground like that."

Klaus and Sunny hurried to help Violet with the suitcase, but even with the three of them carrying it the weight made them stagger. It was misery enough that Count Olaf had reappeared in their lives, just when they were feeling so comfortable and safe with Uncle Monty. But to actually be helping this awful person enter their home was almost more than they could bear. Olaf followed closely behind them and the three children could smell his stale breath as they brought the suitcase indoors and set it on the carpet beneath the painting of the entwined snakes.

"Thank you, orphans," Olaf said, shutting the front door behind him. "Now, Dr. Montgomery said my room would be waiting upstairs. I suppose I can carry my luggage from here. Now run along. We'll have lots of time to get to know one another later."

"We already know you, Count Olaf," Violet said. "You obviously haven't changed a bit."

"You haven't changed, either," Olaf said. "It is clear to me, Violet, that you are as stubborn as ever. And Klaus, you are still wearing those idiotic glasses from reading too many books. And I see that little Sunny here still has nine toes instead of ten."

"Fut!" Sunny shrieked, which probably meant something like "I do not!"

"What are you talking about?" Klaus said

impatiently. "She has ten toes, just like everybody else."

"Really?" Olaf said. "That's odd. I remember that she lost one of her toes in an accident." His eyes shone even brighter, as if he were telling a joke, and he reached into the pocket of his shabby coat and brought out a long knife, such as one might use for slicing bread. "I seem to recall there was a man who was so confused by being called repeatedly by the wrong name that he accidentally dropped a knife on her little foot and severed one of her toes."

Violet and Klaus looked at Count Olaf, and then at the bare foot of their little sister. "You wouldn't dare," Klaus said.

"Let's not discuss what I would or would not dare to do," Olaf said. "Let us discuss, rather, what I am to be called for as long as we are together in this house."

"We'll call you Stephano, if you insist on threatening us," Violet said, "but we won't be together in this house for long."

Stephano opened his mouth to say something, but Violet was not interested in continuing the conversation. She turned on her heel and marched primly through the enormous door of the Reptile Room, followed by her siblings. If you or I had been there, we would have thought that the Baudelaire orphans weren't scared at all, speaking so bravely like that to Stephano and then simply walking away, but once the children reached the far end of the room, their true emotions showed clearly on their faces. The Baudelaires were terrified. Violet put her hands over her face and leaned against one of the reptile cages. Klaus sank into a chair, trembling so hard that his feet rattled against the marble floor. And Sunny curled up into a little ball on the floor, so tiny you might have missed her if you walked into the room. For several moments, none of the children spoke, just listened to the muffled sounds of Stephano walking up the stairs and their own heartbeats pounding in their ears.

"How did he find us?" Klaus asked. His voice was a hoarse whisper, as if he had a sore throat. "How did he get to be Uncle Monty's assistant? What is he doing here?"

"He vowed that he'd get his hands on the Baudelaire fortune," Violet said, taking her hands away from her face and picking up Sunny, who was shivering. "That was the last thing he said to me before he escaped. He said he'd get our fortune if it was the last thing he ever did." Violet shuddered, and did not add that he'd also said that once he got their fortune, he'd do away with all three of the Baudelaire siblings. She did not need to add it. Violet, Klaus, and Sunny all knew that if he figured out a way to seize their fortune, he would slit the throats of the Baudelaire orphans as easily as you or I might eat a small butter cookie.

"What can we do?" Klaus asked. "Uncle Monty won't be back for hours."

"Maybe we can call Mr. Poe," Violet said. "It's the middle of business hours, but maybe he could leave the bank for an emergency."

"He wouldn't believe us," Klaus said. "Remember when we tried to tell him about Count Olaf when we lived there? He took such a long time to realize the truth, it was almost too late. I think we should run away. If we leave right now, we could probably get to town in time to catch a train far away from here."

Violet pictured the three of them, all alone, walking along Lousy Lane beneath the sour apple trees, with the bitter smell of horseradish encircling them. "Where would we go?" she asked.

"Anywhere," Klaus said. "Anywhere but here. We could go far away where Count Olaf wouldn't find us, and change our names so no one would know who we were."

"We haven't any money," Violet pointed out. "How could we live by ourselves?"

"We could get jobs," Klaus replied. "I could work in a library, maybe, and you could work in some sort of mechanical factory. Sunny probably couldn't get a job at her age, but in a few years she could."

The three orphans were quiet. They tried to picture leaving Uncle Monty and living by themselves, trying to find jobs and take care of each other. It was a very lonely prospect. The Baudelaire children sat in sad silence awhile, and they were each thinking the same thing: They wished that their parents had never been killed in the fire, and that their lives had never been turned topsy-turvy the way they had. If only the Baudelaire parents were still alive, the youngsters wouldn't even have heard of Count Olaf, let alone have him settling into their home and undoubtedly making evil plans.

"We can't leave," Violet said finally. "Count Olaf found us once, and I'm sure he'd find us again, no matter how far we went. Plus, who knows where Count Olaf's assistants are? Perhaps they've surrounded the house right now, keeping watch in case we're on to him."

Klaus shivered. He hadn't been thinking of

Olaf's assistants. Besides scheming to get his hands on the Baudelaire fortune, Olaf was the leader of a terrible theater troupe, and his fellow actors were always ready to help him with his plans. They were a gruesome crew, each more terrifying than the next. There was a bald man with a long nose, who always wore a black robe. There were two women who always had ghostly white powder on their faces. There was a person so large and blank-looking that you couldn't tell if it was a man or a woman. And there was a skinny man with two hooks where his hands should have been. Violet was right. Any of these people could be lurking outside Uncle Monty's house, waiting to catch them if they tried to escape.

"I think we should just wait for Uncle Monty to come back, and tell him what has happened," Violet said. "He'll believe us. If we tell him about the tattoo, he'll at least ask *Stephano* for an explanation." Violet's tone of voice when she said "Stephano" indicated her utter scorn for Olaf's disguise.

"Are you sure?" Klaus said. "After all, Uncle Monty is the one who hired *Stephano*." Klaus's tone of voice when *he* said "Stephano" indicated that he shared his sister's feelings. "For all we know, Uncle Monty and Stephano have planned something together."

"Minda!" Sunny shrieked, which probably meant something like "Don't be ridiculous, Klaus!"

Violet shook her head. "Sunny's right. I can't believe that Uncle Monty would be in cahoots with Olaf. He's been so kind and generous to us, and besides, if they were working together, Olaf wouldn't insist on using a different name."

"That's true," Klaus said thoughtfully. "So we wait for Uncle Monty."

"We wait," Violet agreed.

"Tojoo," Sunny said solemnly, and the siblings looked at one another glumly. Waiting is one of life's hardships. It is hard enough to wait for chocolate cream pie while burnt roast beef is still on your plate. It is plenty difficult to wait for Halloween when the tedious month of September is still ahead of you. But to wait for one's adopted uncle to come home while a greedy and violent man is upstairs was one of the worst waits the Baudelaires had ever experienced. To get their mind off it, they tried to continue with their work, but the children were too anxious to get anything done. Violet tried to fix a hinged door on one of the traps, but all she could concentrate on was the knot of worry in her stomach. Klaus tried to read about protecting oneself from thorny Peruvian plants, but thoughts of Stephano kept clouding his brain. And Sunny tried to bite rope, but she had a cold chill of fear running through her teeth and she soon gave up. She didn't even feel like playing with the Incredibly Deadly Viper. So the Baudelaires spent the rest of the afternoon sitting silently in the Reptile Room, looking out the window for Uncle Monty's jeep and listening to the occasional noise from upstairs. They didn't even want to think about what Stephano might be unpacking.

Finally, as the snake-shaped hedges began to cast long, skinny shadows in the setting sun, the three children heard an approaching engine, and the jeep pulled up. A large canoe was strapped to the roof of the jeep, and the backseat was piled with Monty's purchases. Uncle Monty got out, struggling under the weight of several shopping bags, and saw the children through the glass walls of the Reptile Room. He smiled at them. They smiled back, and in that instant when they smiled was created another moment of regret for them. Had they not paused to smile at Monty but instead gone dashing out to the car, they might have had a brief moment alone with him. But by the time they reached the entry hall, he was already talking to Stephano.

"I didn't know what kind of toothbrush you preferred," Uncle Monty was saying apologetically, "so I got you one with extra-firm bristles because that's the kind I like. Peruvian food tends to be sticky, so you need to have at least one extra toothbrush whenever you go there."

"Extra-firm bristles are fine with me," Stephano said, speaking to Uncle Monty but looking at the orphans with his shiny, shiny eyes. "Shall I carry in the canoe?"

"Yes, but my goodness, you can't carry it all by yourself," Uncle Monty said. "Klaus, please help Stephano, will you?"

"Uncle Monty," Violet said, "we have something very important to tell you."

"I'm all ears," Uncle Monty said, "but first let me show you the wasp repellent I picked up. I'm so glad Klaus read up on the insect situation in Peru, because the other repellents I have would have been no use at all." Uncle Monty rooted through one of the bags on his arm as the children waited impatiently for him to finish. "This one contains a chemical called—"

"Uncle Monty," Klaus said, "what we have to tell you really can't wait."

"Klaus," Uncle Monty said, his eyebrows rising in surprise, "it's not polite to interrupt when your uncle is talking. Now, please help Stephano with the canoe, and we'll talk about anything you want in a few moments."

Klaus sighed, but followed Stephano out the open door. Violet watched them walking toward the jeep as Uncle Monty put down the shopping bags and faced her. "I can't remember what I was saying about the repellent," he said, a little crossly. "I hate losing my train of thought."

"What we have to tell you," Violet began, but she stopped when something caught her eye. Monty was facing away from the door, so he couldn't see what Stephano was doing, but Violet saw Stephano stop at the snake-shaped hedges, reach into his coat pocket, and take out the long knife. Its blade caught the light of the setting sun and it glowed brightly, like a lighthouse. As you probably know, lighthouses serve as warning signals, telling ships where the shore is so they don't run into it. The shining knife was a warning, too.

Klaus looked at the knife, and then at Stephano, and then at Violet. Violet looked at Klaus, and then at Stephano, and then at Monty. Sunny looked at everyone. Only Monty didn't notice what was going on, so intent was he on remembering whatever he was babbling about wasp repellent. "What we have to tell you," Violet began again, but she couldn't continue. Stephano didn't say a word. He didn't have to. Violet knew that if she breathed one word about his true identity, Stephano would hurt her brother, right there at the snake-shaped hedges. Without saying a word, the nemesis of the Baudelaire orphans had sent a very clear warning.

Five

That night felt like the longest and most terrible the Baudelaire orphans had ever had, and they'd had plenty. There was one night, shortly after Sunny was born, that all three children had a horrible flu, and tossed and turned in the grasp of a terrible fever, while their father tried to soothe them all at once, placing cold washcloths on their sweaty brows. The night after their parents had been killed, the three children had stayed at Mr. Poe's house, and had stayed up all night, too miserable and confused to even try to sleep. And of course, they had spent many a long and terrible night while living with Count Olaf.

But this particular night seemed worse. From the moment of Monty's arrival until bedtime, Stephano kept the children under his constant surveillance, a phrase which here means "kept watching them so they couldn't possibly talk to Uncle Monty alone and reveal that he was really Count Olaf," and Uncle Monty was too preoccupied to think that anything unusual was going on. When they brought in the rest of Uncle Monty's purchases, Stephano carried bags with only one hand, keeping the other one in his coat pocket where the long knife was hidden, but Uncle Monty was too excited about all the new supplies to ask about it. When they went into the kitchen to prepare dinner, Stephano smiled menacingly at the children as he sliced mushrooms, but Uncle Monty was too busy making sure the stroganoff sauce didn't boil to even notice that Stephano was using his own threatening knife for the chopping. Over dinner, Stephano told funny stories and praised Monty's scientific work, and Uncle Monty was so flattered he didn't even think to guess that Stephano was holding a knife under the table, rubbing the blade gently against Violet's knee for the entire meal. And when Uncle Monty announced that he would spend the evening showing his new assistant around the Reptile Room, he was too eager to realize that the Baudelaires simply went up to bed without a word.

For the first time, having individual bedrooms seemed like a hardship rather than a luxury, for without one another's company the orphans felt even more lonely and helpless. Violet stared at the paper tacked to her wall and tried to imagine what Stephano was planning. Klaus sat in his large cushioned chair and turned on his brass reading lamp but was too worried to even open a book. Sunny stared at her hard objects but didn't bite a single one of them.

All three children thought of walking down the hall to Uncle Monty's room and waking him up to tell him what was wrong. But to get to his bedroom, they would have to walk past the room in which Stephano was staying, and all night long Stephano kept watch in a chair placed in front of his open door. When the orphans opened their doors to peer down the dark hallway, they saw Stephano's pale, shaved head, which seemed to be floating above his body in the darkness. And they could see his knife, which Stephano was moving slowly like the pendulum of a grandfather clock. Back and forth it went, back and forth, glinting in the dim light, and the sight was so fearsome they didn't dare try walking down the hallway.

Finally, the light in the house turned the pale blue-gray of early dawn, and the Baudelaire children walked blearily down the stairs to breakfast, tired and achy from their sleepless night. They sat around the table where they had eaten cake on their first morning at the house, and picked listlessly at their food. For the first time since their arrival at Uncle Monty's, they were not eager to enter the Reptile Room and begin the day's work.

"I suppose we have to go in now," Violet said finally, putting aside her scarcely nibbled toast. "I'm sure Uncle Monty has already started working, and is expecting us."

"And I'm sure that Stephano is there, too," Klaus said, staring glumly into his cereal bowl. "We'll never get a chance to tell Uncle Monty what we know about him."

"Yinga," Sunny said sadly, dropping her untouched raw carrot to the floor.

"If only Uncle Monty knew what we know," Violet said, "and Stephano knew that he knew what we know. But Uncle Monty doesn't know what we know, and Stephano knows that he doesn't know what we know."

"I know," Klaus said.

"I know you know," Violet said, "but what we don't know is what Count Olaf—I mean *Stephano*—is really up to. He's after our fortune, certainly, but how can he get it if we're under Uncle Monty's care?"

"Maybe he's just going to wait until you're of age, and then steal the fortune," Klaus said.

"Four years is a long time to wait," Violet said. The three orphans were quiet, as each remembered where they had been four years ago. Violet had been ten, and had worn her hair very short. She remembered that sometime around her tenth birthday she had invented a new kind of pencil sharpener. Klaus had been about eight, and he remembered how interested he had been in comets, reading all the astronomy books his parents had in their library. Sunny, of course, had not been born four years ago, and she sat and tried to remember what that was like. Very dark, she thought, with nothing to bite. For all three youngsters, four years did seem like a very long time.

"Come on, come on, you are moving very slowly this morning," Uncle Monty said, bursting into the room. His face seemed even brighter than usual, and he was holding a small bunch of folded papers in one hand. "Stephano has only worked here one day, and he's already in the Reptile Room. In fact, he was up before I was—I ran into him on my way down the stairs. He's an eager beaver. But you three— you're moving like the Hungarian Sloth Snake, whose top speed is half an inch per hour! We have lots to do today, and I'd like to catch the six o'clock showing of *Zombies in the Snow* tonight, so let's try to hurry, hurry, hurry."

Violet looked at Uncle Monty, and realized that this might be their only opportunity to talk to him alone, without Stephano around, but he seemed so wound up they weren't sure if he would listen to them. "Speaking of Stephano," she said timidly, "we'd like to talk to you about him."

Uncle Monty's eyes widened, and he looked

around him as if there were spies in the room before leaning in to whisper to the children. "I'd like to talk to you, too," he said. "I have my suspicions about Stephano, and I'd like to discuss them with you."

The Baudelaire orphans looked at one another in relief. "You do?" Klaus said.

"Of course," Uncle Monty said. "Last night I began to get very suspicious about this new assistant of mine. There's something a little spooky about him, and I—" Uncle Monty looked around again, and began speaking even softer, so the children had to hold their breaths to hear him. "And I think we should discuss it outside. Shall we?"

The children nodded in agreement, and rose from the table. Leaving their dirty breakfast dishes behind, which is not a good thing to do in general but perfectly acceptable in the face of an emergency, they walked with Uncle Monty to the front entryway, past the painting of two snakes entwined together, out the front door, and onto the lawn, as if they wanted to talk to the snake-shaped hedges instead of to one another.

"I don't mean to be vainglorious," Uncle Monty began, using a word which here means "braggy," "but I really am one of the most widely respected herpetologists in the world."

Klaus blinked. It was an unexpected beginning for the conversation. "Of course you are," he said, "but—"

"And because of this, I'm sad to say," Uncle Monty continued, as if he had not heard, "many people are jealous of me."

"I'm sure that's true," Violet said, puzzled.

"And when people are jealous," Uncle Monty said, shaking his head, "they will do anything. They will do crazy things. When I was getting my herpetology degree, my roommate was so envious of a new toad I had discovered that he stole and ate my only specimen. I had to X-ray his stomach, and use the X-rays rather than the toad in my presentation. And something tells me we may have a similar situation here."

What was Uncle Monty talking about?

"I'm afraid I don't quite follow you," Klaus said, which is the polite way of saying "What are you talking about, Uncle Monty?"

"Last night, after you went to bed, Stephano asked me a few too many questions about all the snakes and about my upcoming expedition. And do you know why?"

"I think so," Violet began, but Uncle Monty interrupted her.

"It is because this man who is calling himself Stephano," he said, "is really a member of the Herpetological Society, and he is here to try and find the Incredibly Deadly Viper so he can preempt my presentation. Do you three know what the word 'preempt' means?"

"No," Violet said, "but—"

"It means that I think this Stephano is going to steal my snake," Uncle Monty said, "and present it to the Herpetological Society. Because it is a new species, there's no way I can prove I discovered it. Before we know it, the Incredibly Deadly Viper will be called the Stephano Snake, or something dreadful like that. And if he's planning that, just think what he will do to our Peruvian expedition. Each toad we catch, each venom sample we put into a test tube, each snake interview we record—every scrap of work we do—will fall into the hands of this Herpetological Society spy."

"He's not a Herpetological Society spy," Klaus said impatiently, "he's Count Olaf!"

"I know just what you mean!" Uncle Monty said excitedly. "This sort of behavior is indeed as dastardly as that terrible man's. That is why I'm doing this." He raised one hand and waved the folded papers in the air. "As you know," he said, "tomorrow we are leaving for Peru. These are our tickets for the five o'clock voyage on the *Prospero*, a fine ship that will take us across the sea to South America. There's a ticket for me, one for Violet, one for Klaus, one for Stephano, but not one for Sunny because we're going to hide her in a suitcase to save money."

"Deepo!"

"I'm kidding about that. But I'm not kidding about this." Uncle Monty, his face flushed with excitement, took one of the folded papers and began ripping it into tiny pieces. "This is Stephano's ticket. He's not going to Peru with us after all. Tomorrow morning, I'm going to tell him that he needs to stay here and look after my specimens instead. That way we can run a successful expedition in peace."

"But Uncle Monty—" Klaus said.

"How many times must I remind you it's not polite to interrupt?" Uncle Monty interrupted, shaking his head. "In any case, I know what you're worried about. You're worried what will happen if he stays here alone with the Incredibly Deadly Viper. But don't worry. The Viper will join us on the expedition, traveling in one of our snake carrying cases. I don't know why you're looking so glum, Sunny. I thought you'd be happy to have the Viper's company. So don't look so worried, bambini. As you can see, your Uncle Monty has the situation in hand."

When somebody is a little bit wrong—say, when a waiter puts nonfat milk in your espresso macchiato, instead of lowfat milk—it is often quite easy to explain to them how and why they are wrong. But if somebody is surpassingly wrong—say, when a waiter bites your nose instead of taking your order—you can often be so surprised that you are unable to say anything at all. Paralyzed by how wrong the waiter is, your mouth would hang slightly open and your eyes would blink over and over, but you would be unable to say a word. This is what the Baudelaire children did. Uncle Monty was so wrong about Stephano, in thinking he was a herpetological spy rather than Count Olaf, that the three siblings could scarcely think of a way to tell him so.

"Come now, my dears," Uncle Monty said. "We've wasted enough of the morning on talk. We have to—*ow!*" He interrupted himself with a cry of surprise and pain, and fell to the ground.

"Uncle Monty!" Klaus cried. The Baudelaire children saw that a large, shiny object was on top of him, and realized a moment later what the object was: it was the heavy brass reading lamp, the one standing next to the large cushioned chair in Klaus's room.

"*Ow!*" Uncle Monty said again, pulling the lamp off him. "That really hurt. My shoulder may be sprained. It's a good thing it didn't land on my head, or it really could have done some damage."

"But where did it come from?" Violet asked.

"It must have fallen from the window," Uncle Monty said, pointing up to where Klaus's room was. "Whose room is that? Klaus, I believe it is yours. You must be more careful. You can't dangle heavy objects out the window like that. Look what almost happened."

"But that lamp wasn't anywhere near my window," Klaus said. "I keep it in the alcove, so I can read in that large chair."

"Really, Klaus," Uncle Monty said, standing up and handing him the lamp. "Do you honestly expect me to believe that the lamp danced over to the window and leaped onto my shoulder? Please put this back in your room, in a safe place, and we'll say no more about it."

"But—" Klaus said, but his older sister interrupted him.

"I'll help you, Klaus," Violet said. "We'll find a place for it where it's safe."

"Well, don't be too long," Uncle Monty said, rubbing his shoulder. "We'll see you in the Reptile Room. Come, Sunny."

Walking through the entry hall, the four parted ways at the stairs, with Uncle Monty and Sunny going to the enormous door of the Reptile Room, and Violet and Klaus carrying the heavy brass lamp up to Klaus's room.

"You know *very well*," Klaus hissed to his sister, "that I was *not careless* with this lamp."

"Of course I know that," Violet whispered. "But there's no use trying to explain that to

Uncle Monty. He thinks Stephano is a herpe-tological spy. You know as well as I do that Stephano was responsible for this."

"How clever of you to figure that out," said a voice at the top of the stairs, and Violet and Klaus were so surprised they almost dropped the lamp. It was Stephano, or, if you prefer, it was Count Olaf. It was the bad guy. "But then, you've always been clever children," he contin-ued. "A little too clever for my taste, but you won't be around for long, so I'm not troubled by it."

"You're not very clever yourself, " Klaus said fiercely. "This heavy brass lamp almost hit us, but if anything happens to my sisters or me, you'll never get your hands on the Baudelaire fortune."

"Dear me, dear me," Stephano said, his grimy teeth showing as he smiled. "If I wanted to harm *you*, orphan, your blood would already be pouring down these stairs like a waterfall. No, I'm not going to harm a hair on any Baudelaire head—not here in this house. You needn't be afraid of me, little ones, until we find ourselves in a location where crimes are more difficult to trace."

"And where would that be?" Violet asked. "We plan to stay right here until we grow up."

"Really?" Stephano said, in that sneaky, sneaky voice. "Why, I had the impression we were leaving the country tomorrow."

"Uncle Monty tore up your ticket," Klaus replied triumphantly. "He was suspicious of you, so he changed his plans and now you're not going with us."

Stephano's smile turned into a scowl, and his stained teeth seemed to grow bigger. His eyes grew so shiny that it hurt Violet and Klaus to look at them. "I wouldn't rely on that," he said, in a terrible, terrible voice. "Even the best plans can change if there's an accident." He pointed one spiky finger at the brass reading lamp. "And accidents happen all the time."

CHAPTER Six

Bad circumstances have a way of ruining things that would otherwise be pleasant. So it was with the Baudelaire orphans and the movie *Zombies in the Snow*. All afternoon, the three children had sat and worried in the Reptile Room, under the mocking stare of Stephano and the oblivious— the word "oblivious" here means "not aware that Stephano was really Count Olaf and thus being in a great deal of danger"—chatter of Uncle Monty. So by the time it was evening, the siblings

were in no mood for cinematic entertainment. Uncle Monty's jeep was really too small to hold him, Stephano and the three orphans, so Klaus and Violet shared a seat, and poor Sunny had to sit on Stephano's filthy lap, but the Baudelaires were too preoccupied to even notice their discomfort.

The children sat all in a row at the multiplex, with Uncle Monty to one side, while Stephano sat in the middle and hogged the popcorn. But the children were too anxious to eat any snacks, and too busy trying to figure out what Stephano planned to do to enjoy *Zombies in the Snow*, which was a fine film. When the zombies first rose out of the snowbanks surrounding the tiny Alpine fishing village, Violet tried to imagine a way in which Stephano could get aboard the *Prospero* without a ticket and accompany them to Peru. When the town fathers constructed a barrier of sturdy oak, only to have the zombies chomp their way through it, Klaus was concerned with exactly what Stephano had meant when he spoke about accidents. And when Gerta, the little milkmaid, made friends with the zombies and asked them to please stop eating the villagers, Sunny, who was of course scarcely old enough to comprehend the orphans' situation, tried to think up a way to defeat Stephano's plans, whatever they were. In the final scene of the movie, the zombies and villagers celebrated May Day together, but the three Baudelaire orphans were too nervous and afraid to enjoy themselves one bit. On the way home, Uncle Monty tried to talk to the silent, worried children sitting in the back, but they hardly said a word in reply and eventually he fell silent.

When the jeep pulled up to the snake-shaped hedges, the Baudelaire children dashed out and ran to the front door without even saying good night to their puzzled guardian. With heavy hearts they climbed the stairs to their bed-rooms, but when they reached their doors they could not bear to part.

"Could we all spend the night in the same room?" Klaus asked Violet timidly. "Last night I felt as if I were in a jail cell, worrying all by myself."

"Me too," Violet admitted. "Since we're not going to sleep, we might as well not sleep in the same place."

"Tikko," Sunny agreed, and followed her siblings into Violet's room. Violet looked around the bedroom and remembered how excited she had been to move into it just a short while ago. Now, the enormous window with the view of the snake-shaped hedges seemed depressing rather than inspiring, and the blank pages tacked to her wall, rather than being convenient, seemed only to remind her of how anxious she was.

"I see you haven't worked much on your inventions," Klaus said gently. "I haven't been reading at all. When Count Olaf is around, it sure puts a damper on the imagination."

"Not always," Violet pointed out. "When we lived with him, you read all about nuptial law to find out about his plan, and I invented a grappling hook to put a stop to it."

"In this situation, though," Klaus said glumly, "we don't even know what Count Olaf is up to. How can we formulate a plan if we don't know *his* plan?"

"Well, let's try to hash this out," Violet said, using an expression which here means "talk about something at length until we completely understand it." "Count Olaf, calling himself Stephano, has come to this house in disguise and is obviously after the Baudelaire fortune."

"And," Klaus continued, "once he gets his hands on it, he plans to kill us."

"Tadu," Sunny murmured solemnly, which probably meant something along the lines of "It's a loathsome situation in which we find ourselves."

"However," Violet said, "if he harms us,

there's no way he can get to our fortune. That's why he tried to marry me last time."

"Thank God that didn't work," Klaus said, shivering. "Then Count Olaf would be my brother-in-law. But this time he's not planning to marry you. He said something about an accident."

"And about heading to a location where crimes are more difficult to trace," Violet said, remembering his words. "That must mean Peru. But Stephano isn't going to Peru. Uncle Monty tore up his ticket."

"Doog!" Sunny shrieked, in a generic cry of frustration, and pounded her little fist on the floor. The word "generic" here means "when one is unable to think of anything else to say," and Sunny was not alone in this. Violet and Klaus were of course too old to say things like "Doog!" but they wished they weren't. They wished they could figure out Count Olaf's plan. They wished their situation didn't seem as mysterious and hopeless as it did, and they wished they were young enough to simply shriek "Doog!" and pound their fists on the floor. And most of all, of course, they wished that their parents were alive and that the Baudelaires were all safe in the home where they had been born.

And as fervently as the Baudelaire orphans wished their circumstances were different, I wish that I could somehow change the circumstances of this story for you. Even as I sit here, safe as can be and so very far from Count Olaf, I can scarcely bear to write another word. Perhaps it would be best if you shut this book right now and never read the rest of this horrifying story. You can imagine, if you wish, that an hour later, the Baudelaire orphans suddenly figured out what Stephano was up to and were able to save Uncle Monty's life. You can picture the police arriving with all their flashing lights and sirens, and dragging Stephano away to jail for the rest of his life. You can pretend, even though it is not so, that the Baudelaires are living happily with Uncle Monty to this day. Or

best of all, you can conjure up the illusion that
the Baudelaire parents have not been killed,
and that the terrible fire and Count Olaf and
Uncle Monty and all the other unfortunate
events are nothing more than a dream, a figment
of the imagination.

But this story is not a happy one, and I am not
happy to tell you that the Baudelaire orphans
sat dumbly in Violet's room—the word "dumbly"
here means "without speaking," rather than "in
a stupid way"—for the rest of the night. Had
someone peeped through the bedroom window
as the morning sun rose, they would have seen
the three children huddled together on the bed,
their eyes wide open and dark with worry. But
nobody peeped through the window. Somebody
knocked on the door, four loud knocks as if
something were being nailed shut.

The children blinked and looked at one
another. "Who is it?" Klaus called out, his voice
crackly from being silent so long.

Instead of an answer, whoever it was simply

turned the knob and the door swung slowly open. There stood Stephano, with his clothes all rumpled and his eyes shining brighter than they ever had before.

"Good morning," he said. "It's time to leave for Peru. There is just room for three orphans and myself in the jeep, so get a move on."

"We told you yesterday that you weren't going," Violet said. She hoped her voice sounded braver than she felt.

"It is your Uncle Monty who isn't going," Stephano said, and raised the part of his forehead where his eyebrow should have been.

"Don't be ridiculous," Klaus said. "Uncle Monty wouldn't miss this expedition for the world."

"Ask him," Stephano said, and the Baudelaires saw a familiar expression on his face. His mouth scarcely moved, but his eyes were shining as if he'd just told a joke. "Why don't you ask him? He's down in the Reptile Room."

"We *will* ask him," Violet said. "Uncle Monty

has no intention of letting you take us to Peru alone." She rose from the bed, took the hands of her siblings, and walked quickly past Stephano who was smirking in the doorway. "We *will* ask him," Violet said again, and Stephano gave a little bow as the children walked out of the room.

The hallway was strangely quiet, and blank as the eyes of a skull. "Uncle Monty?" Violet called, at the end of the hallway. Nobody answered.

Aside from a few creaks on the steps, the whole house was eerily quiet, as if it had been deserted for many years. "Uncle Monty?" Klaus called, at the bottom of the stairs. They heard nothing.

Standing on tiptoe, Violet opened the enormous door of the Reptile Room and for a moment, the orphans stared into the room as if hypnotized, entranced by the odd blue light which the sunrise made as it shone through the glass ceiling and walls. In the dim glow, they could see only silhouettes of the various reptiles as they moved around in their cages, or slept, curled into shapeless dark masses.

Their footsteps echoing off the glimmering walls, the three siblings walked through the Reptile Room, toward the far end, where Uncle Monty's library lay waiting for them. Even though the dark room felt mysterious and strange, it was a comforting mystery, and a safe strangeness. They remembered Uncle Monty's promise: that if they took time to learn the facts, no harm would come to them here in the Reptile Room. However, you and I remember that Uncle Monty's promise was laden with dramatic irony, and now, here in the early-morning gloom of the Reptile Room, that irony was going to come to fruition, a phrase which here means "the Baudelaires were finally to learn of it." For just as they reached the books, the three siblings could see a large, shadowy mass huddled in the far corner. Nervously, Klaus switched on one of the reading lamps to get a better look.

The shadowy mass was Uncle Monty. His mouth was slightly agape, as if he were surprised, and his eyes were wide open, but he didn't appear to see them. His face, usually so rosy, was very, very pale, and under his left eye were two small holes, right in a line, the sort of mark made by the two fangs of a snake.

"Divo soom?" Sunny asked, and tugged at his pants leg. Uncle Monty did not move. As he had promised, no harm had come to the Baudelaire orphans in the Reptile Room, but great harm had come to Uncle Monty.

C H A P T E R
Seven

"*My,* my, my, my, my," said a
voice from behind them, and
the Baudelaire orphans turned
to find Stephano standing
there, the black suitcase with
the shiny silver padlock in his
hands and a look of brum-
magem surprise on his face.
"Brummagem" is such a rare
word for "fake" that even
Klaus didn't know what it
meant, but the children did
not have to be told that
Stephano was pretending to be

surprised. "What a terrible accident has happened here. Snakebite. Whoever discovers this
will be most upset."

"You—" Violet began to say, but her throat
fluttered, as if the fact of Uncle Monty's death
were food that tasted terrible. "You—" she said
again.

Stephano took no notice. "Of course, after
they discover that Dr. Montgomery is dead,
they'll wonder what became of those repulsive
orphans he had lying around the house. But
they'll be long gone. Speaking of which, it's
time to leave. The *Prospero* sails at five o'clock
from Hazy Harbor and I'd like to be the first
passenger aboard. That way I'll have time for a
bottle of wine before lunch."

"How could you?" Klaus whispered hoarsely.
He couldn't take his eyes off Uncle Monty's
pale, pale face. "How could you do this? How
could you murder him?"

"Why, Klaus, I'm surprised," Stephano said,
and walked over to Uncle Monty's body. "A

smarty-pants boy like you should be able to figure out that your chubby old uncle died from
snakebite, not from murder. Look at those teeth
marks. Look at his pale, pale face. Look at these
staring eyes."

"*Stop it!*" Violet said. "*Don't talk like that!*"

"You're right!" Stephano said. "There's no
time for chitchat! We have a ship to catch! Let's
move!"

"We're not going anywhere with you," Klaus
said. His face was pinched with the effort of
focusing on their predicament rather than going
to pieces. "We will stay here until the police
come."

"And how do you suppose the police will
know to come?" Stephano said.

"We will call them," Klaus said, in what he
hoped was a firm tone of voice, and began to
walk toward the door.

Stephano dropped his suitcase, the shiny
silver padlock making a clattering sound as it
hit the marble floor. He took a few steps and

blocked Klaus's way, his eyes wide and red with fury. "I am *so tired*," Stephano snarled, "of having to *explain* everything to you. You're supposed to be *so very smart*, and yet you always seem to forget about *this!*" He reached into his pocket and pulled out the jagged knife. "This is my knife. It is very sharp and very eager to hurt you— almost as eager as I am. If you don't do what I say, you will suffer bodily harm. Is that clear enough for you? Now, get in the damn jeep."

It is, as you know, very, very rude and usually unnecessary to use profanity, but the Baudelaire orphans were too terrified to point this out to Stephano. Taking a last look at their poor Uncle Monty, the three children followed Stephano to the door of the Reptile Room to get in the damn jeep. To add insult to injury—a phrase which here means "forcing somebody to do an unpleasant task when they're already very upset"— Stephano forced Violet to carry his suitcase out of the house, but she was too lost in her own thoughts to care. She was remembering the last

conversation she and her siblings had had with
Uncle Monty, and thinking with a cold rush of
shame that it hadn't really been a conversation
at all. You will recall, of course, that on the ride
home from seeing *Zombies in the Snow*, the children had been so worried about Stephano that
they hadn't said a word to Uncle Monty, and
that when the jeep had arrived at the house, the
Baudelaire orphans had dashed upstairs to hash
out the situation, without even saying good
night to the man who now lay dead under a
sheet in the Reptile Room. As the youngsters
reached the jeep, Violet tried to remember if
they had even thanked him for taking them
to the movies, but the night was all a blur. She
thought that she, Klaus, and Sunny had probably said "Thank you, Uncle Monty," when
they were standing together at the ticket booth,
but she couldn't be sure. Stephano opened the
door of the jeep and gestured with the knife,
ushering Klaus and Sunny into the tiny backseat and Violet, the black suitcase heavy on her

lap, into the front seat beside him. The orphans had a brief hope that the engine would not start when Stephano turned the key in the ignition, but this was a futile hope. Uncle Monty took good care of his jeep, and it started right up.

Violet, Klaus, and Sunny looked behind them as Stephano began to drive alongside the snake-shaped hedges. At the sight of the Reptile Room, which Uncle Monty had filled so carefully with his specimens and in which he was now a sort of specimen himself, the weight of the Baudelaires' despair was too much for them and they quietly began to cry. It is a curious thing, the death of a loved one. We all know that our time in this world is limited, and that eventually all of us will end up underneath some sheet, never to wake up. And yet it is always a surprise when it happens to someone we know. It is like walking up the stairs to your bedroom in the dark, and thinking there is one more stair than there is. Your foot falls down, through the air, and there is a sickly moment of dark surprise as you try and readjust the way you thought of things. The Baudelaire orphans were crying not only for their Uncle Monty, but for their own parents, and this dark and curious feeling of falling that accompanies any great loss.

What was to happen to them? Stephano had heartlessly slaughtered the man who was supposed to be watching over the Baudelaires, and now they were all alone. What would Stephano do to them? He was supposed to be left behind when they went to Peru, and now he would be leaving with them on the *Prospero*. And what terrible things would happen in Peru? Would anybody rescue them there? Would Stephano get his hands on the fortune? And what would happen to the three children afterward? These are frightening questions, and if you are thinking about such matters, they require your full attention, and the orphans were so immersed in thinking about them that they didn't realize that Stephano was about to collide with another automobile until the moment of impact.

There was a horrible tearing sound of metal and glass as a black car crashed into Uncle Monty's jeep, throwing the children to the floor with a jarring *thump* that felt as though it left the Baudelaire stomachs up on the seat. The black suitcase lurched into Violet's shoulder and then forward into the windshield, which immediately cracked in a dozen places so it looked like a spiderweb. Stephano gave a cry of surprise and turned the steering wheel this way and that, but the two vehicles were locked together and, with another *thump*, veered off the road into a small pile of mud. It is a rare occurrence when a car accident can be called a stroke of good fortune, but that was most certainly the case here. With the snake-shaped hedges still clearly visible behind them, the Baudelaires' journey toward Hazy Harbor had stopped.

Stephano gave another sharp cry, this one of rage. "Blasted furnaces of hell!" he shouted, as Violet rubbed her shoulder to make sure she wasn't seriously hurt. Klaus and Sunny got up cautiously from the jeep floor and looked out the cracked windshield. There appeared to be only one person in the other car, but it was hard to tell, as that vehicle had clearly suffered much more damage than Monty's jeep. Its entire front had pleated itself together, like an accordion, and one hubcap was spinning noisily on the pavement of Lousy Lane, making blurry circles as if it were a giant coin somebody had dropped. The driver was dressed in gray and making a rough hacking sound as he opened the crumpled door of the car and struggled his way out. He made the hacking sound again, and then reached into a pocket of his suit and pulled out a white handkerchief.

"It's Mr. Poe!" Klaus cried.

It *was* Mr. Poe, coughing away as usual, and the children were so delighted to see him that they found themselves smiling despite their horrible circumstances. "Mr. Poe! Mr. Poe!" Violet cried, reaching around Stephano's suitcase to open the passenger door.

Stephano reached out an arm and grabbed her sore shoulder, turning his head slowly so that each child saw his shiny eyes. "This changes *nothing*!" he hissed at them. "This is a bit of luck for you, but it is your last. The three of you will be back in this car with me and heading toward Hazy Harbor in time to catch the *Prospero*, I promise you."

"We'll see about that," Violet replied, opening the door and sliding out from beneath the suitcase. Klaus opened his door and followed her, carrying Sunny. "Mr. Poe! Mr. Poe!"

"Violet?" Mr. Poe asked. "Violet Baudelaire? Is that you?"

"Yes, Mr. Poe," Violet said. "It's all of us, and we're so grateful you ran into us like this."

"Well, I wouldn't say that," Mr. Poe said. "This was clearly the other driver's fault. *You* ran into *me*."

"How dare you!" Stephano shouted, and got out of the car himself, wrinkling his nose at the smell of horseradish that filled the air. He stomped over to where Mr. Poe was standing, but halfway there the children saw his face change from one of pure rage to one of brummagem confusion and sadness. "I'm sorry," he said, in a high, fluttery voice. "This whole thing is my fault. I'm so distressed by what has happened that I wasn't paying any attention to the rules of the road. I hope you're not hurt, Mr. Foe."

"It's *Poe*," Mr. Poe said. "My name is *Poe*. I'm not hurt. Luckily, it looks like nobody was hurt. I wish the same could be said for my car. But who are you and what are you doing with the Baudelaire children?"

"I'll tell you who he is," Klaus said. "He's—"

"Please, Klaus," Mr. Poe admonished, a word which here means "reprimanded Klaus even though he was interrupting for a very good reason." "It is not polite to interrupt."

"My name is Stephano," Stephano said, shaking Mr. Poe's hand. "I am—I mean I *was*—Dr. Montgomery's assistant."

"What do you mean *was?*" Mr. Poe asked sternly. "Were you fired?"

"No. Dr. Montgomery—oh, excuse me—" Stephano turned away and pretended to dab at his eyes as if he were too sad to continue. Facing away from Mr. Poe, he gave the orphans a big wink before continuing. "I'm sorry to tell you there's been a horrible accident, Mr. Doe. Dr. Montgomery is dead."

"Poe," Mr. Poe said. "He's dead? That's terrible. What has happened?"

"I don't know," Stephano said. "It looks like snakebite to me, but I don't know anything about snakes. That's why I was going into town, to get a doctor. The children seemed too upset to be left alone."

"He's not taking us to get a doctor!" Klaus shouted. "He's taking us to Peru!"

"You see what I mean?" Stephano said to Mr. Poe, patting Klaus's head. "The children are obviously very distressed. Dr. Montgomery was going to take them to Peru today."

"Yes, I know," Mr. Poe said. "That's why I hurried over here this morning, to finally bring them their luggage. Klaus, I know you're confused and upset over this accident, but please try to understand that if Dr. Montgomery is really dead, the expedition is canceled."

"But Mr. Poe—" Klaus said indignantly.

"Please," Mr. Poe said. "This is a matter for adults to discuss, Klaus. Clearly, a doctor needs to be called."

"Well, why don't you drive on up to the house," Stephano said, "and I'll take the children and find a doctor."

"*José!*" Sunny shrieked, which probably meant something like "No way!"

"Why don't we all go to the house," Mr. Poe said, "and *call* for a doctor?"

Stephano blinked, and for a second his face grew angry again before he was able to calm himself and answer smoothly. "Of course," he said. "I should have called earlier. Obviously I'm not thinking as clearly as you. Here, children, get back in the jeep, and Mr. Poe will follow us."

"We're not getting back in that car with you," Klaus said firmly.

"*Please*, Klaus," Mr. Poe said. "Try to understand. There's been a serious accident. All other discussions will have to be put aside. The only trouble is, I'm not sure my car will start. It's very smashed up."

"Try the ignition," Stephano said. Mr. Poe nodded, and walked back to his car. He sat in the driver's seat and turned the key. The engine made a rough, wet noise—it sounded quite a bit like Mr. Poe's coughs—but it did not start.

"I'm afraid the engine is quite dead," Mr. Poe called out.

"And before long," Stephano muttered to the children, "you will be too."

"I'm sorry," Mr. Poe said. "I couldn't hear you."

Stephano smiled. "I said, that's too bad. Well, why don't I take the orphans back to the house, and you walk behind us? There isn't room for everyone."

Mr. Poe frowned. "But the children's suitcases are here. I don't want to leave them unattended. Why don't we put the luggage into your car, and the children and I will walk back to the house?"

Stephano frowned. "Well, one of the children should ride with me, so I won't get lost."

Mr. Poe smiled. "But you can see the house from here. You won't get lost."

"Stephano doesn't want us to be alone with you," Violet said, finally speaking up. She had been waiting for the proper moment to make her case. "He's afraid that we'll tell you who he really is, and what he's really up to."

"What's she talking about?" Mr. Poe asked Stephano.

"I have no idea, Mr. Toe," Stephano replied, shaking his head and looking at Violet fiercely.

Violet took a deep breath. "This man is not Stephano," she said, pointing at him. "He's Count Olaf, and he's here to take us away."

"Who am I?" Stephano asked. "What am I doing?"

Mr. Poe looked Stephano up and down, and then shook his head. "Forgive the children," he said. "They are very upset. Count Olaf is a terrible man who tried to steal their money, and the youngsters are very frightened of him."

"Do I look like this Count Olaf?" Stephano asked, his eyes shining.

"No, you don't," Mr. Poe said. "Count Olaf had one long eyebrow, and a clean-shaven face. You have a beard, and if you don't mind my saying so, no eyebrows at all."

"He shaved his eyebrow," Violet said, "and grew a beard. Anyone can see that."

"And he has the tattoo!" Klaus cried. "The eye tattoo, on his ankle! Look at the tattoo!"

Mr. Poe looked at Stephano, and shrugged apologetically. "I'm sorry to ask you this," he said, "but the children seem so upset, and before we discuss anything further I'd like to set their minds at ease. Would you mind showing me your ankle?"

"I'd be happy to," Stephano said, giving the children a toothy smile. "Right or left?"

Klaus closed his eyes and thought for a second. "Left," he said.

Stephano placed his left foot on the bumper of Uncle Monty's jeep. Looking at the Baudelaire orphans with his shiny, shiny eyes, he began to raise the leg of his stained striped pants. Violet, Klaus, Sunny, and Mr. Poe all kept their eyes on Stephano's ankle.

The pant leg went up, like a curtain rising to begin a play. But there was no tattoo of an eye to be seen. The Baudelaire orphans stared at a patch of smooth skin, as blank and pale as poor Uncle Monty's face.

Eight

While the jeep sputtered ahead of them, the Baudelaire orphans trudged back toward Uncle Monty's house, the scent of horseradish in their nostrils and a feeling of frustration in their hearts. It is very unnerving to be proven wrong, particularly when you are really right and the person who is really wrong is the one who is proving you wrong and proving himself, wrongly, right. Right?

"I don't know how he got rid of his tattoo," Klaus said stubbornly to Mr. Poe, who was coughing into his handkerchief, "but that's definitely Count Olaf."

"Klaus," Mr. Poe said, when he had stopped coughing, "this is getting very tiresome, going over this again and again. We have just seen Stephano's unblemished ankle. 'Unblemished' means—"

"We *know* what 'unblemished' means," Klaus said, watching Stephano get out of Uncle Monty's jeep and walk quickly into the house. "'Without tattoos.' But it *is* Count Olaf. Why can't you see it?"

"All I can see," Mr. Poe said, "is what's in front of me. I see a man with no eyebrows, a beard, and no tattoo, and that's not Count Olaf. Anyway, even if by some chance this Stephano wishes you harm, you have nothing to fear. It is quite shocking that Dr. Montgomery has died, but we're not simply going to hand over you and your fortune to his assistant. Why, this man can't even remember my name!"

Klaus looked at his siblings and sighed. It

would be easier, they realized, to argue with the snake-shaped hedge than with Mr. Poe when he had made up his mind. Violet was about to try reasoning with him one more time when a horn honked behind them. The Baudelaires and Mr. Poe got out of the way of the approaching automobile, a small gray car with a very skinny driver. The car stopped in front of the house and the skinny person got out, a tall man in a white coat.

"May we help you?" Mr. Poe called, as he and the children approached.

"I am Dr. Lucafont," the tall man said, pointing to himself with a big, solid hand. "I received a call that there's been a terrible accident involving a snake."

"You're here already?" Mr. Poe asked. "But Stephano has scarcely had time to call, let alone for you to drive here."

"I believe that speed is of the essence in an emergency, don't you?" Dr. Lucafont said. "If an autopsy is to be performed, it should be done immediately."

"Of course, of course," Mr. Poe said quickly. "I was just surprised."

"Where is the body?" Dr. Lucafont asked, walking toward the door.

"Stephano can tell you," Mr. Poe said, opening the door of the house. Stephano was waiting in the entryway, holding a coffeepot.

"I'm going to make some coffee," he said. "Who wants some?"

"I'll have a cup," Dr. Lucafont said. "Nothing like a hearty cup of coffee before starting the day's work."

Mr. Poe frowned. "Shouldn't you take a look at Dr. Montgomery first?"

"Yes, Dr. Lucafont," Stephano said. "Time is of the essence in an emergency, don't you think?"

"Yes, yes, I suppose you're right," Dr. Lucafont said.

"Poor Dr. Montgomery is in the Reptile

Room," Stephano said, gesturing to where the Baudelaires' guardian still lay. "Please do a thorough examination, and *then* you may have some coffee."

"You're the boss," Dr. Lucafont said, opening the door of the Reptile Room with an oddly stiff hand. Stephano led Mr. Poe into the kitchen, and the Baudelaires glumly followed. When one feels useless and unable to help, one can use the expression "feeling like a fifth wheel," because if something has four wheels, such as a wagon or a car, there is no real need for a fifth. As Stephano brewed coffee for the adults, the three children sat down at the kitchen table where they had first had coconut cake with Uncle Monty just a short time ago, and Violet, Klaus, and Sunny felt like fifth, sixth, and seventh wheels on a car that was going the wrong direction—toward Hazy Harbor, and the departing *Prospero*.

"When I spoke to Dr. Lucafont on the phone," Stephano said, "I told him about the accident with your car. When he is done with his medical examination, he will drive you into town to get a mechanic and I will stay here with the orphans."

"No," Klaus said firmly. "We are not staying alone with him for an instant."

Mr. Poe smiled as Stephano poured him a cup of coffee, and looked sternly at Klaus. "Klaus, I realize you are very upset, but it is inexcusable for you to keep treating Stephano so rudely. Please apologize to him at once."

"*No!*" Klaus cried.

"That's quite all right, Mr. Yoe," Stephano said soothingly. "The children are upset over Dr. Montgomery's murder, so I don't expect them to be on their best behavior."

"Murder?" Violet said. She turned to Stephano and tried to look as if she were merely politely curious, instead of enraged. "Why did you say *murder,* Stephano?"

Stephano's face darkened, and his hands

clenched at his sides. It looked like there was nothing he wanted to do more than scratch out Violet's eyes. "I misspoke," he said finally.

"Of course he did," Mr. Poe said, sipping from his cup. "But the children can come with Dr. Lucafont and me if they feel more comfortable that way."

"I'm not sure they will fit," Stephano said, his eyes shining. "It's a very small car. But if the orphans would rather, they could come with me in the jeep and we could follow you and Dr. Lucafont to the mechanic."

The three orphans looked at one another and thought hard. Their situation seemed like a game, although this game had desperately high stakes. The object of the game was not to end up alone with Stephano, for when they did, he would whisk them away on the *Prospero*. What would happen then, when they were alone in Peru with such a greedy and despicable person, they did not want to think about. What they had to think about was stopping it from happening. It seemed incredible that their very lives hinged on a carpooling conversation, but in life it is often the tiny details that end up being the most important.

"Why don't we ride with Dr. Lucafont," Violet said carefully, "and Mr. Poe can ride with Stephano?"

"Whatever for?" Mr. Poe asked.

"I've always wanted to see the inside of a doctor's automobile," Violet said, knowing that this was a fairly lame invention.

"Oh yes, me too," Klaus said. "Please, can't we ride with Dr. Lucafont?"

"I'm afraid not," Dr. Lucafont said from the doorway, surprising everyone. "Not all three of you children, anyway. I have placed Dr. Montgomery's body in my car, which only leaves room for two more passengers."

"Have you completed your examination already?" Mr. Poe asked.

"The preliminary one, yes," Dr. Lucafont said.

"I will have to take the body for some further tests, but my autopsy shows that the doctor died of snakebite. Is there any coffee left for me?"

"Of course," Stephano answered, and poured him a cup.

"How can you be sure?" Violet asked the doctor.

"What do you mean?" Dr. Lucafont said quizzically. "I can be sure there's coffee left because I see it right here."

"What I think Violet means," Mr. Poe said, "is how can you be sure that Dr. Montgomery died of snakebite?"

"In his veins, I found the venom of the Mamba du Mal, one of the world's most poisonous snakes."

"Does this mean that there's a poisonous snake loose in this house?" Mr. Poe asked.

"No, no," Dr. Lucafont said. "The Mamba du Mal is safe in its cage. It must have gotten out, bitten Dr. Montgomery, and locked itself up again."

"*What?*" Violet asked. "That's a ridiculous theory. A snake cannot operate a lock by itself."

"Perhaps other snakes helped it," Dr. Lucafont said calmly, sipping his coffee. "Is there anything here to eat? I had to rush over here without my breakfast."

"Your story does seem a little odd," Mr. Poe said. He looked questioningly at Dr. Lucafont, who was opening a cupboard and peering inside.

"Terrible accidents, I have found, are often odd," he replied.

"It can't have been an accident," Violet said. "Uncle Monty is—" She stopped. "Uncle Monty *was* one of the world's most respected herpetologists. He never would have kept a poisonous snake in a cage it could open itself."

"If it wasn't an accident," Dr. Lucafont said, "then someone would have had to do this on purpose. Obviously, you three children didn't kill him, and the only other person in the house was Stephano."

"And I," Stephano added quickly, "hardly know anything about snakes. I've only been working here for two days and scarcely had time to learn anything."

"It certainly appears to be an accident," Mr. Poe said. "I'm sorry, children. Dr. Montgomery seemed like an appropriate guardian for you."

"He was more than that," Violet said quietly. "He was much, much more than an appropriate guardian."

"That's Uncle Monty's food!" Klaus cried out suddenly, his face contorted in anger. He pointed at Dr. Lucafont, who had taken a can out of the cupboard. *"Stop eating his food!"*

"I was only going to have a few peaches," Dr. Lucafont said. With one of his oddly solid hands, he held up a can of peaches Uncle Monty had bought only yesterday.

"Please," Mr. Poe said gently to Dr. Lucafont. "The children are very upset. I'm sure you can understand that. Violet, Klaus, Sunny, why don't you excuse yourselves for a little while? We have much to discuss, and you are obviously too overwrought to participate. Now, Dr. Lucafont, let's try and figure this out. You have room for three passengers, including Dr. Montgomery's body. And you, Stephano, have room for three passengers as well."

"So it's very simple," Stephano said. "You and the corpse will go in Dr. Lucafont's car, and I will drive behind you with the children."

"*No,*" Klaus said firmly.

"Baudelaires," Mr. Poe said, just as firmly, "will you three please excuse yourselves?"

"Afoop!" Sunny shrieked, which probably meant "No."

"Of course we will," Violet said, giving Klaus and Sunny a significant look, and taking her siblings' hands, she half-led them, half-dragged them out of the kitchen. Klaus and Sunny looked up at their older sister, and saw that something about her had changed. Her face looked more determined than grief-stricken, and she walked quickly, as if she were late for something.

You will remember, of course, that even years later, Klaus would lie awake in bed, filled with regret that he didn't call out to the driver of the taxicab who had brought Stephano into their lives once more. But in this respect Violet was luckier than her brother. For unlike Klaus, who was so surprised when he first recognized Stephano that the moment to act passed him by, Violet realized, as she heard the adults drone on and on, that the time to act was now. I cannot say that Violet, years later, slept easily when she looked back on her life—there were too many miserable times for any of the Baudelaires to be peaceful sleepers—but she was always a bit proud of herself that she realized she and her siblings should in fact excuse themselves from the kitchen and move to a more helpful location.

"What are we doing?" Klaus asked. "Where are we going?" Sunny, too, looked questioningly at her sister, but Violet merely shook her head in answer, and walked faster, toward the door of the Reptile Room.

When Violet opened the enormous door
of the Reptile Room, the reptiles
were still there in their cages, the
books were still on their shelves,
and the morning sun was still
streaming through the glass walls, but the
place simply wasn't the same. Even though
Dr. Lucafont had removed Uncle Monty's
body, the Reptile Room was not as invit-
ing as it used to be, and probably never
would be. What happens in a certain
place can stain your feelings for that
location, just as ink can stain a white
sheet. You can wash it, and wash it, and

still never forget what has transpired, a word which here means "happened and made everybody sad."

"I don't want to go in," Klaus said. "Uncle Monty died in here."

"I know we don't want to be here," Violet said, "but we have work to do."

"Work?" Klaus asked. "What work?"

Violet gritted her teeth. "We have work to do," she said, "that Mr. Poe should be doing, but as usual, he is well intentioned but of no real help." Klaus and Sunny sighed as she spoke out loud a sentiment all three siblings had never said, but always felt, since Mr. Poe had taken over their affairs. "Mr. Poe doesn't believe that Stephano and Count Olaf are the same person. And he believes that Uncle Monty's death was an accident. We have to prove him wrong on both counts."

"But Stephano doesn't have the tattoo," Klaus pointed out. "And Dr. Lucafont found the venom of the Mamba du Mal in Monty's veins."

"I know, I know," Violet said impatiently. "The three of us know the truth, but in order to convince the adults, we have to find evidence and proof of Stephano's plan."

"If only we'd found evidence and proof earlier," Klaus said glumly. "Then maybe we could have saved Uncle Monty's life."

"We'll never know about that," Violet said quietly. She looked around at the Reptile Room, which Monty had worked on his whole life. "But if we put Stephano behind bars for his murder, we'll at least be able to prevent him from harming anyone else."

"Including us," Klaus pointed out.

"Including us," Violet agreed. "Now, Klaus, find all of Uncle Monty's books that might contain information about the Mamba du Mal. Let me know when you find anything."

"But all that research could take days," Klaus said, looking at Monty's considerable library.

"Well, we don't have days," Violet said firmly. "We don't even have hours. At five o'clock, the *Prospero* leaves Hazy Harbor, and Stephano is going to do everything he can to make sure we're on that ship. And if we end up alone in Peru with him—"

"All right, all right," Klaus said. "Let's get started. Here, you take this book."

"I'm not taking any book," Violet said. "While you're in the library, I'm going up to Stephano's room to see if I can find any clues."

"Alone?" Klaus asked. "In his room?"

"It'll be perfectly safe," Violet said, although she knew nothing of the kind. "Get cracking with the books, Klaus. Sunny, watch the door and bite anybody who tries to get in."

"Ackroid!" Sunny said, which probably meant something like "Roger!"

Violet left, and true to her word, Sunny sat near the door with her teeth bared. Klaus walked to the far end of the room where the library was, carefully avoiding the aisle where the poisonous snakes were kept. He didn't even want to look at the Mamba du Mal or any other deadly reptile. Even though Klaus knew that Uncle Monty's death was the fault of Stephano and not really of the snake, he could not bear to look at the reptile who had put an end to the happy times he and his sisters had enjoyed. Klaus sighed, and opened a book, and as at so many other times when the middle Baudelaire child did not want to think about his circumstances, he began to read.

It is now necessary for me to use the rather hackneyed phrase "meanwhile, back at the ranch." The word "hackneyed" here means "used by so, so many writers that by the time Lemony Snicket uses it, it is a tiresome cliché." "Meanwhile, back at the ranch" is a phrase used to link what is going on in one part of the story to what is going on in another part of the story, and it has nothing to do with cows or with horses or with any people who work in rural areas where ranches are, or even with ranch dressing, which is creamy and put on salads. Here, the phrase "meanwhile, back at the ranch" refers to what Violet was doing while Klaus and Sunny were in the Reptile Room. For as Klaus began his research in Uncle Monty's library, and Sunny guarded the door with her sharp teeth, Violet was up to something I am sure will be of interest to you.

Meanwhile, back at the ranch, Violet went to listen at the kitchen door, trying to catch what the adults were saying. As I'm sure you know, the key to good eavesdropping is not getting caught, and Violet moved as quietly as she could, trying not to step on any creaky parts of the floor. When she reached the door of the kitchen, she took her hair ribbon out of her pocket and dropped it on the floor, so if anyone opened the door she could claim that she was kneeling down to pick it up, rather than to eavesdrop. This was a trick she had learned when she was very small, when she would listen at her parents' bedroom door to hear what they might be planning for her birthday, and like all good tricks, it still worked.

"But Mr. Poe, if Stephano rides with me in my car, and you drive Dr. Montgomery's jeep," Dr. Lucafont was saying, "then how will you know the way?"

"I see your point," Mr. Poe said. "But I don't think Sunny will be willing to sit on Dr. Montgomery's lap, if he's dead. We'll have to work out another way."

"I've got it," Stephano said. "I will drive the children in Dr. Lucafont's car, and Dr. Lucafont can go with you and Dr. Montgomery in Dr. Montgomery's jeep."

"I'm afraid that won't work," Dr. Lucafont said gravely. "The city laws won't allow anybody else to drive my car."

"And we haven't even discussed the issue of the children's luggage," Mr. Poe said.

Violet stood up, having heard enough to know she had enough time to go up to Stephano's room. Quietly, quietly, Violet walked up the staircase and down the hallway toward Stephano's door, where he had sat holding the knife that fearsome night. When she reached his door, Violet stopped. It was amazing, she thought, how everything having to do with Count Olaf was frightening. He was such a terrible person that merely the sight of his bedroom door could get her heart pounding. Violet found herself half hoping that Stephano would bound up the stairs and stop her, just so she wouldn't have to open this door and go into the room where he slept. But then Violet thought of her own safety, and the safety of her two siblings. If one's safety is threatened, one often finds courage one didn't know one had, and the eldest Baudelaire found she could be brave enough to open the door. Her shoulder still aching from the car collision, Violet turned the brass handle of the door and walked inside.

The room, as Violet suspected, was a dirty mess. The bed was unmade and had cracker crumbs and bits of hair all over it. Discarded newspapers and mail-order catalogs lay on the floor in untidy piles. On top of the dresser was a small assortment of half-empty wine bottles. The closet door was open, revealing a bunch of rusty wire coathangers that shivered in the drafty room. The curtains over the windows were all bunched up and encrusted with something flaky, and as Violet drew closer she realized with faint horror that Stephano had blown his nose on them.

But although it was disgusting, hardened phlegm was not the sort of evidence Violet was hoping for. The eldest Baudelaire orphan stood in the center of the room and surveyed the sticky disorder of the bedroom. Everything was horrendous, nothing was helpful. Violet rubbed her sore shoulder and remembered when she and her siblings were living with Count Olaf and found themselves locked in his tower room. Although it was frightening to be trapped in his inner sanctum—a phrase which here means "filthy room in which evil plans are devised"—it turned out to be quite useful, because they were able to read up on nuptial law and work their way out of their predicament. But here, in Stephano's inner sanctum at Uncle Monty's house, all Violet could find were signs of uncleanliness. Somewhere Stephano must have left a trail of evidence that Violet could find and use to convince Mr. Poe, but where was it? Disheartened—and afraid she had spent too much time in Stephano's bedroom—Violet went quietly back downstairs.

"No, no, no," Mr. Poe was saying, when she stopped to listen at the kitchen door again. "Dr. Montgomery can't drive. He's dead. There must be a way to do this."

"I've told you over and over," Stephano said, and Violet could tell that he was growing angry. "The easiest way is for me to take the three children into town, while you follow with Dr. Lucafont and the corpse. What could be simpler?"

"Perhaps you're right," Mr. Poe said with a sigh, and Violet hurried into the Reptile Room.

"Klaus, Klaus," she cried. "Tell me you've found something! I went to Stephano's room but there's nothing there to help us, and I think Stephano's going to get us alone in his car."

Klaus smiled for an answer and began to read out loud from the book he was holding. "'The Mamba du Mal,'" he read, "'is one of the deadliest snakes in the hemisphere, noted for its strangulatory grip, used in conjunction with its deadly venom, giving all of its victims a tenebrous hue, which is ghastly to behold.'"

"Strangulatory? Conjunction? Tenebrous? Hue?" Violet repeated. "I have no idea what you're talking about."

"I didn't either," Klaus admitted, "until I looked up some of the words. 'Strangulatory' means 'having to do with strangling.' 'In conjunction' means 'together.' 'Tenebrous' means 'dark.' And 'hue' means 'color.' So the Mamba du Mal is noted for strangling people while it bites them, leaving their corpses dark with bruises."

"Stop! Stop!" Violet cried, covering her ears. "I don't want to hear any more about what happened to Uncle Monty!"

"You don't understand," Klaus said gently. "That *isn't* what happened to Uncle Monty."

"But Dr. Lucafont said there was the venom of the Mamba du Mal in Monty's veins," she said.

"I'm sure there was," Klaus said, "but the snake didn't put it there. If it had, Uncle Monty's body would have been dark with bruises. But you and I remember that it was as pale as can be."

Violet started to speak, and then stopped, remembering the pale, pale face of Uncle Monty when they discovered him. "That's true," she said. "But then how was he poisoned?"

"Remember how Uncle Monty said he kept the venoms of all his poisonous snakes in test tubes, to study them?" Klaus said. "I think Stephano took the venom and injected it into Uncle Monty."

"Really?" Violet shuddered. "That's awful."

"Okipi!" Sunny shrieked, apparently in agreement.

"When we tell Mr. Poe about this," Klaus said confidently, "Stephano will be arrested for Uncle Monty's murder and sent to jail. No longer will he try to whisk us away to Peru, or threaten us with knives, or make us carry his suitcase, or anything like that."

Violet looked at her brother, her eyes wide with excitement. "Suitcase!" she said. "His suitcase!"

"What are you talking about?" Klaus said quizzically, and Violet was about to explain when there was a knock on the door.

"Come in," Violet called, signaling to Sunny not to bite Mr. Poe as he walked in.

"I hope you are feeling a bit calmer," Mr. Poe said, looking at each of the children in turn, "and no longer entertaining the thought that Stephano is Count Olaf." When Mr. Poe used the word "entertaining" here he meant "thinking," rather than "singing or dancing or putting on skits."

"Even if he's not Count Olaf," Klaus said carefully, "we think he may be responsible for Uncle Monty's death."

"Nonsense!" Mr. Poe exclaimed, as Violet shook her head at her brother. "Uncle Monty's death was a terrible accident, and nothing more."

Klaus held up the book he was reading. "But while you were in the kitchen, we were reading about snakes, and—"

"Reading about snakes?" Mr. Poe said. "I should think you'd want to read about any-thing *but* snakes, after what happened to Dr. Montgomery."

"But I found out something," Klaus said, "that—"

"It doesn't matter what you found out about snakes," Mr. Poe said, taking out a handker-chief. The Baudelaires waited while he coughed into it before returning it to his pocket. "It doesn't matter," he said again, "what you found out about snakes. Stephano doesn't know anything about snakes. He told us that himself."

"But—" Klaus said, but he stopped when he saw Violet. She shook her head at him again, just slightly. It was a signal, telling him not to say anything more to Mr. Poe. He looked at his sister, and then at Mr. Poe, and shut his mouth.

Mr. Poe coughed slightly into his handkerchief and looked at his wristwatch. "Now that we have settled that matter, there is the issue of riding in the car. I know that the three of you were eager to see the inside of a doctor's automobile, but we've discussed it over and over and there's simply no way it can work. You three are going to ride with Stephano into town, while I will ride with Dr. Lucafont and your Uncle Monty. Stephano and Dr. Lucafont are unloading all the bags now and we will leave in a few minutes. If you will excuse me, I have to call the Herpetological Society and tell them the bad news." Mr. Poe coughed once more into his handkerchief and left the room.

"Why didn't you want me to tell Mr. Poe what I read?" Klaus asked Violet, when he was sure Mr. Poe was out of earshot, a word which here means "close enough to hear him." Violet didn't answer. She was looking through the glass wall of the Reptile Room, watching Dr. Lucafont and Stephano walk past the snake-shaped hedges to Uncle Monty's jeep. Stephano opened the jeep door, and Dr. Lucafont began to carry suitcases out of the backseat in his strangely stiff hands. "Violet, why didn't you want me to tell Mr. Poe what I read?"

"When the adults come to fetch us," Violet said, ignoring Klaus's question, "keep them in the Reptile Room until I get back."

"But how will I do that?" Klaus asked.

"Create a distraction," Violet answered impatiently, still looking out the window at the little pile of suitcases Dr. Lucafont was making.

"What distraction?" Klaus asked anxiously. "How?"

"For goodness' sake, Klaus," his older sister replied. "You have read hundreds of books. Surely you must have read something about creating a distraction."

Klaus thought for a second. "In order to win the Trojan War," he said, "the ancient Greeks hid soldiers inside an enormous wooden horse. That was sort of a distraction. But I don't have time to build a wooden horse."

"Then you'll have to think of something else," Violet said, and began to walk toward the door, still gazing out the window. Klaus and Sunny looked first at their sister, and then out the window of the Reptile Room in the direction she was looking. It is remarkable that different people will have different thoughts when they look at the same thing. For when the two younger Baudelaires looked at the pile of suitcases, all they thought was that unless they did something quickly, they would end up alone in Uncle Monty's jeep with Stephano. But from the way Violet was staring as she walked out of the Reptile Room, she was obviously thinking something else. Klaus and Sunny could not imagine what it was, but somehow their sister had reached a different conclusion as she looked at her own brown suitcase, or perhaps the beige one that held Klaus's things, or the tiny gray one that was Sunny's, or maybe the large black one, with the shiny silver padlock, that belonged to Stephano.

CHAPTER
Ten

When you were very small, perhaps someone
read to you the insipid story—the word "insipid"
here means "not worth reading to someone"—
of the Boy Who Cried Wolf. A very dull boy, you
may remember, cried "Wolf!" when there was
no wolf, and the gullible villagers ran to rescue
him only to find the whole thing was a joke.
Then he cried "Wolf!" when it wasn't a joke,
and the villagers didn't come running, and the
boy was eaten and the story, thank goodness,
was over.

The story's moral, of course, ought to be "Never live somewhere where wolves are running around loose," but whoever read you the story probably told you that the moral was not to lie. This is an absurd moral, for you and I both know that sometimes not only is it good to lie, it is necessary to lie. For example, it was perfectly appropriate, after Violet left the Reptile Room, for Sunny to crawl over to the cage that held the Incredibly Deadly Viper, unlatch the cage, and begin screaming as loudly as she could even though nothing was really wrong.

There is another story concerning wolves that somebody has probably read to you, which is just as absurd. I am talking about Little Red Riding Hood, an extremely unpleasant little girl who, like the Boy Who Cried Wolf, insisted on intruding on the territory of dangerous animals. You will recall that the wolf, after being treated very rudely by Little Red Riding Hood, ate the little girl's grandmother and put on her clothing as a disguise. It is this aspect of the story that is the most ridiculous, because one would think that even a girl as dim-witted as Little Red Riding Hood could tell in an instant the difference between her grandmother and a wolf dressed in a nightgown and fuzzy slippers. If you know somebody very well, like your grandmother or your baby sister, you will know when they are real and when they are fake. This is why, as Sunny began to scream, Violet and Klaus could tell immediately that her scream was absolutely fake.

"That scream is absolutely fake," Klaus said to himself, from the other end of the Reptile Room.

"That scream is absolutely fake," Violet said to herself, from the stairs as she went up to her room.

"My Lord! Something is terribly wrong!" Mr. Poe said to himself, from the kitchen where he was talking on the phone. "Good-bye," he said into the receiver, hung up, and ran out of the kitchen to see what the matter was.

"What's the matter?" Mr. Poe asked Stephano and Dr. Lucafont, who had finished unloading the suitcases and were entering the house. "I heard some screams coming from the Reptile Room."

"I'm sure it's nothing," Stephano said.

"You know how children are," Dr. Lucafont said.

"We can't have another tragedy on our hands," Mr. Poe said, and rushed to the enormous door of the Reptile Room. "Children! Children!"

"In here!" Klaus cried. "Come quickly!" His voice was rough and low, and anyone who didn't know Klaus would think he was very frightened. If you *did* know Klaus, however, you would know that when he was very frightened his voice became tense and squeaky, as it did when he discovered Uncle Monty's body. His voice became rough and low when he was try-ing not to laugh. It is a very good thing that Klaus managed not to laugh as Mr. Poe, Stephano, and

Dr. Lucafont came into the Reptile Room. It would have spoiled everything.

Sunny was lying down on the marble floor, her tiny arms and legs waving wildly as if she were trying to swim. Her facial expression was what made Klaus want to chuckle. Sunny's mouth was wide open, showing her four sharp teeth, and her eyes were blinking rapidly. She was trying to appear to be very frightened, and if you didn't know Sunny it would have seemed genuine. But Klaus *did* know Sunny, and knew that when she was very frightened, her face grew all puckered and silent, as it did when Stephano had threatened to cut off one of her toes. To anyone but Klaus, Sunny looked as if she were very frightened, particularly because of who she was with. For wrapped around Sunny's small body was a snake, as dark as a coal mine and as thick as a sewer pipe. It was looking at Sunny with shiny green eyes, and its mouth was open as if it were about to bite her.

"The Incredibly Deadly Viper!" Klaus cried. "It's going to bite her!" Klaus screamed, and Sunny opened her mouth and eyes even wider to seem even more scared. Dr. Lucafont's mouth opened too, and Klaus saw him start to say something, but he was unable to find words. Stephano, who of course could not have cared less about Sunny's well-being, at least looked surprised, but it was Mr. Poe who absolutely panicked.

There are two basic types of panicking: standing still and not saying a word, and leaping all over the place babbling anything that comes into your head. Mr. Poe was the leaping-and-babbling kind. Klaus and Sunny had never seen the banker move so quickly or talk in such a high-pitched voice. "Goodness!" he cried. "Golly! Good God! Blessed Allah! Zeus and Hera! Mary and Joseph! Nathaniel Hawthorne! Don't touch her! Grab her! Move closer! Run away! Don't move! Kill the snake! Leave it alone! Give it some food! Don't let it bite her!

Lure the snake away! Here, snakey! Here, snakey snakey!"

The Incredibly Deadly Viper listened patiently to Mr. Poe's speech, never taking its eyes off of Sunny, and when Mr. Poe paused to cough into his handkerchief, it leaned over and bit Sunny on the chin, right where it had bitten her when the two friends had first met. Klaus tried not to grin, but Dr. Lucafont gasped, Stephano stared, and Mr. Poe began leaping and babbling again.

"It's bitten her!" he cried. "It bit her! It bited her! Calm down! Get moving! Call an ambulance! Call the police! Call a scientist! Call my wife! This is terrible! This is awful! This is ghastly! This is phantasmagorical! This is—"

"This is nothing to worry about," Stephano interrupted smoothly.

"What do you mean, nothing to worry about?" Mr. Poe asked incredulously. "Sunny was just bitten by—what's the name of the snake, Klaus?"

"The Incredibly Deadly Viper," Klaus answered promptly.

"The Incredibly Deadly Viper!" Mr. Poe repeated, pointing to the snake as it held on to Sunny's chin with its teeth. Sunny gave another fake shriek of fear. "How can you say it's nothing to worry about?"

"Because the Incredibly Deadly Viper is completely harmless," Stephano said. "Calm yourself, Poe. The snake's name is a misnomer that Dr. Montgomery created for his own amusement."

"Are you sure?" Mr. Poe asked. His voice got a little lower, and he moved a bit more slowly as he began to calm down.

"Of course I'm sure," Stephano said, and Klaus recognized a look on his face he remembered from living at Count Olaf's. It was a look of sheer vanity, a word which here means "Count Olaf thinking he's the most incredible person who ever lived." When the Baudelaire orphans had been under Olaf's care, he had often acted this way, always happy to show off his skills, whether he was onstage with his atrocious theater company or up in his tower room making nasty plans. Stephano smiled, and continued to speak to Mr. Poe, eager to show off. "The snake is perfectly harmless—friendly, even. I read up on the Incredibly Deadly Viper, and many other snakes, in the library section of the Reptile Room as well as Dr. Montgomery's private papers."

Dr. Lucafont cleared his throat. "Uh, boss—" he said.

"Don't interrupt me, Dr. Lucafont," Stephano said. "I studied books on all the major species. I looked carefully at sketches and charts. I took careful notes and looked them over each night before I went to sleep. If I may say so, I consider myself to be quite the expert on snakes."

"Aha!" Sunny cried, disentangling herself from the Incredibly Deadly Viper.

"Sunny! You're unharmed!" Mr. Poe cried.

"Aha!" Sunny cried again, pointing at Stephano. The Incredibly Deadly Viper blinked its green eyes triumphantly.

Mr. Poe looked at Klaus, puzzled. "What does your sister mean by 'Aha'?" he asked.

Klaus sighed. He felt, sometimes, as if he had spent half his life explaining things to Mr. Poe. "By 'Aha,'" he said, "she means 'One minute' Stephano claims he knows nothing about snakes, the next he claims he is an expert! By 'Aha' she means 'Stephano has been lying to us.' By 'Aha' she means 'we've finally exposed his dishonesty to you!' By 'Aha' she means *'Aha!'*"

CHAPTER
Eleven

Meanwhile, back at the ranch, Violet was upstairs, surveying her bedroom with a critical eye. She took a deep breath, and then tied her hair in a ribbon, to keep it out of her eyes. As you and I and everyone who is familiar with Violet know, when she ties her hair back like that, it is because she needs to think up an invention. And right now she needed to think of one quickly.

Violet had realized, when her brother had talked about Stephano ordering them to carry his suitcase into the

house, that the evidence she had been looking for was undoubtedly in that very suitcase.
And now, while her siblings were distracting the adults in the Reptile Room, would
be her only opportunity to open the suitcase
and retrieve proof of Stephano's evil plot.
But her aching shoulder was a reminder that
she couldn't simply open the suitcase—it was
locked, with a lock as shiny as Stephano's
scheming eyes. I confess that if I were in Violet's
place, with only a few minutes to open a locked
suitcase, instead of on the deck of my friend
Bela's yacht, writing this down, I probably
would have given up hope. I would have sunk
to the floor of the bedroom and pounded
my fists against the carpet wondering why in
the world life was so unfair and filled with
inconveniences.

Luckily for the Baudelaires, however, Violet
was made of sterner stuff, and she took a good
look around her bedroom for anything that

might help her. There wasn't much in the way of inventing materials. Violet longed for a good room in which to invent things, filled with wires and gears and all of the necessary equipment to invent really top-notch devices. Uncle Monty was in fact in possession of many of these supplies, but, to Violet's frustration as she thought of this, they were located in the Reptile Room. She looked at the pieces of butcher paper tacked to the wall, where she had hoped to sketch out inventions as she lived in Uncle Monty's house. The trouble had begun so quickly that Violet had only a few scribblings on one of the sheets, which she had written by the light of a floorlamp on her first night here. Violet's eyes traveled to the floorlamp as she remembered that evening, and when she reached the electric socket she had an idea.

We all know, of course, that we should never, ever, ever, ever, ever, ever, ever, ever, ever, ever,

ever, ever, ever, ever, ever, ever, ever, ever, ever,
ever, ever, ever, ever, ever, ever, ever, ever, ever,
ever, ever, ever, ever, ever, ever, ever, ever, ever,
ever, ever, ever, ever, ever, ever, ever, ever, ever,
ever, ever, ever, ever, ever, ever, ever, ever, ever,
ever, ever, ever, ever, ever, ever, ever, ever, ever,
ever, ever, ever, ever, ever, ever, ever, ever, ever,
ever, ever, ever, ever, ever, ever, ever, ever, ever,
ever, ever, ever, ever, ever, ever, ever, ever, ever,
ever, ever, ever, ever, ever, ever, ever, ever, ever,
ever, ever, ever, ever, ever, ever, ever, ever, ever,
ever, ever, ever, ever, ever, ever, ever, ever, ever,
ever, ever, ever, ever, ever, ever, ever, ever, ever,
ever, ever, ever, ever, ever, ever, ever, ever, ever,
ever, ever, ever, ever, ever, ever, ever, ever, ever,
ever, ever, ever, ever, ever, ever, ever, ever, ever,
ever, ever, ever, ever, ever, ever, ever, ever, ever,
ever, ever, ever, ever, ever, ever, ever, ever, ever,
ever, ever, ever, ever, ever, ever, ever, ever, ever,
ever, ever, ever, ever, ever, ever, ever, ever, ever,
ever, ever, ever, ever, ever, ever, ever, ever, ever,
ever, ever, ever, ever, ever, ever, ever, ever, ever,

ever, *ever* fiddle around in any way with electric devices. *Never.* There are two reasons for this. One is that you can get electrocuted, which is not only deadly but very unpleasant, and the other is that you are not Violet Baudelaire, one of the few people in the world who know how to handle such things. And even Violet was very careful and nervous as she unplugged the lamp and took a long look at the plug itself. It might work.

Hoping that Klaus and Sunny were continuing to stall the adults successfully, Violet wiggled the two prongs of the plug this way and that until at last they came loose from their plastic casing. She now had two small metal strips. Violet then took one of the thumbtacks out of the butcher paper, letting the paper curl down the wall as if it were lazy. With the sharp end of the tack she poked and prodded the two pieces of metal until one was hooked around the other, and then forced the thumbtack between the two pieces so the sharp end stuck straight out. The result looked like a piece of metal you might not notice if it lay in the street, but in fact what Violet had made was a crude—the word "crude" here means "roughly made at the last minute" rather than "rude or ill-mannered"— lockpick. Lockpicks, as you probably know, are devices that work as if they were proper keys, usually used by bad guys to rob houses or escape from jail, but this was one of the rare times when a lockpick was being used by a good guy: Violet Baudelaire.

Violet walked quietly back down the stairs, holding her lockpick in one hand and crossing her fingers with the other. She tiptoed past the enormous door of the Reptile Room and hoped that her absence would not be noticed as she slipped outside. Deliberately averting her eyes from Dr. Lucafont's car to avoid catching even a glimpse of Uncle Monty's body, the eldest Baudelaire walked toward the pile of suitcases. She looked first at the old ones belonging to the Baudelaires. Those suitcases contained, she

remembered, lots of ugly, itchy clothing that
Mrs. Poe had bought for them soon after their
parents died. For a few seconds, Violet found
herself staring at the suitcases, remembering
how effortless her life had been before all this
trouble had set upon them, and how surprising
it was to find herself in such miserable circumstances now. This may not be surprising to us,
because we know how disastrous the lives of the
Baudelaire orphans are, but Violet's misfortune
was constantly surprising to her and it took her
a minute to push thoughts of their situation out
of her head and to concentrate on what she had
to do.

She knelt down to get closer to Stephano's
suitcase, held the shiny silver padlock in one
hand, took a deep breath, and stuck the lockpick into the keyhole. It went inside, but when
she tried to turn it around, it scarcely budged,
only scraped a little at the inside of the keyhole.
It needed to move more smoothly or it would
never work. Violet took her lockpick out and

wet it with her mouth, grimacing at the stale taste of the metal. Then she stuck the lockpick into the keyhole again and tried to move it. It wiggled slightly and then lay still.

Violet took the lockpick out and thought very, very hard, retying her hair in the ribbon. As she cleared the hair from her eyes, though, she felt a sudden prickle on her skin. It was unpleasant and familiar. It was the feeling of being watched. She looked quickly behind her, but saw only the snake-shaped hedges on the lawn. She looked to the side and saw only the driveway leading down to Lousy Lane. But then she looked straight ahead, through the glass walls of the Reptile Room.

It had never occurred to her that people could see in through the Reptile Room's walls as clearly as they could see out, but when she looked up Violet could see, through the cages of reptiles, the figure of Mr. Poe leaping up and down excitedly. You and I know, of course, that Mr. Poe was panicking over Sunny and the Incredibly

Deadly Viper, but all Violet knew was that whatever ruse her siblings had devised was still working. The prickle on her skin was not explained, however, until she looked a little closer, just to the right of Mr. Poe, and saw that Stephano was looking right back at her.

Her mouth fell open in surprise and panic. She knew that any second now, Stephano would invent an excuse to leave the Reptile Room and come find her, and she hadn't even opened the suitcase. Quickly, quickly, quickly, she had to find some way to make her lockpick work. She looked down at the damp gravel of the driveway, and up at the dim, yellowish afternoon sun. She looked at her own hands, smudged with dust from picking apart the electric plug, and that's when she thought of something.

Jumping to her feet, Violet sprinted back into the house as if Stephano were already after her and pushed her way through the door into the kitchen. Shoving a chair to the floor in her haste, she grabbed a bar of soap from the dripping sink. She rubbed the slippery substance carefully over her lockpick until the entire invention had a thin, slick coating. Her heart pounding in her chest, she ran back outside, taking a hurried look through the walls of the Reptile Room. Stephano was saying something to Mr. Poe—he was bragging about his expertise of snakes, but Violet had no way of knowing that—and Violet took this moment to kneel down and stick the lockpick back into the keyhole of the padlock. It spun quickly all the way around and then snapped in two, right in her hands. There was a faint sputter of sound as one half fell to the grass, the other one sticking in the keyhole like a jagged tooth. Her lockpick was destroyed.

Violet closed her eyes for a moment in despair, and then pulled herself to her feet, using the suitcase to gain her balance. When she put her hand on the suitcase, however, the padlock swung open, and the case tipped open and spilled everything all over the ground. Violet fell back down in surprise. Somehow, as the lock-pick turned, it must have unstuck the lock. Sometimes even in the most unfortunate of lives there will occur a moment or two of good fortune.

It is very difficult, experts have told us, to find a needle in a haystack, which is why "needle in a haystack" has become a rather hackneyed phrase meaning "something that is difficult to find." The reason it is difficult to find a needle in a haystack, of course, is that out of all the things in a haystack, the needle is only one of them. If, however, you were looking for *anything* in a haystack, that wouldn't be difficult at all, because once you started sifting through the haystack you would most certainly find something: hay, of course, but also dirt, bugs, a few farming tools, and maybe even a man who had escaped from prison and was hiding there. When Violet searched through the contents of Stephano's suitcase, it was more like looking for *anything* in a haystack, because she didn't know exactly what she wanted to find. Therefore it was actually fairly easy to find useful items of evidence: a glass vial with a sealed rubber cap, as one might find in a scientific laboratory; a syringe with a sharp needle, like the one your doctor uses to give you shots; a small bunch of folded papers; a card laminated in plastic; a powder puff and small hand mirror.

Even though she knew she had only a few more moments, Violet separated these items from the smelly clothes and the bottle of wine that were also in the suitcase, and looked at all her evidence very carefully, concentrating on each item as if they were small parts out of which she was going to make a machine. And in a way, they were. Violet Baudelaire needed to arrange these pieces of evidence to defeat Stephano's evil plan and bring justice and peace into the lives of the Baudelaire orphans for the first time since their parents perished in the terrible fire. Violet gazed at each piece of evidence, thinking very hard, and before too long, her face lit up the way it always did when all the pieces of something were fit together properly and the machine worked just the way it should.

I promise you that this is the last time that I will use the phrase "meanwhile, back at the ranch," but I can think of no other way to return to the moment when Klaus has just explained to Mr. Poe what Sunny had meant by shouting "Aha!" and now everyone in the Reptile Room was staring at Stephano. Sunny looked triumphant. Klaus looked defiant. Mr. Poe looked furious. Dr. Lucafont looked worried. You

couldn't tell how the Incredibly Deadly Viper looked, because the facial expressions of snakes are difficult to read. Stephano looked back at all these people silently, his face fluttering as he tried to decide whether to come clean, a phrase which here means "admit that he's really Count Olaf and up to no good," or perpetuate his deception, a phrase which here means "lie, lie, lie."

"Stephano," Mr. Poe said, and coughed into his handkerchief. Klaus and Sunny waited impatiently for him to continue. "Stephano, explain yourself. You have just told us that you are an expert on snakes. Previously, however, you told us you knew nothing of snakes, and therefore couldn't have been involved in Dr. Montgomery's death. What is going on?"

"When I told you I knew nothing of snakes," Stephano said, "I was being modest. Now, if you will excuse me, I have to go outside for a moment, and—"

"You weren't being modest!" Klaus cried.

"You were *lying!* And you are lying now! You're nothing but a liar and murderer!"

Stephano's eyes grew wide and his face clouded in anger. "You have no evidence of that," he said.

"Yes we do," said a voice in the doorway, and everyone turned around to find Violet standing there, with a smile on her face and evidence in her arms. Triumphantly, she walked across the Reptile Room to the far end, where the books Klaus had been reading about the Mamba du Mal were still stacked in a pile. The others followed her, walking down the aisles of reptiles. Silently, she arranged the objects in a line on top of a table: the glass vial with the sealed rubber cap, the syringe with the sharp needle, the small bunch of folded papers, a card laminated in plastic, the powder puff and the small hand mirror.

"What is all this?" Mr. Poe said, gesturing to the arrangement.

"This," Violet said, "is evidence, which I

found in Stephano's suitcase."

"My suitcase," Stephano said, "is private property, which you are not allowed to touch. It's very rude of you, and besides, it was locked."

"It was an emergency," Violet said calmly, "so I picked the lock."

"How did you do that?" Mr. Poe asked. "Nice girls shouldn't know how to do such things."

"My sister *is* a nice girl," Klaus said, "and she knows how to do all sorts of things."

"Roofik!" Sunny agreed.

"Well, we'll discuss that later," Mr. Poe said. "In the meantime, please continue."

"When Uncle Monty died," Violet began, "my siblings and I were very sad, but we were also very suspicious."

"We weren't suspicious!" Klaus exclaimed. "If someone is suspicious, it means they're not sure! We were *positive* that Stephano killed him!"

"Nonsense!" Dr. Lucafont said. "As I explained to all of you, Montgomery Montgomery's death was an accident. The Mamba du Mal escaped from its cage and bit him, and that's all there is to it."

"I beg your pardon," Violet said, "but that is *not* all there is to it. Klaus read up on the Mamba du Mal, and found out how it kills its victims."

Klaus walked over to the stack of books and opened the one on top. He had marked his place with a small piece of paper, so he found what he was looking for right away. "'The Mamba du Mal,'" he read out loud, "'is one of the deadliest snakes in the hemisphere, noted for its strangulatory grip, used in conjunction with its deadly venom, giving all of its victims a tenebrous hue, which is ghastly to behold.'" He put the book down, and turned to Mr. Poe. "'Strangulatory' means—"

"We *know* what the words mean!" Stephano shouted.

"Then you must know," Klaus said, "that the Mamba du Mal did not kill Uncle Monty. His body didn't have a tenebrous hue. It was as pale as could be."

"That's true," Mr. Poe said, "but it doesn't necessarily indicate that Dr. Montgomery was murdered."

"Yes," Dr. Lucafont said. "Perhaps, just this once, the snake didn't feel like bruising its victim."

"It is more likely," Violet said, "that Uncle Monty was killed with these items." She held up the glass vial with the sealed rubber cap. "This vial is labeled 'Venom du Mal,' and it's obviously from Uncle Monty's cabinet of venom samples." She then held up the syringe with the sharp needle. "Stephano—Olaf—took this syringe and injected the venom into Uncle Monty. Then he poked an extra hole, so it would look like the snake had bitten him."

"But I loved Dr. Montgomery," Stephano said. "I would have had nothing to gain from his death."

Sometimes, when someone tells a ridiculous

lie, it is best to ignore it entirely. "When I turn eighteen, as we all know," Violet continued, ignoring Stephano entirely, "I inherit the Baudelaire fortune, and Stephano intended to get that fortune for himself. It would be easier to do so if we were in a location that was more difficult to trace, such as Peru." Violet held up the small bunch of folded papers. "These are tickets for the *Prospero*, leaving Hazy Harbor for Peru at five o'clock today. That's where Stephano was taking us when we happened to run into you, Mr. Poe."

"But Uncle Monty tore up Stephano's ticket to Peru," Klaus said, looking confused. "I saw him."

"That's true," Violet said. "That's why he had to get Uncle Monty out of the way. He killed Uncle Monty—" Violet stopped for a minute and shuddered. "He killed Uncle Monty, and took this laminated card. It's Monty's membership card for the Herpetological Society. Stephano planned to pose as Uncle Monty to get on board the *Prospero,* and whisk us away to Peru."

"But I don't understand," Mr. Poe said. "How did Stephano even know about your fortune?"

"Because he's really Count Olaf," Violet said, exasperated that she had to explain what she and her siblings and you and I knew the moment Stephano arrived at the house. "He may have shaved his head, and trimmed off his eyebrows, but the only way he could get rid of the tattoo on his left ankle was with this powder puff and hand mirror. There's makeup all over his left ankle, to hide the eye, and I'll bet if we rub it with a cloth we can see the tattoo."

"That's absurd!" Stephano cried.

"We'll see about that," Mr. Poe replied. "Now, who has a cloth?"

"Not me," Klaus said.

"Not me," Violet said.

"Guweel!" Sunny said.

"Well, if nobody has a cloth, we might as well forget the whole thing," Dr. Lucafont said, but

Mr. Poe held up a finger to tell him to wait. To the relief of the Baudelaire orphans, he reached into his pocket and withdrew his handkerchief.

"Your left ankle, please," he said sternly to Stephano.

"But you've been coughing into that all day!" Stephano said. "It has germs!"

"If you are really who the children say you are," Mr. Poe said, "then germs are the least of your problems. Your left ankle, please."

Stephano—and this is the last time, thank goodness, we'll have to call him by his phony name—gave a little growl, and pulled his left pants leg up to reveal his ankle. Mr. Poe knelt down and rubbed at it for a few moments. At first, nothing appeared to happen, but then, like a sun shining through clouds at the end of a terrible rainstorm, the faint outline of an eye began to appear. Clearer and clearer it grew until it was as dark as it had been when the orphans first saw it, back when they had lived with Count Olaf.

Violet, Klaus, and Sunny all stared at the eye, and the eye stared back. For the first time in their lives, the Baudelaire orphans were happy to see it.

If this were a book written to entertain small children, you would know what would happen next. With the villain's identity and evil plans exposed, the police would arrive on the scene and place him in a jail for the rest of his life, and the plucky youngsters would go out for pizza and live happily ever after. But this book is about the Baudelaire orphans, and you and I know that these three unfortunate children living happily ever after is about as likely as Uncle Monty returning to life. But it seemed to the Baudelaire orphans, as the tattoo became evident, that at least a little bit of Uncle Monty had come back to them as they proved Count Olaf's treachery once and for all.

"That's the eye, all right," Mr. Poe said, and stopped rubbing Count Olaf's ankle. "You are most definitely Count Olaf, and you are most definitely under arrest."

"And I am most definitely shocked," Dr. Lucafont said, clapping his oddly solid hands to his head.

"As am I," Mr. Poe agreed, grabbing Count Olaf's arm in case he tried to run anywhere. "Violet, Klaus, Sunny—please forgive me for not believing you earlier. It just seemed too far-fetched that he would have searched you out, disguised himself as a laboratory assistant, and concocted an elaborate plan to steal your fortune."

"I wonder what happened to Gustav, Uncle Monty's *real* lab assistant?" Klaus wondered out loud. "If Gustav hadn't quit, then Uncle Monty never would have hired Count Olaf."

Count Olaf had been quiet this whole time, ever since the tattoo had appeared. His shiny eyes had darted this way and that, watching everyone carefully the way a lion will watch a herd of antelope, looking for the one that would be best to kill and eat. But at the mention of Gustav's name, he spoke up.

"Gustav didn't quit," he said in his wheezy voice. "Gustav is *dead!* One day when he was out collecting wildflowers I drowned him in the Swarthy Swamp. Then I forged a note saying he quit." Count Olaf looked at the three children as if he were going to run over and strangle them, but instead he stood absolutely still, which somehow was even scarier. "But that's nothing compared to what I will do to you, orphans. You have won this round of the game, but I will return for your fortune, and for your precious skin."

"This is not a game, you horrible man," Mr.

Poe said. "Dominos is a game. Water polo is a game. Murder is a crime, and you will go to jail for it. I will drive you to the police station in town right this very minute. Oh, drat, I can't. My car is wrecked. Well, I'll take you down in Dr. Montgomery's jeep, and you children can follow along in Dr. Lucafont's car. I guess you'll be able to see the inside of a doctor's automobile, after all."

"It might be easier," Dr. Lucafont said, "to put Stephano in my car, and have the children follow behind. After all, Dr. Montgomery's body is in my car, so there's no room for all three children, anyway."

"Well," Mr. Poe said, "I'd hate to disappoint the children after they've had such a trying time. We can move Dr. Montgomery's body to the jeep, and—"

"We couldn't care less about the inside of a doctor's automobile," Violet said impatiently. "We only made that up so we wouldn't be trapped alone with Count Olaf."

"You shouldn't tell lies, orphans," Count Olaf said.

"I don't think you are in a position to give moral lectures to children, Olaf," Mr. Poe said sternly. "All right, Dr. Lucafont, *you* take him."

Dr. Lucafont grabbed Count Olaf's shoulder with one of his oddly stiff hands, and led the way out of the Reptile Room and to the front door, stopping at the doorway to give Mr. Poe and the three children a thin smile.

"Say good-bye to the orphans, Count Olaf," Dr. Lucafont said.

"Good-bye," Count Olaf said.

"Good-bye," Violet said.

"Good-bye," Klaus said.

Mr. Poe coughed into his handkerchief and gave a sort of disgusted half-wave at Count Olaf, indicating good-bye. But Sunny didn't say anything. Violet and Klaus looked down at her, surprised that she hadn't said "Yeet!" or "Libo!" or any of her various terms for "good-bye." But Sunny was staring at Dr. Lucafont with a determined look in her eye, and in a moment she had leaped into the air and bitten him on the hand.

"Sunny!" Violet said, and was about to apologize for her behavior when she saw Dr. Lucafont's whole hand come loose from his arm and fall to the floor. As Sunny clamped down on it with her four sharp teeth, the hand made a crackling sound, like breaking wood or plastic rather than skin or bone. And when Violet looked at the place where Dr. Lucafont's hand had been, she saw no blood or indication of a wound, but a shiny, metal hook. Dr. Lucafont looked at the hook, too, and then at Violet, and grinned horribly. Count Olaf grinned too, and in a second the two of them had darted out the door.

"The hook-handed man!" Violet shouted. "He's not a doctor! He's one of Count Olaf's henchmen!" Instinctively, Violet grabbed the air where the two men had been standing, but of course they weren't there. She opened the front door wide and saw the two of them sprinting through the snake-shaped hedges.

"After them!" Klaus shouted, and the three Baudelaires started to run through the door. But Mr. Poe stepped in front of them and blocked their way.

"No!" he cried.

"But it's the hook-handed man!" Violet shouted. "He and Olaf will get away!"

"I can't let you run out after two dangerous criminals," Mr. Poe replied. "I am responsible for the safety of you children, and I will not have any harm come to you."

"Then *you* go after them!" Klaus cried. "But hurry!"

Mr. Poe began to step out the door, but he stopped when he heard the roar of a car engine starting up. The two ruffians—a word which here means "horrible people"—had reached Dr. Lucafont's car, and were already driving away.

"Get in the jeep!" Violet exclaimed. "Follow them!"

"A grown man," Mr. Poe said sternly, "does not get involved in a car chase. This is a job for the police. I'll go call them now, and maybe they can set up roadblocks."

The Baudelaire youngsters watched Mr. Poe shut the door and race to the telephone, and their hearts sank. They knew it was no use. By the time Mr. Poe was through explaining the situation to the police, Count Olaf and the hook-handed man were sure to be long gone. Suddenly exhausted, Violet, Klaus, and Sunny walked to Uncle Monty's enormous staircase and sat down on the bottom step, listening to the faint sound of Mr. Poe talking on the phone. They knew that trying to find Count Olaf and the hook-handed man, particularly when it grew dark, would be like trying to find a needle in a haystack.

Despite their anxiety over Count Olaf's escape, the three orphans must have fallen asleep for a few hours, for the next thing they knew, it was nighttime and they were still on the bottom step. Somebody had placed a blanket over them, and as they stretched themelves, they saw three men in overalls walking out of the Reptile Room, carrying some of the reptiles in their cages. Behind them walked a chubby man in a brightly colored plaid suit, who stopped when he saw they were awake.

"Hey, kids," the chubby man said in a loud, booming voice. "I'm sorry if I woke you up, but my team has to move quickly."

"Who are you?" Violet asked. It is confusing to fall asleep in the daytime and wake up at night.

"What are you doing with Uncle Monty's reptiles?" Klaus asked. It is also confusing to realize you have been sleeping on stairs, rather than in a bed or sleeping bag.

"Dixnik?" Sunny asked. It is always confusing why anyone would choose to wear a plaid suit.

"The name's Bruce," Bruce said. "I'm the

director of marketing for the Herpetological Society. Your friend Mr. Poe called me to come and retrieve the snakes now that Dr. Montgomery has passed on. 'Retrieve' means 'take away.'"

"We *know* what the word 'retrieve' means," Klaus said, "but why are you taking them? Where are they going?"

"Well, you three are the orphans, right? You'll be moving on to some other relative who won't die on you like Montgomery did. And these snakes need to be taken care of, so we're giving them away to other scientists, zoos, and retirement homes. Those we can't find homes for we'll have put to sleep."

"But they're Uncle Monty's collection!" Klaus cried. "It took him years to find all these reptiles! You can't just scatter them to the winds!"

"It's the way it has to be," Bruce said smoothly. He was still talking in a very loud voice, for no apparent reason.

"Viper!" Sunny shouted, and began to crawl toward the Reptile Room.

"What my sister means," Violet explained, "is that she's very close friends with one of the snakes. Could we take just one with us—the Incredibly Deadly Viper?"

"First off, *no*," Bruce said. "That guy Poe said all the snakes now belong to us. And second off, if you think I'm going to let small children near the Incredibly Deadly Viper, think again."

"But the Incredibly Deadly Viper is harmless," Violet said. "Its name is a misnomer."

Bruce scratched his head. "A what?"

"That means 'a wrong name,'" Klaus explained. "Uncle Monty discovered it, so he got to name it."

"But this guy was supposed to be brilliant," Bruce said. He reached into a pocket in his plaid jacket and pulled out a cigar. "Giving a snake a wrong name doesn't sound brilliant to me. It sounds idiotic. But then, what can you expect from a man whose own name was Montgomery Montgomery?"

"It is not nice," Klaus said, "to lampoon someone's name like that."

"I don't have time to ask you what 'lampoon' means," Bruce said. "But if the baby here wants to wave bye-bye to the Incredibly Deadly Viper, she'd better do it soon. It's already outside."

Sunny began to crawl toward the front door, but Klaus was not through talking to Bruce. "Our Uncle Monty *was* brilliant," he said firmly.

"He was a brilliant man," Violet agreed, "and we will always remember him as such."

"Brilliant!" Sunny shrieked, in mid-crawl, and her siblings smiled down at her, surprised she had uttered a word that everyone could understand.

Bruce lit his cigar and blew smoke into the air, then shrugged. "It's nice you feel that way, kid," he said. "Good luck wherever they put you." He looked at a shiny diamond watch on his wrist, and turned to talk to the men in overalls. "Let's get a move on. In five minutes we have to be back on that road that smells like ginger."

"It's *horseradish*," Violet corrected, but Bruce had already walked away. She and Klaus looked at each other, and then began following Sunny outside to wave good-bye to their reptile friends. But as they reached the door, Mr. Poe walked into the room and blocked them again.

"I see you're awake," he said. "Please go upstairs and go to sleep, then. We have to get up very early in the morning."

"We just want to say good-bye to the snakes," Klaus said, but Mr. Poe shook his head.

"You'll get in Bruce's way," he replied. "Plus, I would think you three would never want to see a snake again."

The Baudelaire orphans looked at one another and sighed. Everything in the world seemed wrong. It was wrong that Uncle Monty was dead. It was wrong that Count Olaf and the hook-handed man had escaped. It was wrong for Bruce to think of Monty as a person with a silly name, instead of a brilliant scientist. And it was wrong to assume that the children never wanted to see a snake again. The snakes, and indeed everything in the Reptile Room, were the last reminders the Baudelaires had of the few happy days they'd spent there at the house—the few happy days they'd had since their parents had perished. Even though they understood that Mr. Poe wouldn't let them live alone with the reptiles, it was all wrong never to see them again, without even saying good-bye.

Ignoring Mr. Poe's instructions, Violet, Klaus, and Sunny rushed out the front door where the men in overalls were loading the cages into a van with "Herpetological Society" written on the back. It was a full moon, and the moonlight reflected off the glass walls of the Reptile Room as though it were a large jewel with a bright, bright shine—*brilliant*, one might say. When Bruce had used the word "brilliant" about

Uncle Monty, he meant "having a reputation for cleverness or intelligence." But when the children used the word—and when they thought of it now, staring at the Reptile Room glowing in the moonlight—it meant more than that. It meant that even in the bleak circumstances of their current situation, even throughout the series of unfortunate events that would happen to them for the rest of their lives, Uncle Monty and his kindness would shine in their memories. Uncle Monty was brilliant, and their time with him was brilliant. Bruce and his men from the Herpetological Society could dismantle Uncle Monty's collection, but nobody could ever dismantle the way the Baudelaires would think of him.

"Good-bye, good-bye!" the Baudelaire orphans called, as the Incredibly Deadly Viper was loaded into the truck. "Good-bye, good-bye!" they called, and even though the Viper was Sunny's special friend, Violet and Klaus found themselves crying along with their sister, and when the Incredibly Deadly Viper looked up to see them, they saw that it was crying too, tiny shiny tears falling from its green eyes. The Viper was brilliant, too, and as the children looked at one another, they saw their own tears and the way they shone.

"You're brilliant," Violet murmured to Klaus, "reading up on the Mamba du Mal."

"You're brilliant," Klaus murmured back, "getting the evidence out of Stephano's suitcase."

"Brilliant!" Sunny said again, and Violet and Klaus gave their baby sister a hug. Even the youngest Baudelaire was brilliant, for distracting the adults with the Incredibly Deadly Viper.

"Good-bye, good-bye!" the brilliant Baudelaires called, and waved to Uncle Monty's reptiles. They stood together in the moonlight, and kept waving, even when Bruce shut the doors of the van, even as the van drove past the snake-shaped hedges and down the driveway to Lousy Lane, and even when it turned a corner and disappeared into the dark.

To My Kind Editor,

I am writing to you from the shores of Lake Lachrymose, where I am examining the remains of Aunt Josephine's house in order to completely understand everything that happened when the Baudelaire orphans found themselves here.

Please go to the Café Kafka at 4 P.M. next Wednesday and order a pot of jasmine tea from the tallest waiter on duty. Unless my enemies have succeeded, he will bring you a large envelope instead. Inside the envelope, you will find my description of these horrific events, entitled THE WIDE WINDOW, as well as a sketch of Curdled Cave, a small bag of shattered glass, and the menu from the Anxious Clown restaurant. There will also be a test tube containing one (1) Lachrymose Leech, so that Mr. Helquist can draw an accurate illustration. UNDER NO CIRCUMSTANCES should this test tube be opened.

Remember, you are my last hope that the tales of the Baudelaire orphans can finally be told to the general public.

With all due respect,

Lemony Snicket

Lemony Snicket

THE WIDE WINDOW

For Beatrice—
I would much prefer it if you were alive and well.

If you didn't know much about the Baudelaire orphans, and you saw them sitting on their suitcases at Damocles Dock, you might think that they were bound for an exciting adventure. After all, the three children had just disembarked from the Fickle Ferry, which had driven them across Lake Lachrymose to live with their Aunt Josephine, and in most cases such a situation would lead to thrillingly good times.

But of course you would be dead wrong. For although Violet, Klaus, and Sunny Baudelaire were about to experience events that would be both exciting and memorable, they would not be exciting and memorable like having your fortune told or going to a rodeo. Their adventure would be exciting and memorable like being chased by a werewolf through a field of thorny bushes at midnight with nobody around to help you. If you are interested in reading a story filled with thrillingly good times, I am sorry to inform you that you are most certainly reading the wrong book, because the Baudelaires experience very few good times over the course of their gloomy and miserable lives. It is a terrible thing, their misfortune, so terrible that I can scarcely bring myself to write about it. So if you do not want to read a story of tragedy and sadness, this is your very last chance to put this book down, because the misery of the Baudelaire orphans begins in the very next paragraph.

"Look what I have for you," Mr. Poe said, grinning from ear to ear and holding out a small paper bag. "Peppermints!" Mr. Poe was a banker who had been placed in charge of handling the affairs of the Baudelaire orphans after their parents died. Mr. Poe was kindhearted, but it is not enough in this world to be kindhearted, particularly if you are responsible for keeping children out of danger. Mr. Poe had known the three children since they were born, and could never remember that they were allergic to peppermints.

"Thank you, Mr. Poe," Violet said, and took the paper bag and peered inside. Like most fourteen-year-olds, Violet was too well mannered to mention that if she ate a peppermint she would break out in hives, a phrase which here means "be covered in red, itchy rashes for a few hours." Besides, she was too occupied with inventing thoughts to pay much attention to Mr. Poe. Anyone who knew Violet would know that when her hair was tied up in a ribbon to keep it out of her eyes, the way it was now, her thoughts were filled with wheels, gears, levers, and other necessary things for inventions. At this particular moment she was thinking of how she could improve the engine of the Fickle Ferry so it wouldn't belch smoke into the gray sky.

"That's very kind of you," said Klaus, the middle Baudelaire child, smiling at Mr. Poe and thinking that if he had even one lick of a peppermint, his tongue would swell up and he would scarcely be able to speak. Klaus took his glasses off and wished that Mr. Poe had bought him a book or a newspaper instead. Klaus was a voracious reader, and when he had learned about his allergy at a birthday party when he was eight, he had immediately read all his parents' books about allergies. Even four years later he could recite the chemical formulas that caused his tongue to swell up.

"Toi!" Sunny shrieked. The youngest Baudelaire was only an infant, and like many infants, she spoke mostly in words that were tricky to understand. By "Toi!" she probably meant "I have never eaten a peppermint because I suspect that I, like my siblings, am allergic to them," but it was hard to tell. She may also have meant "I wish I could bite a peppermint, because I like to bite things with my four sharp teeth, but I don't want to risk an allergic reaction."

"You can eat them on your cab ride to Mrs. Anwhistle's house," Mr. Poe said, coughing into his white handkerchief. Mr. Poe always seemed to have a cold and the Baudelaire orphans were accustomed to receiving information from him between bouts of hacking and wheezing. "She apologizes for not meeting you at the dock, but she says she's frightened of it."

"Why would she be frightened of a dock?" Klaus asked, looking around at the wooden piers and sailboats.

"She's frightened of anything to do with Lake Lachrymose," Mr. Poe said, "but she didn't say why. Perhaps it has to do with her husband's death. Your Aunt Josephine—she's not really your aunt, of course; she's your second cousin's sister-in-law, but asked that you call her Aunt Josephine—your Aunt Josephine lost her husband recently, and it may be possible that he drowned or died in a boat accident. It didn't seem polite to ask how she became a dowager. Well, let's put you in a taxi."

"What does that word mean?" Violet asked.

Mr. Poe looked at Violet and raised his eyebrows. "I'm surprised at you, Violet," he said. "A girl of your age should know that a taxi is a car which will drive you someplace for a fee. Now, let's gather your luggage and walk to the curb."

"'Dowager,'" Klaus whispered to Violet, "is a fancy word for 'widow.'"

"Thank you," she whispered back, picking up her suitcase in one hand and Sunny in the other. Mr. Poe was waving his handkerchief in the air to signal a taxi to stop, and in no time at all the cabdriver piled all of the Baudelaire suitcases into the trunk and Mr. Poe piled the Baudelaire children into the back seat.

"I will say good-bye to you here," Mr. Poe said. "The banking day has already begun, and I'm afraid if I go with you out to Aunt

Josephine's I will never get anything done. Please give her my best wishes, and tell her that I will keep in touch regularly." Mr. Poe paused for a moment to cough into his handkerchief before continuing. "Now, your Aunt Josephine is a bit nervous about having three children in her house, but I assured her that you three were very well behaved. Make sure you mind your manners, and, as always, you can call or fax me at the bank if there's any sort of problem. Although I don't imagine anything will go wrong *this* time."

When Mr. Poe said *"this* time," he looked at the children meaningfully as if it were their fault that poor Uncle Monty was dead. But the Baudelaires were too nervous about meeting their new caretaker to say anything more to Mr. Poe except "So long."

"So long," Violet said, putting the bag of peppermints in her pocket.

"So long," Klaus said, taking one last look at Damocles Dock.

"Frul!" Sunny shrieked, chewing on her seat belt buckle.

"So long," Mr. Poe replied, "and good luck to you. I will think of the Baudelaires as often as I can."

Mr. Poe gave some money to the taxi driver and waved good-bye to the three children as the cab pulled away from the dock and onto a gray, cobblestoned street. There was a small grocery store with barrels of limes and beets out front. There was a clothing store called Look! It Fits!, which appeared to be undergoing renovations. There was a terrible-looking restaurant called the Anxious Clown, with neon lights and balloons in the window. But mostly, there were many stores and shops that were all closed up, with boards or metal gratings over the windows and doors.

"The town doesn't seem very crowded," Klaus remarked. "I was hoping we might make some new friends here."

"It's the off-season," the cabdriver said. He

was a skinny man with a skinny cigarette hanging out of his mouth, and as he talked to the children he looked at them through the rear-view mirror. "The town of Lake Lachrymose is a resort, and when the nice weather comes it's as crowded as can be. But around now, things here are as dead as the cat I ran over this morning. To make new friends, you'll have to wait until the weather gets a little better. Speaking of which, Hurricane Herman is expected to arrive in town in a week or so. You better make sure you have enough food up there in the house."

"A hurricane on a lake?" Klaus asked. "I thought hurricanes only occurred near the ocean."

"A body of water as big as Lake Lachrymose," the driver said, "can have anything occur on it. To tell you the truth, I'd be a little nervous about living on top of this hill. Once the storm hits, it'll be very difficult to drive all the way down into town."

Violet, Klaus, and Sunny looked out the window and saw what the driver meant by "all the way down." The taxi had turned one last corner and arrived at the scraggly top of a tall, tall hill, and the children could see the town far, far below them, the cobblestone road curling around the buildings like a tiny gray snake, and the small square of Damocles Dock with specks of people bustling around it. And out beyond the dock was the inky blob of Lake Lachrymose, huge and dark as if a monster were standing over the three orphans, casting a giant shadow below them. For a few moments the children stared into the lake as if hypnotized by this enormous stain on the landscape.

"The lake is so enormous," Klaus said, "and it looks so deep. I can almost understand why Aunt Josephine is afraid of it."

"The lady who lives up here," the cabdriver asked, "is afraid of the lake?"

"That's what we've been told," Violet said.

The cabdriver shook his head and brought

the cab to a halt. "I don't know how she can stand it, then."

"What do you mean?" Violet asked.

"You mean you've never been to this house?" he asked.

"No, never," Klaus replied. "We've never even met our Aunt Josephine before."

"Well, if your Aunt Josephine is afraid of the water," the cabdriver said, "I can't believe she lives here in this house."

"What are you talking about?" Klaus asked.

"Well, take a look," the driver answered, and got out of the cab.

The Baudelaires took a look. At first, the three youngsters saw only a small boxy square with a peeling white door, and it looked as if the house was scarcely bigger than the taxi which had taken them to it. But as they piled out of the car and drew closer, they saw that this small square was the only part of the house that was on top of the hill. The rest of it—a large pile of boxy squares, all stuck together like ice cubes—

hung over the side, attached to the hill by long metal stilts that looked like spider legs. As the three orphans peered down at their new home, it seemed as if the entire house were holding on to the hill for dear life.

The taxi driver took their suitcases out of the trunk, set them in front of the peeling white door, and drove down the hill with a *toot!* of his horn for a good-bye. There was a soft squeak as the peeling white door opened, and from behind the door appeared a pale woman with her white hair piled high on top of her head in a bun.

"Hello," she said, smiling thinly. "I'm your Aunt Josephine."

"Hello," Violet said, cautiously, and stepped forward to meet her new guardian. Klaus stepped forward behind her, and Sunny crawled forward behind him, but all three Baudelaires were walking carefully, as if their weight would send the house toppling down from its perch.

The orphans couldn't help wondering how a woman who was so afraid of Lake Lachrymose could live in a house that felt like it was about to fall into its depths.

"*This* is the radiator," Aunt Josephine said, pointing to a radiator with a pale and skinny finger. "Please don't ever touch it. You may find yourself very cold here in my home. I never turn on the radiator, because I am frightened that it might explode, so it often gets chilly in the evenings."

Violet and Klaus looked at one another briefly, and Sunny looked at both of them. Aunt Josephine was giving them a tour of their new home and so far appeared to be afraid of everything in it, from the welcome mat—which, Aunt Josephine explained, could cause someone to trip and break their neck—to the sofa in the living room, which she said could fall over at any time and crush them flat.

"This is the telephone," Aunt Josephine said, gesturing to the telephone. "It should only be used in emergencies, because there is a danger of electrocution."

"Actually," Klaus said, "I've read quite a bit about electricity. I'm pretty sure that the telephone is perfectly safe."

Aunt Josephine's hands fluttered to her white hair as if something had jumped onto her head. "You can't believe everything you read," she pointed out.

"I've built a telephone from scratch," Violet said. "If you'd like, I could take the telephone apart and show you how it works. That might make you feel better."

"I don't think so," Aunt Josephine said, frowning.

"Delmo!" Sunny offered, which probably meant something along the lines of "If you wish, I will bite the telephone to show you that it's harmless."

"Delmo?" Aunt Josephine asked, bending over to pick up a piece of lint from the faded flowery carpet. "What do you mean by 'delmo'? I consider myself an expert on the English language, and I have no idea what the word 'delmo' means. Is she speaking some other language?"

"Sunny doesn't speak fluently yet, I'm afraid," Klaus said, picking his little sister up. "Just baby talk, mostly."

"Grun!" Sunny shrieked, which meant something like "I object to your calling it baby talk!"

"Well, I will have to teach her proper English," Aunt Josephine said stiffly. "I'm sure you all need some brushing up on your grammar, actually. Grammar is the greatest joy in life, don't you find?"

The three siblings looked at one another. Violet was more likely to say that inventing things was the greatest joy in life, Klaus thought reading was, and Sunny of course took no greater pleasure than in biting things. The Baudelaires thought of grammar—all those rules about how to write and speak the English language—the way they thought of banana bread: fine, but nothing to make a fuss about. Still, it seemed rude to contradict Aunt Josephine.

"Yes," Violet said finally. "We've always loved grammar."

Aunt Josephine nodded, and gave the Baudelaires a small smile. "Well, I'll show you to your room and continue the rest of the tour after dinner. When you open this door, just push on the wood here. Never use the doorknob. I'm always afraid that it will shatter into a million pieces and that one of them will hit my eye."

The Baudelaires were beginning to think that they would not be allowed to touch a single object in the whole house, but they smiled at Aunt Josephine, pushed on the wood, and opened the door to reveal a large, well-lit room with blank white walls and a plain blue carpet on the floor. Inside were two good-sized beds and one good-sized crib, obviously for Sunny, each covered in a plain blue bedspread, and at the foot of each bed was a large trunk, for storing things. At the other end of the room was a large closet for everyone's clothes, a small window for looking out, and a medium-sized pile of tin cans for no apparent purpose.

"I'm sorry that all three of you have to share a room," Aunt Josephine said, "but this house isn't very big. I tried to provide you with everything you would need, and I do hope you will be comfortable."

"I'm sure we will," Violet said, carrying her suitcase into the room. "Thank you very much, Aunt Josephine."

"In each of your trunks," Aunt Josephine said, "there is a present."

Presents? The Baudelaires had not received presents for a long, long time. Smiling, Aunt Josephine walked to the first trunk and opened it. "For Violet," she said, "there is a lovely new doll with plenty of outfits for it to wear." Aunt Josephine reached inside and pulled out a plastic doll with a tiny mouth and wide, staring eyes. "Isn't she adorable? Her name is Pretty Penny."

"Oh, thank you," said Violet, who at fourteen was too old for dolls and had never particularly liked dolls anyway. Forcing a smile on her face, she took Pretty Penny from Aunt Josephine and patted it on its little plastic head.

"And for Klaus," Aunt Josephine said, "there is a model train set." She opened the second trunk and pulled out a tiny train car. "You can set up the tracks in that empty corner of the room."

"What fun," said Klaus, trying to look excited. Klaus had never liked model trains, as they were a lot of work to put together and when you were done all you had was something that went around and around in endless circles.

"And for little Sunny," Aunt Josephine said,

reaching into the smallest trunk, which sat at the foot of the crib, "here is a rattle. See, Sunny, it makes a little noise."

Sunny smiled at Aunt Josephine, showing all four of her sharp teeth, but her older siblings knew that Sunny despised rattles and the irritating sounds they made when you shook them. Sunny had been given a rattle when she was very small, and it was the only thing she was not sorry to lose in the enormous fire that had destroyed the Baudelaire home.

"It is so generous of you," Violet said, "to give us all of these things." She was too polite to add that they weren't things they particularly liked.

"Well, I am very happy to have you here," Aunt Josephine said. "I love grammar so much. I'm excited to be able to share my love of grammar with three nice children like yourselves. Well, I'll give you a few minutes to settle in and then we'll have some dinner. See you soon."

"Aunt Josephine," Klaus asked, "what are these cans for?"

"Those cans? For burglars, naturally," Aunt Josephine said, patting the bun of hair on top of her head. "You must be as frightened of burglars as I am. So every night, simply place these tin cans right by the door, so that when burglars come in, they'll trip over the cans and you'll wake up."

"But what will we do then, when we're awake in a room with an angry burglar?" Violet asked. "I would prefer to sleep through a burglary."

Aunt Josephine's eyes grew wide with fear. "Angry burglars?" she repeated. "*Angry burglars?* Why are you talking about *angry burglars?* Are you trying to make us all even more frightened than we already are?"

"Of course not," Violet stuttered, not pointing out that Aunt Josephine was the one who had brought up the subject. "I'm sorry. I didn't mean to frighten you."

"Well, we'll say no more about it," Aunt Josephine said, looking nervously at the tin cans as if a burglar were tripping on them at that very minute. "I'll see you at the dinner table in a few minutes."

Their new guardian shut the door, and the Baudelaire orphans listened to her footsteps padding down the hallway before they spoke.

"Sunny can have Pretty Penny," Violet said, handing the doll to her sister. "The plastic is hard enough for chewing, I think."

"And you can have the model trains, Violet," Klaus said. "Maybe you can take apart the engines and invent something."

"But that leaves you with a rattle," Violet said. "That doesn't seem fair."

"Schu!" Sunny shrieked, which probably meant something along the lines of "It's been a long time since anything in our lives has felt fair."

The Baudelaires looked at one another with bitter smiles. Sunny was right. It wasn't fair that their parents had been taken away from them. It wasn't fair that the evil and revolting Count Olaf was pursuing them wherever they went, caring for nothing but their fortune. It wasn't fair that they moved from relative to relative, with terrible things happening at each of their new homes, as if the Baudelaires were riding on some horrible bus that stopped only at stations of unfairness and misery. And, of course, it certainly wasn't fair that Klaus only had a rattle to play with in his new home.

"Aunt Josephine obviously worked very hard to prepare this room for us," Violet said sadly. "She seems to be a good-hearted person. We shouldn't complain, even to ourselves."

"You're right," Klaus said, picking up his rattle and giving it a halfhearted little shake. "We shouldn't complain."

"Twee!" Sunny shrieked, which probably meant something like "Both of you are right. We shouldn't complain."

Klaus walked over to the window and looked out at the darkening landscape. The sun was beginning to set over the inky depths of Lake Lachrymose, and a cold evening wind was beginning to blow. Even from the other side of the glass Klaus could feel a small chill. "I want to complain, anyway," he said.

"Soup's on!" Aunt Josephine called from the kitchen. "Please come to dinner!"

Violet put her hand on Klaus's shoulder and gave it a little squeeze of comfort, and without another word the three Baudelaires headed back down the hallway and into the dining room. Aunt Josephine had set the table for four, providing a large cushion for Sunny and another pile of tin cans in the corner of the room, just in case burglars tried to steal their dinner.

"Normally, of course," Aunt Josephine said, "'soup's on' is an idiomatic expression that has nothing to do with soup. It simply means that dinner is ready. In this case, however, I've actually made soup."

"Oh good," Violet said. "There's nothing like hot soup on a chilly evening."

"Actually, it's not hot soup," Aunt Josephine said. "I never cook anything hot because I'm afraid of turning the stove on. It might burst into flames. I've made chilled cucumber soup for dinner."

The Baudelaires looked at one another and tried to hide their dismay. As you probably know, chilled cucumber soup is a delicacy that is best enjoyed on a very hot day. I myself once enjoyed it in Egypt while visiting a friend of mine who works as a snake charmer. When it is well prepared, chilled cucumber soup has a delicious, minty taste, cool and refreshing as if you are drinking something as well as eating it. But on a cold day, in a drafty room, chilled cucumber soup is about as welcome as a swarm of wasps at a bat mitzvah. In dead silence, the three children sat down at the table with their Aunt Josephine and did their best to force down the cold, slimy concoction. The only sound was of Sunny's four teeth chattering on her soup spoon as she ate her frigid dinner. As I'm sure you know, when no one is speaking at the dinner table, the meal seems to take hours, so it felt like much, much later when Aunt Josephine broke the silence.

"My dear husband and I never had children," she said, "because we were afraid to. But I do want you to know that I'm very happy that you're here. I am often very lonely up on this hill by myself, and when Mr. Poe wrote to me about your troubles I didn't want you to be as lonely as I was when I lost my dear Ike."

"Was Ike your husband?" Violet asked.

Aunt Josephine smiled, but she didn't look at Violet, as if she were talking more to herself than to the Baudelaires. "Yes," she said, in a far-away voice, "he was my husband, but he was much more than that. He was my best friend, my partner in grammar, and the only person I knew who could whistle with crackers in his mouth."

"Our mother could do that," Klaus said, smiling. "Her specialty was Mozart's fourteenth symphony."

"Ike's was Beethoven's fourth quartet," Aunt

Josephine replied. "Apparently it's a family characteristic."

"I'm sorry we never got to meet him," Violet said. "He sounds wonderful."

"He *was* wonderful," Aunt Josephine said, stirring her soup and blowing on it even though it was ice cold. "I was so sad when he died. I felt like I'd lost the two most special things in my life."

"Two?" Violet asked. "What do you mean?"

"I lost Ike," Aunt Josephine said, "and I lost Lake Lachrymose. I mean, I didn't really lose it, of course. It's still down in the valley. But I grew up on its shores. I used to swim in it every day. I knew which beaches were sandy and which were rocky. I knew all the islands in the middle of its waters and all the caves along-side its shore. Lake Lachrymose felt like a friend to me. But when it took poor Ike away from me I was too afraid to go near it anymore. I stopped swimming in it. I never went to the beach again. I even put away all my books about it. The only way I can bear to look at it is from the Wide Window in the library."

"Library?" Klaus asked, brightening. "You have a library?"

"Of course," Aunt Josephine said. "Where else could I keep all my books on grammar? If you've all finished with your soup, I'll show you the library."

"I couldn't eat another bite," Violet said truthfully.

"Irm!" Sunny shrieked in agreement.

"No, no, Sunny," Aunt Josephine said. "'Irm' is not grammatically correct. You mean to say, 'I have also finished my supper.'"

"Irm," Sunny insisted.

"My goodness, you do need grammar lessons," Aunt Josephine said. "All the more reason to go to the library. Come, children."

Leaving behind their half-full soup bowls, the Baudelaires followed Aunt Josephine down the hallway, taking care not to touch any of the doorknobs they passed. At the end of the hallway,

Aunt Josephine stopped and opened an ordinary-looking door, but when the children stepped through the door they arrived in a room that was anything but ordinary.

The library was neither square nor rectangular, like most rooms, but curved in the shape of an oval. One wall of the oval was devoted to books—rows and rows and rows of them, and every single one of them was about grammar. There was an encyclopedia of nouns placed in a series of simple wooden bookshelves, curved to fit the wall. There were very thick books on the history of verbs, lined up in metal bookshelves that were polished to a bright shine. And there were cabinets made of glass, with adjective manuals placed inside them as if they were for sale in a store instead of in someone's house. In the middle of the room were some comfortable-looking chairs, each with its own footstool so one could stretch out one's legs while reading.

But it was the other wall of the oval, at the

far end of the room, that drew the children's attention. From floor to ceiling, the wall was a window, just one enormous curved pane of glass, and beyond the glass was a spectacular view of Lake Lachrymose. When the children stepped forward to take a closer look, they felt as if they were flying high above the dark lake instead of merely looking out on it.

"This is the only way I can stand to look at the lake," Aunt Josephine said in a quiet voice. "From far away. If I get much closer I remember my last picnic on the beach with my darling Ike. I warned him to wait an hour after eating before he went into the lake, but he only waited forty-five minutes. He thought that was enough."

"Did he get cramps?" Klaus asked. "That's what's supposed to happen if you don't wait an hour before you swim."

"That's one reason," Aunt Josephine said, "but in Lake Lachrymose, there's another one. If you don't wait an hour after eating, the

Lachrymose Leeches will smell food on you, and attack."

"Leeches?" Violet asked.

"Leeches," Klaus explained, "are a bit like worms. They are blind and live in bodies of water, and in order to feed, they attach themselves to you and suck your blood."

Violet shuddered. "How horrible."

"Swoh!" Sunny shrieked, which probably meant something along the lines of "Why in the world would you go swimming in a lake full of leeches?"

"The Lachrymose Leeches," Aunt Josephine said, "are quite different from regular leeches. They each have six rows of very sharp teeth, and one very sharp nose—they can smell even the smallest bit of food from far, far away. The Lachrymose Leeches are usually quite harmless, preying only on small fish. But if they smell food on a human they will swarm around him and—and . . ." Tears came to Aunt Josephine's eyes, and she took out a pale pink handkerchief and dabbed them away. "I apologize, children. It is not grammatically correct to end a sentence with the word 'and', but I get so upset when I think about Ike that I cannot talk about his death."

"We're sorry we brought it up," Klaus said quickly. "We didn't mean to upset you."

"That's all right," Aunt Josephine said, blowing her nose. "It's just that I prefer to think of Ike in other ways. Ike always loved the sunshine, and I like to imagine that wherever he is now, it's as sunny as can be. Of course, nobody knows what happens to you after you die, but it's nice to think of my husband someplace very, very hot, don't you think?"

"Yes I do," Violet said. "It is very nice." She swallowed. She wanted to say something else to Aunt Josephine, but when you have only known someone for a few hours it is difficult to know what they would like to hear. "Aunt Josephine," she said timidly, "have you thought of moving someplace else? Perhaps if you lived somewhere far from Lake Lachrymose, you might feel better."

"We'd go with you," Klaus piped up.

"Oh, I could never sell this house," Aunt Josephine said. "I'm terrified of realtors."

The three Baudelaire youngsters looked at one another surreptitiously, a word which here means "while Aunt Josephine wasn't looking." None of them had ever heard of a person who was frightened of realtors.

There are two kinds of fears: rational and irrational—or, in simpler terms, fears that make sense and fears that don't. For instance, the Baudelaire orphans have a fear of Count Olaf, which makes perfect sense, because he is an evil man who wants to destroy them. But if they were afraid of lemon meringue pie, this would be an irrational fear, because lemon meringue pie is delicious and has never hurt a soul. Being afraid of a monster under the bed is perfectly rational, because there may in fact be a monster under your bed at any time, ready to eat you all up, but a fear of realtors is an irrational fear. Realtors, as I'm sure you know, are people who assist in the buying and selling of houses. Besides occasionally wearing an ugly yellow coat, the worst a realtor can do to you is show you a house that you find ugly, and so it is completely irrational to be terrified of them.

As Violet, Klaus, and Sunny looked down at the dark lake and thought about their new lives with Aunt Josephine, they experienced a fear themselves, and even a worldwide expert on fear would have difficulty saying whether this was a rational fear or an irrational fear. The Baudelaires' fear was that misfortune would soon befall them. On one hand, this was an irrational fear, because Aunt Josephine seemed like a good person, and Count Olaf was nowhere to be seen. But on the other hand, the Baudelaires had experienced so many terrible things that it seemed rational to think that another catastrophe was just around the corner.

There is a way of looking at life called "keeping things in perspective." This simply means "making yourself feel better by comparing the things that are happening to you right now against other things that have happened at a different time, or to different people." For instance, if you were upset about an ugly pimple on the end of your nose, you might try to feel better by keeping your pimple in perspective. You might compare your pimple situation to that of someone who was being eaten by a bear, and when you looked in the mirror at your ugly pimple, you could say to yourself, "Well, at least I'm not being eaten by a bear."

You can see at once why keeping things in perspective rarely works very well, because it is hard to concentrate on somebody else being eaten by a bear when you are staring at your own ugly pimple. So it was with the Baudelaire orphans in the days that followed. In the morning, when the children joined Aunt Josephine for a breakfast of orange juice and untoasted bread, Violet thought to herself, "Well, at least we're not being forced to cook for Count Olaf's disgusting theater troupe." In the afternoon, when Aunt Josephine would take them to the library and teach them all about grammar, Klaus thought to himself, "Well, at least Count Olaf isn't about to whisk us away to Peru." And in the evening, when the children joined Aunt Josephine for a dinner of orange juice and untoasted bread, Sunny thought to herself, "Zax!" which meant something along the lines of "Well, at least there isn't a sign of Count Olaf anywhere."

But no matter how much the three siblings compared their life with Aunt Josephine to the miserable things that had happened to them before, they couldn't help but be dissatisfied with their circumstances. In her free time, Violet would dismantle the gears and switches from the model train set, hoping to invent something that could prepare hot food without frightening Aunt Josephine, but she couldn't help wishing that Aunt Josephine would simply turn on the stove. Klaus would sit in one of the chairs in the library with his feet on a footstool, reading about grammar until the sun went down, but when he looked out at the gloomy lake he couldn't help wishing that they were still living with Uncle Monty and all of his reptiles. And Sunny would take time out from her schedule and bite the head of Pretty Penny, but she couldn't help wishing that their parents were still alive and that she and her siblings were safe and sound in the Baudelaire home.

Aunt Josephine did not like to leave the house very much, because there were so many things outside that frightened her, but one day the children told her what the cabdriver had said about Hurricane Herman approaching, and she agreed to take them into town in order to buy groceries. Aunt Josephine was afraid to drive in automobiles, because the doors might get stuck, leaving her trapped inside, so they walked the long way down the hill. By the time the Baudelaires reached the market their legs were sore from the walk.

"Are you sure that you won't let us cook for you?" Violet asked, as Aunt Josephine reached into the barrel of limes. "When we lived with Count Olaf, we learned how to make puttanesca sauce. It was quite easy and perfectly safe."

Aunt Josephine shook her head. "It is my responsibility as your caretaker to cook for you, and I am eager to try this recipe for cold lime stew. Count Olaf certainly does sound evil. Imagine forcing children to stand near a stove!"

"He was very cruel to us," Klaus agreed, not adding that being forced to cook had been the least of their problems when they lived with Count Olaf. "Sometimes I still have nightmares about the terrible tattoo on his ankle. It always scared me."

Aunt Josephine frowned, and patted her bun. "I'm afraid you made a grammatical mistake, Klaus," she said sternly. "When you said, 'It always scared me,' you sounded as if you meant that his ankle always scared you, but you meant his tattoo. So you should have said, 'The tattoo always scared me.' Do you understand?"

"Yes, I understand," Klaus said, sighing. "Thank you for pointing that out, Aunt Josephine."

"Niku!" Sunny shrieked, which probably meant something like "It wasn't very nice to point out Klaus's grammatical mistake when he was talking about something that upset him."

"No, no, Sunny," Aunt Josephine said firmly, looking up from her shopping list. "'Niku' isn't a word. Remember what we said about using correct English. Now, Violet, would you please get some cucumbers? I thought I would make chilled cucumber soup again sometime next week."

Violet groaned inwardly, a phrase which here means "said nothing but felt disappointed at the prospect of another chilly dinner," but she smiled at Aunt Josephine and headed down an aisle of the market in search of cucumbers. She looked wistfully at all the delicious food on the shelves that required turning on the stove in order to prepare it. Violet hoped that some-day she could cook a nice hot meal for Aunt Josephine and her siblings using the invention she was working on with the model train engine. For a few moments she was so lost in her invent-ing thoughts that she didn't look where she was going until she walked right into someone.

"Excuse m—" Violet started to say, but when

she looked up she couldn't finish her sentence. There stood a tall, thin man with a blue sailor hat on his head and a black eye patch covering his left eye. He was smiling eagerly down at her as if she were a brightly wrapped birthday present that he couldn't wait to rip open. His fingers were long and bony, and he was leaning awkwardly to one side, a bit like Aunt Josephine's house dangling over the hill. When Violet looked down, she saw why: There was a thick stump of wood where his left leg should have been, and like most people with peg legs, this man was leaning on his good leg, which caused him to tilt. But even though Violet had never seen anyone with a peg leg before, this was not why she couldn't finish her sentence. The reason why had to do with something she *had* seen before—the bright, bright shine in the man's one eye, and above it, just one long eyebrow.

When someone is in disguise, and the disguise is not very good, one can describe it as a transparent disguise. This does not mean that the person is wearing plastic wrap or glass or anything else transparent. It merely means that people can see through his disguise—that is, the disguise doesn't fool them for a minute. Violet wasn't fooled for even a second as she stood staring at the man she'd walked into. She knew at once it was Count Olaf.

"Violet, what are you doing in this aisle?" Aunt Josephine said, walking up behind her. "This aisle contains food that needs to be heated, and you know—" When she saw Count Olaf she stopped speaking, and for a second Violet thought that Aunt Josephine had recognized him, too. But then Aunt Josephine smiled, and Violet's hopes were dashed, a word which here means "shattered."

"Hello," Count Olaf said, smiling at Aunt Josephine. "I was just apologizing for running into your sister here."

Aunt Josephine's face grew bright red, seeming even brighter under her white hair. "Oh, no," she said, as Klaus and Sunny came down the aisle to see what all the fuss was about. "Violet is not my sister, sir. I am her legal guardian."

Count Olaf clapped one hand to his face as if Aunt Josephine had just told him she was the tooth fairy. "I cannot believe it," he said. "Madam, you don't look nearly old enough to be anyone's guardian."

Aunt Josephine blushed again. "Well, sir, I have lived by the lake my whole life, and some people have told me that it keeps me looking youthful."

"I would be happy to have the acquaintance of a local personage," Count Olaf said, tipping his blue sailor hat and using a silly word which here means "person." "I am new to this town, and beginning a new business, so I am eager to make new acquaintances. Allow me to introduce myself."

"Klaus and I are happy to introduce you," Violet said, with more bravery than I would have had when faced with meeting Count Olaf again. "Aunt Josephine, this is Count—"

"No, no, Violet," Aunt Josephine interrupted. "Watch your grammar. You should have said 'Klaus and I *will be* happy to introduce you,' because you haven't introduced us yet."

"But—" Violet started to say.

"Now, Veronica," Count Olaf said, his one eye shining brightly as he looked down at her. "Your guardian is right. And before you make any other mistakes, allow me to introduce myself. My name is Captain Sham, and I have a new business renting sailboats out on Damocles Dock. I am happy to make your acquaintance, Miss—?"

"I am Josephine Anwhistle," Aunt Josephine said. "And these are Violet, Klaus, and little Sunny Baudelaire."

"Little Sunny," Captain Sham repeated, sounding as if he were eating Sunny rather than greeting her. "It's a pleasure to meet all of you. Perhaps someday I can take you out on the lake for a little boat ride."

"Ging!" Sunny shrieked, which probably meant something like "I would rather eat dirt."

"We're not going anywhere with you," Klaus said.

Aunt Josephine blushed again, and looked sharply at the three children. "The children seem to have forgotten their manners as well as their grammar," she said. "Please apologize to Captain Sham at once."

"He's not Captain Sham," Violet said impatiently. "He's Count Olaf."

Aunt Josephine gasped, and looked from the anxious faces of the Baudelaires to the calm face of Captain Sham. He had a grin on his face, but his smile had slipped a notch, a phrase which here means "grown less confident as he waited to see if Aunt Josephine realized he was really Count Olaf in disguise."

Aunt Josephine looked him over from head to toe, and then frowned. "Mr. Poe told me to be on the watch for Count Olaf," she said finally, "but he did also say that you children tended to see him everywhere."

"We see him everywhere," Klaus said tiredly, "because he *is* everywhere."

"Who is this Count Omar person?" Captain Sham asked.

"Count *Olaf*," Aunt Josephine said, "is a terrible man who—"

"—is standing right in front of us," Violet finished. "I don't care what he calls himself. He has the same shiny eyes, the same single eyebrow—"

"But plenty of people have those characteristics," Aunt Josephine said. "Why, my mother-in-law had not only one eyebrow, but also only one ear."

"The tattoo!" Klaus said. "Look for the tattoo! Count Olaf has a tattoo of an eye on his left ankle."

Captain Sham sighed, and, with difficulty, lifted his peg leg so everyone could get a clear look at it. It was made of dark wood that was polished to shine as brightly as his eye, and attached to his left knee with a curved metal hinge. "But I don't even have a left ankle," he said, in a whiny voice. "It was all chewed away by the Lachrymose Leeches."

Aunt Josephine's eyes welled up, and she placed a hand on Captain Sham's shoulder. "Oh, you poor man," she said, and the children knew at once that they were doomed. "Did you hear what Captain Sham said?" she asked them.

Violet tried one more time, knowing it would probably be futile, a word which here means "filled with futility." "He's not Captain Sham," she said. "He's—"

"You don't think he would allow the Lachrymose Leeches to chew off his leg," Aunt Josephine said, "just to play a prank on you? Tell us, Captain Sham. Tell us how it happened."

"Well, I was sitting on my boat, just a few weeks ago," Captain Sham said. "I was eating some pasta with puttanesca sauce, and I spilled some on my leg. Before I knew it, the leeches were attacking."

"That's just how it happened with my husband," Aunt Josephine said, biting her lip. The Baudelaires, all three of them, clenched their fists in frustration. They knew that Captain Sham's story about the puttanesca sauce was as phony as his name, but they couldn't prove it.

"Here," Captain Sham said, pulling a small card out of his pocket and handing it to Aunt Josephine. "Take my business card, and next time you're in town perhaps we could enjoy a cup of tea."

"That sounds delightful," Aunt Josephine said, reading his card. "'Captain Sham's Sailboats. Every boat has it's own sail.' Oh, Captain, you have made a very serious grammatical error here."

"What?" Captain Sham said, raising his eyebrow.

"This card says 'it's,' with an apostrophe. I-T-apostrophe-S always means 'it is.' You don't mean to say 'Every boat has it is own sail.' You mean simply I-T-S, 'belonging to it.' It's a very common mistake, Captain Sham, but a dreadful one."

Captain Sham's face darkened, and it looked for a minute like he was going to raise his peg leg again and kick Aunt Josephine with all his might. But then he smiled and his face cleared. "Thank you for pointing that out," he said finally.

"You're welcome," Aunt Josephine said. "Come, children, it's time to pay for our groceries. I hope to see you soon, Captain Sham."

Captain Sham smiled and waved good-bye, but the Baudelaires watched as his smile turned to a sneer as soon as Aunt Josephine had turned her back. He had fooled her, and there was nothing the Baudelaires could do about it. They spent the rest of the afternoon trudging back up the hill carrying their groceries, but the heaviness of cucumbers and limes was nothing compared to the heaviness in the orphans' hearts. All the way up the hill, Aunt Josephine talked about Captain Sham and what a nice man he was and how much she hoped they would see him again, while the children knew he was really Count Olaf and a terrible man and hoped they would never see him for the rest of their lives.

There is an expression that, I am sad to say, is appropriate for this part of the story. The expression is "falling for something hook, line, and sinker," and it comes from the world of fishing. The hook, the line, and the sinker are all parts of a fishing rod, and they work together to lure fish out of the ocean to their doom. If somebody is falling for something hook, line, and sinker, they are believing a bunch of lies and may find themselves doomed as a result. Aunt Josephine was falling for Captain Sham's lies hook, line, and sinker, but it was Violet, Klaus, and Sunny who were feeling doomed. As they walked up the hill in silence, the children looked down at Lake Lachrymose and felt the chill of doom fall over their hearts. It made the three siblings feel cold and lost, as if they were not simply looking at the shadowy lake, but had been dropped into the middle of its depths.

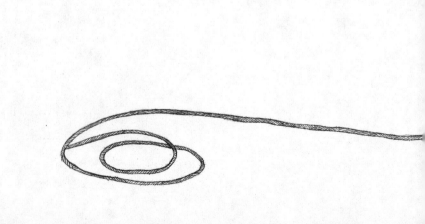

That night, the Baudelaire children sat at the table with Aunt Josephine and ate their dinner with a cold pit in their stomachs. Half of the pit came from the chilled lime stew that Aunt Josephine had prepared. But the other half—if not more than half—came from the knowledge that Count Olaf was in their lives once again.

"That Captain Sham is certainly a charming person," Aunt Josephine said, putting a piece of lime rind in her

mouth. "He must be very lonely, moving to a new town and losing a leg. Maybe we could have him over for dinner."

"We keep trying to tell you, Aunt Josephine," Violet said, pushing the stew around on her plate so it would look like she'd eaten more than she actually had. "He's not Captain Sham. He's Count Olaf in disguise."

"I've had enough of this nonsense," Aunt Josephine said. "Mr. Poe told me that Count Olaf had a tattoo on his left ankle and one eyebrow over his eyes. Captain Sham doesn't have a left ankle and only has one eye. I can't believe you would dare to disagree with a man who has eye problems."

"I have eye problems," Klaus said, pointing to his glasses, "and you're disagreeing with me."

"I will thank you not to be impertinent," Aunt Josephine said, using a word which here means "pointing out that I'm wrong, which annoys me." "It is very annoying. You will have to accept, once and for all, that Captain Sham is *not* Count Olaf." She reached into her pocket and pulled out the business card. "Look at his card. Does it say Count Olaf? No. It says Captain Sham. The card does have a serious grammatical error on it, but it is nevertheless proof that Captain Sham is who he says he is."

Aunt Josephine put the business card down on the dinner table, and the Baudelaires looked at it and sighed. Business cards, of course, are not proof of anything. Anyone can go to a print shop and have cards made that say anything they like. The king of Denmark can order business cards that say he sells golf balls. Your dentist can order business cards that say she is your grandmother. In order to escape from the castle of an enemy of mine, I once had cards printed that said I was an admiral in the French navy. Just because something is typed—whether it is typed on a business card or typed in a newspaper or book—this does not mean that it is true. The three siblings were well aware of this simple fact but could not find the words to convince Aunt Josephine. So they merely looked at Aunt Josephine, sighed, and silently pretended to eat their stew.

It was so quiet in the dining room that everyone jumped—Violet, Klaus, Sunny, and even Aunt Josephine—when the telephone rang. "My goodness!" Aunt Josephine said. "What should we do?"

"Minka!" Sunny shrieked, which probably meant something like "Answer it, of course!"

Aunt Josephine stood up from the table, but didn't move even as the phone rang a second time. "It might be important," she said, "but I don't know if it's worth the risk of electrocution."

"If it makes you feel more comfortable," Violet said, wiping her mouth with her napkin, "I will answer the phone." Violet stood up and walked to the phone in time to answer it on the third ring.

"Hello?" she asked.

"Is this Mrs. Anwhistle?" a wheezy voice asked.

"No," Violet replied. "This is Violet Baude-laire. May I help you?"

"Put the old woman on the phone, orphan," the voice said, and Violet froze, realizing it was Captain Sham. Quickly, she stole a glance at Aunt Josephine, who was now watching Violet nervously.

"I'm sorry," Violet said into the phone. "You must have the wrong number."

"Don't play with me, you wretched girl—" Captain Sham started to say, but Violet hung up the phone, her heart pounding, and turned to Aunt Josephine.

"Someone was asking for the Hopalong Dancing School," she said, lying quickly. "I told them they had the wrong number."

"What a brave girl you are," Aunt Josephine murmured. "Picking up the phone like that."

"It's actually very safe," Violet said.

"Haven't you ever answered the phone, Aunt Josephine?" Klaus asked.

"Ike almost always answered it," Aunt

Josephine said, "and he used a special glove for safety. But now that I've seen you answer it, maybe I'll give it a try next time somebody calls."

The phone rang, and Aunt Josephine jumped again. "Goodness," she said, "I didn't think it would ring again so soon. What an adventurous evening!"

Violet stared at the phone, knowing it was Captain Sham calling back. "Would you like me to answer it again?" she asked.

"No, no," Aunt Josephine said, walking toward the small ringing phone as if it were a big barking dog. "I said I'd try it, and I will." She took a deep breath, reached out a nervous hand, and picked up the phone.

"Hello?" she said. "Yes, this is she. Oh, hello, Captain Sham. How lovely to hear your voice." Aunt Josephine listened for a moment, and then blushed bright red. "Well, that's very nice of you to say, Captain Sham, but—what? Oh, all right. That's very nice of you to say, *Julio*. What?

What? Oh, what a lovely idea. But please hold on one moment."

Aunt Josephine held a hand over the receiver and faced the three children. "Violet, Klaus, Sunny, please go to your room," she said. "Captain Sham—I mean Julio, he asked me to call him by his first name—is planning a surprise for you children, and he wants to discuss it with me."

"We don't want a surprise," Klaus said.

"Of course you do," Aunt Josephine said. "Now run along so I can discuss it without your eavesdropping."

"We're not eavesdropping," Violet said, "but I think it would be better if we stayed here."

"Perhaps you are confused about the meaning of the word 'eavesdropping,'" Aunt Josephine said. "It means 'listening in.' If you stay here, you will be eavesdropping. Please go to your room."

"We *know* what eavesdropping means," Klaus said, but he followed his sisters down the hallway to their room. Once inside, they looked at one another in silent frustration. Violet put aside pieces of the toy caboose that she had planned to examine that evening to make room on her bed for the three of them to lie beside one another and frown at the ceiling.

"I thought we'd be safe here," Violet said glumly. "I thought that anybody who was frightened of realtors would never be friendly to Count Olaf, no matter how he was disguised."

"Do you think that he actually let leeches chew off his leg," Klaus wondered, shuddering, "just to hide his tattoo?"

"Choin!" Sunny shrieked, which probably meant "That seems a little drastic, even for Count Olaf."

"I agree with Sunny," Violet said. "I think he told that tale about leeches just to make Aunt Josephine feel sorry for him."

"And it sure worked," Klaus said, sighing. "After he told her that sob story, she fell for his disguise hook, line, and sinker."

"At least she isn't as trusting as Uncle Monty," Violet pointed out. "He let Count Olaf move right into the house."

"At least then we could keep an eye on him," Klaus replied.

"Ober!" Sunny remarked, which meant something along the lines of "Although we still didn't save Uncle Monty."

"What do you think he's up to this time?" Violet asked. "Maybe he plans to take us out in one of his boats and drown us in the lake."

"Maybe he wants to push this whole house off the mountain," Klaus said, "and blame it on Hurricane Herman."

"Haftu!" Sunny said glumly, which probably meant something like "Maybe he wants to put the Lachrymose Leeches in our beds."

"Maybe, maybe, maybe," Violet said. "All these maybes won't get us anywhere."

"We could call Mr. Poe and tell him Count

Olaf is here," Klaus said. "Maybe he could come and fetch us."

"That's the biggest maybe of them all," Violet said. "It's always impossible to convince Mr. Poe of anything, and Aunt Josephine doesn't believe us even though she saw Count Olaf with her own eyes."

"She doesn't even think she saw Count Olaf," Klaus agreed sadly. "She thinks she saw *Captain Sham.*"

Sunny nibbled halfheartedly on Pretty Penny's head and muttered "Poch!" which probably meant "You mean *Julio.*"

"Then I don't see what we can do," Klaus said, "except keep our eyes and ears open."

"Doma," Sunny agreed.

"You're both right," Violet said. "We'll just have to keep a very careful watch."

The Baudelaire orphans nodded solemnly, but the cold pit in their stomachs had not gone away. They all felt that keeping watch wasn't really much of a plan for defending themselves from Captain Sham, and as it grew later and later it worried them more and more. Violet tied her hair up in a ribbon to keep it out of her eyes, as if she were inventing something, but she thought and thought for hours and hours and was unable to invent another plan. Klaus stared at the ceiling with the utmost concentration, as if something very interesting were written on it, but nothing helpful occurred to him as the hour grew later and later. And Sunny bit Pretty Penny's head over and over, but no matter how long she bit it she couldn't think of anything to ease the Baudelaires' worries.

I have a friend named Gina-Sue who is socialist, and Gina-Sue has a favorite saying: "You can't lock up the barn after the horses are gone." It means simply that sometimes even the best of plans will occur to you when it is too late. This, I'm sorry to say, is the case with the Baudelaire orphans and their plan to keep a close watch on Captain Sham, for after hours and hours of worrying they heard an enormous crash of shattering glass, and knew at once that keeping watch hadn't been a good enough plan.

"What was that noise?" Violet said, getting up off the bed.

"It sounded like breaking glass," Klaus said worriedly, walking toward the bedroom door.

"Vestu!" Sunny shrieked, but her siblings did not have time to figure out what she meant as they all hurried down the hallway.

"Aunt Josephine! Aunt Josephine!" Violet called, but there was no answer. She peered up and down the hallway, but everything was quiet. "Aunt Josephine!" she called again. Violet led the way as the three orphans ran into the dining room, but their guardian wasn't there either. The candles on the table were still lit, casting a flickering glow on the business card and the bowls of cold lime stew.

"Aunt Josephine!" Violet called again, and

the children ran back out to the hallway and toward the door of the library. As she ran, Violet couldn't help but remember how she and her siblings had called Uncle Monty's name, early one morning, just before discovering the tragedy that had befallen him. "Aunt Josephine!" she called. "Aunt Josephine!" She couldn't help but remember all the times she had woken up in the middle of the night, calling out the names of her parents as she dreamed, as she so often did, of the terrible fire that had claimed their lives. "Aunt Josephine!" she said, reaching the library door. Violet was afraid that she was calling out Aunt Josephine's name when her aunt could no longer hear it.

"Look," Klaus said, and pointed to the door. A piece of paper, folded in half, was attached to the wood with a thumbtack. Klaus pried the paper loose and unfolded it.

"What is it?" Violet asked, and Sunny craned her little neck to see.

"It's a note," Klaus said, and read it out loud:

Violet, Klaus, and Sunny—
By the time you read this note, my life will be at
it's end. My heart is as cold as Ike and I find
life inbearable. I know your children may not
understand the sad life of a dowadger, or
what would have leaded me to this desperate akt,
but please know that I am much happier this
way. As my last will and testament, I leave you
three in the care of Captain Sham, a kind and
honorable men. Please think of me kindly even
though I'd done this terrible thing.
—Your Aunt Josephine

"Oh no," Klaus said quietly when he was fin-ished reading. He turned the piece of paper over and over as if he had read it incorrectly, as if it said something different. "Oh no," he said again, so faintly that it was as if he didn't even know he was speaking out loud.

Without a word Violet opened the door to the library, and the Baudelaires took a step inside and found themselves shivering. The room was freezing cold, and after one glance the orphans knew why. The Wide Window had shattered. Except for a few shards that still stuck to the window frame, the enormous pane of glass was gone, leaving a vacant hole that looked out into the still blackness of the night.

The cold night air rushed through the hole, rattling the bookshelves and making the children shiver up against one another, but despite the cold the orphans walked carefully to the empty space where the window had been, and looked down. The night was so black that it seemed as if there was absolutely nothing beyond the window. Violet, Klaus, and Sunny stood there for a moment and remembered the fear they had felt, just a few days ago, when they were standing in this very same spot. They knew now that their fear had been rational.

Huddling together, looking down into the blackness, the Baudelaires knew that their plan to keep a careful watch had come too late. They had locked the barn door, but poor Aunt Josephine was already gone.

Violet, Klaus, and Sunny—
By the time you read this note,
my life will be at it's end. My heart
is as cold as Ike and I find life
inbearable. I know your
children may not
understand the sad
life of a dowadger,
or what would have
leaded me to this desperate akt, but
please know that I am much

happier this way. As my last will and testament,
I leave you three in the care of Captain Sham, a
kind and honorable men. Please think of me
kindly even though I'd done this terrible thing.
—*Your Aunt Josephine*

"*Stop it!*" Violet cried. "Stop reading it out loud, Klaus! We already know what it says."

"I just can't believe it," Klaus said, turning the paper around for the umpteenth time. The Baudelaire orphans were sitting glumly around the dining-room table with the cold lime stew in bowls and dread in their hearts. Violet had called Mr. Poe and told him what had happened, and the Baudelaires, too anxious to sleep, had stayed up the whole night waiting for him to arrive on the first Fickle Ferry of the day. The candles were almost completely burned down, and Klaus had to lean forward to read Josephine's note. "There's something funny about this note, but I can't put my finger on it."

"How can you say such a thing?" Violet asked. "Aunt Josephine has thrown herself out of the window. There's nothing funny about it at all."

"Not funny as in a funny joke," Klaus said. "Funny as in a funny smell. Why, in the very first sentence she says 'my life will be at it's end.'"

"And now it is," Violet said, shuddering.

"That's not what I mean," Klaus said impatiently. "She uses it's, I-T-apostrophe-S, which always means 'it is.' But you wouldn't say 'my life will be at it is end.' She means I-T-S, 'belonging to it.'" He picked up Captain Sham's business card, which was still lying on the table. "Remember when she saw this card? 'Every boat has it's own sail.' She said it was a serious grammatical error."

"Who cares about grammatical errors," Violet asked, "when Aunt Josephine has jumped out the window?"

"But Aunt Josephine would have cared,"

Klaus pointed out. "That's what she cared about most: grammar. Remember, she said it was the greatest joy in life."

"Well, it wasn't enough," Violet said sadly. "No matter how much she liked grammar, it says she found her life unbearable."

"But that's another error in the note," Klaus said. "It doesn't say *un*bearable, with a U. It says *in*bearable, with an I."

"*You* are being unbearable, with a U," Violet cried.

"And *you* are being stupid, with an S," Klaus snapped.

"Aget!" Sunny shrieked, which meant something along the lines of "Please stop fighting!" Violet and Klaus looked at their baby sister and then at one another. Oftentimes, when people are miserable, they will want to make other people miserable, too. But it never helps.

"I'm sorry, Klaus," Violet said meekly. "You're not unbearable. Our situation is unbearable."

"I know," Klaus said miserably. "I'm sorry,

too. You're not stupid, Violet. You're very clever. In fact, I hope you're clever enough to get us out of this situation. Aunt Josephine has jumped out the window and left us in the care of Captain Sham, and I don't know what we can do about it."

"Well, Mr. Poe is on his way," Violet said. "He said on the phone that he would be here first thing in the morning, so we don't have long to wait. Maybe Mr. Poe can be of some help."

"I guess so," Klaus said, but he and his sisters looked at one another and sighed. They knew that the chances of Mr. Poe being of much help were rather slim. When the Baudelaires lived with Count Olaf, Mr. Poe was not helpful when the children told him about Count Olaf's cruelty. When the Baudelaires lived with Uncle Monty, Mr. Poe was not helpful when the children told him about Count Olaf's treachery. It seemed clear that Mr. Poe would not be of any help in this situation, either.

One of the candles burned out in a small

puff of smoke, and the children sank down lower in their chairs. You probably know of a plant called the Venus flytrap, which grows in the tropics. The top of the plant is shaped like an open mouth, with toothlike spines around the edges. When a fly, attracted by the smell of the flower, lands on the Venus flytrap, the mouth of the plant begins to close, trapping the fly. The terrified fly buzzes around the closed mouth of the plant, but there is nothing it can do, and the plant slowly, slowly, dissolves the fly into nothing. As the darkness of the house closed in around them, the Baudelaire youngsters felt like the fly in this situation. It was as if the disastrous fire that took the lives of their parents had been the beginning of a trap, and they hadn't even known it. They buzzed from place to place—Count Olaf's house in the city, Uncle Monty's home in the country, and now, Aunt Josephine's house overlooking the lake—but their own misfortune always closed around them, tighter and tighter, and it seemed to the three siblings that before too long they would dissolve away to nothing.

"We could rip up the note," Klaus said finally. "Then Mr. Poe wouldn't know about Aunt Josephine's wishes, and we wouldn't end up with Captain Sham."

"But I already told Mr. Poe that Aunt Josephine left a note," Violet said.

"Well, we could do a forgery," Klaus said, using a word which here means "write something yourself and pretend somebody else wrote it." "We'll write everything she wrote, but we'll leave out the part about Captain Sham."

"Aha!" Sunny shrieked. This word was a favorite of Sunny's, and unlike most of her words, it needed no translation. What Sunny meant was "Aha!", an expression of discovery.

"Of course!" Violet cried. "That's what Captain Sham did! *He* wrote this letter, not Aunt Josephine!"

Behind his glasses, Klaus's eyes lit up. "That explains *it's*!"

"That explains *inbearable*!" Violet said.

"Leep!" Sunny shrieked, which probably meant "Captain Sham threw Aunt Josephine out the window and then wrote this note to hide his crime."

"What a terrible thing to do," Klaus said, shuddering as he thought of Aunt Josephine falling into the lake she feared so much.

"Imagine the terrible things he will do to us," Violet said, "if we don't expose his crime. I can't wait until Mr. Poe gets here so we can tell him what happened."

With perfect timing, the doorbell rang, and the Baudelaires hurried to answer it. Violet led her siblings down the hallway, looking wistfully at the radiator as she remembered how afraid of it Aunt Josephine was. Klaus followed closely behind, touching each doorknob gently in memory of Aunt Josephine's warnings about them shattering into pieces. And when they reached the door, Sunny looked mournfully at the welcome mat that Aunt Josephine thought could cause someone to break their neck. Aunt Josephine had been so careful to avoid anything that she thought might harm her, but harm had still come her way.

Violet opened the peeling white door, and there stood Mr. Poe in the gloomy light of dawn. "Mr. Poe," Violet said. She intended to tell him immediately of their forgery theory, but as soon as she saw him, standing in the doorway with a white handkerchief in one hand and a black briefcase in the other, her words stuck in her throat. Tears are curious things, for like earthquakes or puppet shows they can occur at any time, without any warning and without any good reason. "Mr. Poe," Violet said again, and without any warning she and her siblings burst into tears. Violet cried, her shoulders shaking with sobs, and Klaus cried, the tears making his glasses slip down his nose, and Sunny cried, her open mouth revealing her four teeth. Mr. Poe put down his briefcase and put away his handkerchief. He was not very good at comforting people, but he put his arms around the children the best he could, and murmured "There, there," which is a phrase some people murmur to comfort other people despite the fact that it doesn't really mean anything.

Mr. Poe couldn't think of anything else to say that might have comforted the Baudelaire orphans, but I wish now that I had the power to go back in time and speak to these three sobbing children. If I could, I could tell the Baudelaires that like earthquakes and puppet shows, their tears were occurring not only without warning but without good reason. The youngsters were crying, of course, because they thought Aunt Josephine was dead, and I wish I had the power to go back and tell them that they were wrong. But of course, I cannot. I am not on top of the hill, overlooking Lake Lachrymose, on that gloomy morning. I am sitting in my room, in the middle of the night, writing down this story and looking out my window at the graveyard behind my home. I cannot tell the Baudelaire orphans that they are wrong, but I can tell you, as the orphans cry in Mr. Poe's arms, that Aunt Josephine is not dead.

Not yet.

Chapter Six

Mr. Poe frowned, sat down at the table, and took out his handkerchief. "Forgery?" he repeated. The Baudelaire orphans had shown him the shattered window in the library. They had shown him the note that had been thumb-tacked to the door. And they had shown him the business card with the grammatical mistake on it. "Forgery is a very serious charge," he said sternly, and blew his nose.

"Not as serious as murder," Klaus pointed out. "And that's what Captain Sham did. He murdered Aunt Josephine and forged a note."

"But why would this Captain Sham person,"

Mr. Poe asked, "go to all this trouble just to place you under his care?"

"We've already told you," Violet said, trying to hide her impatience. "Captain Sham is really Count Olaf in disguise."

"These are very serious accusations," Mr. Poe said firmly. "I understand that the three of you have had some terrible experiences, and I hope you're not letting your imagination get the best of you. Remember when you lived with Uncle Monty? You were convinced that his assistant, Stephano, was really Count Olaf in disguise."

"But Stephano *was* Count Olaf in disguise," Klaus exclaimed.

"That's not the point," Mr. Poe said. "The point is that you can't jump to conclusions. If you really think this note is a forgery, then we have to stop talking about disguises and do an investigation. Somewhere in this house, I'm sure we can find something that your Aunt Josephine has written. We can compare the handwriting and see if this note matches up."

The Baudelaire orphans looked at one another. "Of course," Klaus said. "If the note we found on the library door doesn't match Aunt Josephine's handwriting, then it was obviously written by somebody else. We didn't think of that."

Mr. Poe smiled. "You see? You are very intelligent children, but even the most intelligent people in the world often need the help of a banker. Now, where can we find a sample of Aunt Josephine's handwriting?"

"In the kitchen," Violet said promptly. "She left her shopping list in the kitchen when we got home from the market."

"Chuni!" Sunny shrieked, which probably meant "Let's go to the kitchen and get it," and that's exactly what they did. Aunt Josephine's kitchen was very small and had a large white sheet covering the stove and the oven—for safety, Aunt Josephine had explained, during her tour. There was a countertop where she prepared the food, a refrigerator where she stored the food, and a sink where she washed away the food nobody had eaten. To one side of the countertop was a small piece of paper on which Aunt Josephine had made her list, and Violet crossed the kitchen to retrieve it. Mr. Poe turned on the lights, and Violet held the shopping list up to the note to see if they matched.

There are men and women who are experts in the field of handwriting analysis. They are called graphologists, and they attend graphological schools in order to get their degree in graphology. You might think that this situation would call for a graphologist, but there are times when an expert's opinion is unnecessary. For instance, if a friend of yours brought you her pet dog, and said she was concerned because it wasn't laying eggs, you would not have to be a veterinarian to tell her that dogs do not lay eggs and so there was nothing to worry about.

Yes, there are some questions that are so simple that anyone can answer them, and Mr. Poe and the Baudelaire orphans instantly knew the answer to the question "Does the handwriting on the shopping list match the handwriting on the note?" The answer was yes. When Aunt Josephine had written "Vinegar" on the shopping list, she had curved the tips of the V into tiny spirals—the same spirals that decorated the tips of the V in "Violet," on the note. When she had written "Cucumbers" on the shopping list, the Cs were slightly squiggly, like earthworms, and the same earthworms appeared in the words "cold" and "Captain Sham" on the note. When Aunt Josephine had written "Limes" on the shopping list, the *i* was dotted with an oval rather than a circle, just as it was in "my life will be at it's end." There was no doubt that Aunt Josephine had written on both the pieces of paper that Mr. Poe and the Baudelaires were examining.

"I don't think there's any doubt that Aunt Josephine wrote on both these pieces of paper," Mr. Poe said.

"But—" Violet began.

"There are no buts about it," Mr. Poe said. "Look at the curvy V's. Look at the squiggly C's. Look at the oval dots over the I's. I'm no graphologist, but I can certainly tell that these were written by the same person."

"You're right," Klaus said miserably. "I know that Captain Sham is behind this somehow, but Aunt Josephine definitely wrote this note."

"And that," Mr. Poe said, "makes it a legal document."

"Does that mean we have to live with Captain Sham?" Violet asked, her heart sinking.

"I'm afraid so," Mr. Poe replied. "Someone's last will and testament is an official statement of the wishes of the deceased. You were placed in Aunt Josephine's care, so she had the right to assign you to a new caretaker before she leaped out the window. It is very shocking, certainly, but it is entirely legal."

"We won't go live with him," Klaus said fiercely. "He's the worst person on earth."

"He'll do something terrible, I know it,"

Violet said. "All he's after is the Baudelaire fortune."

"Gind!" Sunny shrieked, which meant something like "Please don't make us live with this evil man."

"I know you don't like this Captain Sham person," Mr. Poe said, "but there's not much I can do about it. I'm afraid the law says that that's where you'll go."

"We'll run away," Klaus said.

"You will do nothing of the kind," Mr. Poe said sternly. "Your parents entrusted me to see that you would be cared for properly. You want to honor your parents' wishes, don't you?"

"Well, yes," Violet said, "but—"

"Then please don't make a fuss," Mr. Poe said. "Think of what your poor mother and father would say if they knew you were threatening to run away from your guardian."

The Baudelaire parents, of course, would have been horrified to learn that their children were to be in the care of Captain Sham, but before the children could say this to Mr. Poe, he had moved on to other matters. "Now, I think the easiest thing to do would be to meet with Captain Sham and go over some details. Where is his business card? I'll phone him now."

"On the table, in the dining room," Klaus said glumly, and Mr. Poe left the kitchen to make the call. The Baudelaires looked at Aunt Josephine's shopping list and the suicide note.

"I just can't believe it," Violet said. "I was sure we were on the right track with the forgery idea."

"Me too," Klaus said. "Captain Sham has done something here—I *know* he has—but he's been even sneakier than usual."

"We'd better be smarter than usual, then," Violet replied, "because we've got to convince Mr. Poe before it's too late."

"Well, Mr. Poe said he had to go over some details," Klaus said. "Perhaps that will take a long time."

"I got ahold of Captain Sham," Mr. Poe said, coming back into the kitchen. "He was shocked to hear of Aunt Josephine's death but overjoyed at the prospect of raising you children. We're meeting him in a half hour for lunch at a restaurant in town, and after lunch we'll go over the details of your adoption. By tonight you should be staying in his house. I'm sure you're relieved that this can be sorted out so quickly."

Violet and Sunny stared at Mr. Poe, too dismayed to speak. Klaus was silent too, but he was staring hard at something else. He was staring at Aunt Josephine's note. His eyes were focused in concentration behind his glasses as he stared and stared at it, without blinking. Mr. Poe took his white handkerchief out of his pocket and coughed into it at great length and with great gusto, a word which here means "in a way which produced a great deal of phlegm." But none of the Baudelaires said a word.

"Well," Mr. Poe said finally, "I will call for

a taxicab. There's no use walking down that enormous hill. You children comb your hair and put your coats on. It's very windy out and it's getting cold. I think a storm might be approaching."

Mr. Poe left to make his phone call, and the Baudelaires trudged to their room. Rather than comb their hair, however, Sunny and Violet immediately turned to Klaus. "What?" Violet asked him.

"*What* what?" Klaus answered.

"Don't give me that *what* what," Violet answered. "You've figured something out, that's *what* what. I know you have. You were rereading Aunt Josephine's note for the umpteenth time, but you had an expression as if you had just figured something out. Now, what is it?"

"I'm not sure," Klaus said, looking over the note one more time. "I might have begun figuring something out. Something that could help us. But I need more time."

"But we don't have any time!" Violet cried.

"We're going to have lunch with Captain Sham *right now*!"

"Then we're going to have to make some more time, somehow," Klaus said determinedly.

"Come on, children!" Mr. Poe called from the hallway. "The cab will be here any minute! Get your coats and let's go!"

Violet sighed, but went to the closet and took out all three Baudelaire coats. She handed Klaus his coat, and buttoned Sunny into her coat as she talked to her brother. "How can we make more time?" Violet asked.

"You're the inventor," Klaus answered, buttoning his coat.

"But you can't invent things like time," Violet said. "You can invent things like automatic popcorn poppers. You can invent things like steam-powered window washers. But you can't invent more *time*." Violet was so certain she couldn't invent more time that she didn't even put her hair up in a ribbon to keep it out of her eyes. She merely gave Klaus a look of frustration and confusion, and started to put on her coat. But as she did up the buttons she realized she didn't even need to put her hair up in a ribbon, because the answer was right there with her.

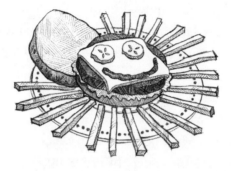

"*Hello*, I'm Larry, your waiter," said Larry, the Baudelaire orphans' waiter. He was a short, skinny man in a goofy clown costume with a name tag pinned to his chest that read LARRY. "Welcome to the Anxious Clown restaurant— where everybody has a good time, whether they like it or not. I can see we have a whole family lunching together today, so allow me to recommend the Extra Fun Special Family Appetizer. It's a bunch of things fried up together and served with a sauce."

"What a wonderful idea," Captain Sham said,

smiling in a way that showed all of his yellow teeth. "An Extra Fun Special Family Appetizer for an extra fun special family—*mine*."

"I'll just have water, thank you," Violet said.

"Same with me," Klaus said. "And a glass of ice cubes for my baby sister, please."

"I'll have a cup of coffee with nondairy creamer," Mr. Poe said.

"Oh, no, Mr. Poe," Captain Sham said. "Let's share a nice big bottle of red wine."

"No, thank you, Captain Sham," Mr. Poe said. "I don't like to drink during banking hours."

"But this is a celebratory lunch," Captain Sham exclaimed. "We should drink a toast to my three new children. It's not every day that a man becomes a father."

"Please, Captain," Mr. Poe said. "It is heartening to see that you are glad to raise the Baudelaires, but you must understand that the children are rather upset about their Aunt Josephine."

There is a lizard called the chameleon that, as you probably know, can change color instantly to blend into its surroundings. Besides being slimy and cold-blooded, Captain Sham resembled the chameleon in that he was chameleonic, a word means "able to blend in with any situation." Since Mr. Poe and the Baudelaires had arrived at the Anxious Clown, Captain Sham had been unable to conceal his excitement at having the children almost in his clutches. But now that Mr. Poe had pointed out that the occasion actually called for sadness, Captain Sham instantly began to speak in a mournful voice. "I am upset, too," he said, brushing a tear away from beneath his eyepatch. "Josephine was one of my oldest and dearest friends."

"You met her *yesterday*," Klaus said, "in the grocery store."

"It does only seem like yesterday," Captain Sham said, "but it was really years ago. She and I met in cooking school. We were oven partners in the Advanced Baking Course."

"You weren't *oven partners*," Violet said, disgusted at Captain Sham's lies. "Aunt Josephine was desperately afraid of turning on the oven. She never would have attended cooking school."

"We soon became friends," Captain Sham said, going on with his story as if no one had interrupted, "and one day she said to me, 'if I ever adopt some orphans and then meet an untimely death, promise me you will raise them for me.' I told her I would, but of course I never thought I would have to keep my promise."

"That's a very sad story," Larry said, and everyone turned to see that their waiter was still standing over them. "I didn't realize this was a sad occasion. In that case, allow me to recommend the Cheer-Up Cheeseburgers. The pickles, mustard, and ketchup make a little smiley face on top of the burger, which is guaranteed to get you smiling, too."

"That sounds like a good idea," Captain Sham said. "Bring us all Cheer-Up Cheeseburgers, Larry."

"They'll be here in a jiffy," the waiter promised, and at last he was gone.

"Yes, yes," Mr. Poe said, "but after we've finished our cheeseburgers, Captain Sham, there are some important papers for you to sign. I have them in my briefcase, and after lunch we'll look them over."

"And then the children will be mine?" Captain Sham asked.

"Well, you will be caring for them, yes," Mr. Poe said. "Of course, the Baudelaire fortune will still be under my supervision, until Violet comes of age."

"What fortune?" Captain Sham asked, his eyebrow curling. "I don't know anything about a fortune."

"Duna!" Sunny shrieked, which meant something along the lines of "Of course you do!"

"The Baudelaire parents," Mr. Poe explained, "left an enormous fortune behind, and the children inherit it when Violet comes of age."

"Well, I have no interest in a fortune,"

Captain Sham said. "I have my sailboats. I wouldn't touch a penny of it."

"Well, that's good," Mr. Poe said, "because you *can't* touch a penny of it."

"We'll see," Captain Sham said.

"What?" Mr. Poe asked.

"Here are your Cheer-Up Cheeseburgers!" Larry sang out, appearing at their table with a tray full of greasy-looking food. "Enjoy your meal."

Like most restaurants filled with neon lights and balloons, the Anxious Clown served terrible food. But the three orphans had not eaten all day, and had not eaten anything warm for a long time, so even though they were sad and anxious they found themselves with quite an appetite. After a few minutes without conversation, Mr. Poe began to tell a very dull story about something that had happened at the bank. Mr. Poe was so busy talking, Klaus and Sunny were so busy pretending to be interested, and Captain Sham was so busy wolfing down his meal, that nobody noticed what Violet was up to.

When Violet had put on her coat to go out into the wind and cold, she had felt the lump of something in her pocket. The lump was the bag of peppermints that Mr. Poe had given the Baudelaires the day they had arrived at Lake Lachrymose, and it had given her an idea. As Mr. Poe droned on and on, she carefully, carefully, took the bag of peppermints out of her coat pocket and opened it. To her dismay, they were the kind of peppermints that are each wrapped up in a little bit of cellophane. Placing her hands underneath the table, she unwrapped three peppermints, using the utmost—the word "utmost," when it is used here, means "most"— care not to make any of those crinkling noises that come from unwrapping candy and are so annoying in movie theaters. At last, she had three bare peppermints sitting on the napkin in her lap. Without drawing attention to herself, she put one on Klaus's lap and one on Sunny's.

When her younger siblings felt something appear in their laps and looked down and saw the peppermints, they at first thought the eldest Baudelaire orphan had lost her mind. But after a moment, they understood.

If you are allergic to a thing, it is best not to put that thing in your mouth, particularly if the thing is cats. But Violet, Klaus, and Sunny all knew that this was an emergency. They needed time alone to figure out Captain Sham's plan, and how to stop it, and although causing allergic reactions is a rather drastic way of getting time by yourself, it was the only thing they could think of. So while neither of the adults at the table were watching, all three children put the peppermints into their mouths and waited.

The Baudelaire allergies are famous for being quick-acting, so the orphans did not have long to wait. In a few minutes, Violet began to break out in red, itchy hives, Klaus's tongue started to swell up, and Sunny, who of course had never eaten a peppermint, broke out in hives *and* had her tongue swell up.

Mr. Poe finally finished telling his story and then noticed the orphans' condition. "Why, children," he said, "you look *terrible*! Violet, you have red patches on your skin. Klaus, your tongue is hanging out of your mouth. Sunny, both things are happening to you."

"There must be something in this food that we're allergic to," Violet said.

"My goodness," Mr. Poe said, watching a hive on Violet's arm grow to the size of a hard-boiled egg.

"Just take deep breaths," Captain Sham said, scarcely looking up from his cheeseburger.

"I feel terrible," Violet said, and Sunny began to wail. "I think we should go home and lie down, Mr. Poe."

"Just lean back in your seat," Captain Sham said sharply. "There's no reason to leave when we're in the middle of lunch."

"Why, Captain Sham," Mr. Poe said, "the

children are quite ill. Violet is right. Come now, I'll pay the bill and we'll take the children home."

"No, no," Violet said quickly. "We'll get a taxi. You two stay here and take care of all the details."

Captain Sham gave Violet a sharp look. "I wouldn't dream of leaving you all alone," he said in a dark voice.

"Well, there is a lot of paperwork to go over," Mr. Poe said. He glanced at his meal, and the Baudelaires could see he was not too eager to leave the restaurant and care for sick children. "We wouldn't be leaving them alone for long."

"Our allergies are fairly mild," Violet said truthfully, scratching at one of her hives. She stood up and led her swollen-tongued siblings toward the front door. "We'll just lie down for an hour or two while you have a relaxing lunch. When you have signed all the papers, Captain Sham, you can just come and retrieve us."

Captain Sham's one visible eye grew as shiny

as Violet had ever seen it. "I'll do that," he replied. "I'll come and retrieve you very, very soon."

"Good-bye, children," Mr. Poe said. "I hope you feel better soon. You know, Captain Sham, there is someone at my bank who has terrible allergies. Why, I remember one time . . ."

"Leaving so soon?" Larry asked the three children as they buttoned up their coats. Outside, the wind was blowing harder, and it had started to drizzle as Hurricane Herman got closer and closer to Lake Lachrymose. But even so, the three children were eager to leave the Anxious Clown, and not just because the garish restaurant—the word "garish" here means "filled with balloons, neon lights, and obnoxious waiters"—was filled with balloons, neon lights, and obnoxious waiters. The Baudelaires knew that they had invented just a little bit of time for themselves, and they had to use every second of it.

CHAPTER Eight

When someone's tongue swells up due to an allergic reaction, it is often difficult to understand what they are saying.

"Bluh bluh bluh bluh bluh," Klaus said, as the three children got out of the taxi and headed toward the peeling white door of Aunt Josephine's house.

"I don't understand what you're saying," Violet said, scratching at a hive on her neck that was the exact shape of the state of Minnesota.

"*Bluh bluh bluh bluh bluh,*" Klaus repeated, or perhaps he was saying something else; I haven't the faintest idea.

"Never mind, never mind," Violet said, opening the door and ushering her siblings inside. "Now you have the time that you need to figure out whatever it is that you're figuring out."

"Bluh bluh bluh," Klaus bluhed.

"I still can't understand you," Violet said. She took Sunny's coat off, and then her own, and dropped them both on the floor. Normally, of course, one should hang up one's coat on a hook or in a closet, but itchy hives are very irritating and tend to make one abandon such matters. "I'm going to assume, Klaus, that you said something in agreement. Now, unless you need us to help you, I'm going to give Sunny and myself a baking soda bath to help our hives."

"Bluh!" Sunny shrieked. She meant to shriek "Gans!" which meant something along the lines of "Good, because my hives are driving me crazy!"

"Bluh," Klaus said, nodding vigorously, and he began hurrying down the hallway. Klaus had not taken off his coat, but it wasn't because of his own irritating allergic condition. It was because he was going someplace cold.

When Klaus opened the door of the library, he was surprised at how much had changed. The wind from the approaching hurricane had blown away the last of the window, and the rain had soaked some of Aunt Josephine's comfortable chairs, leaving dark, spreading stains. A few books had fallen from their shelves and blown over to the window, where water had swollen them. There are few sights sadder than a ruined book, but Klaus had no time to be sad. He knew Captain Sham would come and retrieve the Baudelaires as soon as he could, so he had to get right to work. First he took Aunt Josephine's note out of his pocket and placed it on the table, weighing it down with books so it wouldn't blow away in the wind. Then he crossed quickly to the shelves and began to scan the spines of the books, looking for titles. He chose three: *Basic Rules of Grammar and Punctuation, Handbook for*

Advanced Apostrophe Use, and *The Correct Spelling of Every English Word That Ever, Ever Existed*. Each of the books was as thick as a watermelon, and Klaus staggered under the weight of carrying all three. With a loud *thump* he dropped them on the table. "Bluh bluh bluh, bluh bluh bluh bluh," he mumbled to himself, and found a pen and got to work.

A library is normally a very good place to work in the afternoon, but not if its window has been smashed and there is a hurricane approaching. The wind blew colder and colder, and it rained harder and harder, and the room became more and more unpleasant. But Klaus took no notice of this. He opened all of the books and took copious—the word "copious" here means "lots of"—notes, stopping every so often to draw a circle around some part of what Aunt Josephine had written. It began to thunder outside, and with each roll of thunder the entire house shook, but Klaus kept flipping pages and writing things down. Then, as lightning began to flash outside, he stopped, and stared at the note for a long time, frowning intently. Finally, he wrote two words at the bottom of Aunt Josephine's note, concentrating so hard as he did so that when Violet and Sunny entered the library and called out his name he nearly jumped out of his chair.

"Bluh surprised bluh!" he shrieked, his heart pounding and his tongue a bit less swollen.

"I'm sorry," Violet said. "I didn't mean to surprise you."

"Bluh bluh take a baking soda bluh?" he asked.

"No," Violet replied. "We couldn't take a baking soda bath. Aunt Josephine doesn't have any baking soda, because she never turns on the oven to bake. We just took a regular bath. But that doesn't matter, Klaus. What have *you* been doing, in this freezing room? Why have you drawn circles all over Aunt Josephine's note?"

"Bluhdying grammar," he replied, gesturing to the books.

"Bluh?" Sunny shrieked, which probably meant "gluh?" which meant something along the lines of "Why are you wasting valuable time studying grammar?"

"Bluhcause," Klaus explained impatiently, "I think bluh Josephine left us a message in bluh note."

"She was miserable, and she threw herself out the window," Violet said, shivering in the wind. "What other message could there be?"

"There are too many grammatical mistakes in the bluh," Klaus said. "Aunt Josephine loved grammar, and she'd never make that many mistakes unless she had a bluh reason. So that's what I've been doing bluh—counting up the grammatical mistakes."

"Bluh," Sunny said, which meant something along the lines of "Please continue, Klaus."

Klaus wiped a few raindrops off his glasses and looked down at his notes. "Well, we already know that bluh first sentence uses the wrong 'its.' I think that was to get our attention. But look at the second bluhtence. 'My heart is as cold as Ike and I find life inbearable.'"

"But the correct word is *un*bearable," Violet said. "You told us that already."

"Bluh I think there's more," Klaus said. "'My heart is as cold as Ike' doesn't sound right to me. Remember, Aunt Josephine told us bluh liked to think of her husband someplace very hot."

"That's true," Violet said, remembering. "She said it right here in this very room. She said Ike liked the sunshine and so she imagined him someplace sunny."

"So I think Aunt Bluhsephine meant 'cold as *ice*,'" Klaus said.

"Okay, so we have *ice* and *un*bearable. So far this doesn't mean anything to me," Violet said.

"Me neither," Klaus said. "But look at bluh next part. 'I know your children may not under-stand the sad life of a dowadger.' We don't have any children."

"That's true," Violet said. "I'm not planning to have children until I am considerably older."

"So why would Aunt Josephine say 'your children'? I think she meant '*you* children.' And I looked up 'dowadger' in *The Correct Spelling of Every English Word That Ever, Ever Existed.*"

"Why?" Violet asked. "You already know it's a fancy word for widow."

"It *is* a bluhncy word for widow," Klaus replied, "but it's spelled D-O-W-A-G-E-R. Aunt Josephine added an extra D."

"Cold as *ice*," Violet said, counting on her fingers, "*un*bearable, *you* children, and an extra D in dowager. That's not much of a message, Klaus."

"Let me finish," Klaus said. "I discovered even more grammbluhtical mistakes. When she wrote, 'or what would have leaded me to this desperate akt,' she meant 'what would have *led* me,' and the word 'act,' of course, is spelled with a C."

"Coik!" Sunny shrieked, which meant "Thinking about all this is making me dizzy!"

"Me too, Sunny," Violet said, lifting her sister

up so she could sit on the table. "But let him finish."

"There are just bluh more," Klaus said, holding up two fingers. "One, she calls Captain Sham 'a kind and honorable men,' when she should have said 'a kind and honorable *man*.' And in the last sentence, Aunt Josephine wrote 'Please think of me kindly even though I'd done this terrible thing,' but according to the *Handbook for Advanced Apostrophe Use*, she should have written 'even though *I've* done this terrible thing.'"

"But so what?" Violet asked. "What do all these mistakes mean?"

Klaus smiled, and showed his sisters the two words he had written on the bottom of the note. "Curdled Cave," he read out loud.

"Curdled *veek*?" Sunny asked, which meant "Curdled *what*?"

"Curdled Cave," Klaus repeated. "If you take all the letters involved in the grammatical mistakes, that's what it spells. Look: C for ice instead of Ike. U for unbearable instead of inbearable. The extra R in your children instead of you children, and the extra D in dowager. L-E-D for led instead of leaded. C for act instead of akt. A for man instead of men. And V-E for I've instead of I'd. That spells CURDLED CAVE. Don't you see? Aunt Josephine *knew* she was making grammatical errors, and she knew we'd spot them. She was leaving us a message, and the message is Curdled—"

A great gust of wind interrupted Klaus as it came through the shattered window and shook the library as if it were maracas, a word which describes rattling percussion instruments used in Latin American music. Everything rattled wildly around the library as the wind flew through it. Chairs and footstools flipped over and fell to the floor with their legs in the air. The bookshelves rattled so hard that some of the heaviest books in Aunt Josephine's collection spun off into puddles of rainwater on the floor. And the Baudelaire orphans were jerked violently to the ground as a streak of lightning flashed across the darkening sky.

"Let's get out of here!" Violet shouted over the noise of the thunder, and grabbed her siblings by the hand. The wind was blowing so hard that the Baudelaires felt as if they were climbing an enormous hill instead of walking to the door of the library. The orphans were quite out of breath by the time they shut the library door behind them and stood shivering in the hallway.

"Poor Aunt Josephine," Violet said. "Her library is wrecked."

"But I need to go back in there," Klaus said, holding up the note. "We just found out what Aunt Josephine means by Curdled Cave, and we need a library to find out more."

"Not that library," Violet pointed out. "All that library had were books on grammar. We need her books on Lake Lachrymose."

"Why?" Klaus asked.

"Because I'll bet you anything that's where

Curdled Cave is," Violet said, "in Lake Lachry-mose. Remember she said she knew every island in its waters and every cave on its shore? I bet Curdled Cave is one of those caves."

"But why would her secret message be about some cave?" Klaus asked.

"You've been so busy figuring out the mes-sage," Violet said, "that you don't understand what it means. Aunt Josephine isn't dead. She just wants people to *think* she's dead. But she wanted to tell *us* that she was hiding. We have to find her books on Lake Lachrymose and find out where Curdled Cave is."

"But first we have to know where the books are," Klaus said. "She told us she hid them away, remember?"

Sunny shrieked something in agreement, but her siblings couldn't hear her over a burst of thunder.

"Let's see," Violet said. "Where would you hide something if you didn't want to look at it?"

The Baudelaire orphans were quiet as they thought of places they had hidden things they did not want to look at, back when they had lived with their parents in the Baudelaire home. Violet thought of an automatic harmonica she had invented that had made such horrible noises that she had hidden it so she didn't have to think of her failure. Klaus thought of a book on the Franco-Prussian War that was so difficult that he had hidden it so as not to be reminded that he wasn't old enough to read it. And Sunny thought of a piece of stone that was too hard for even her sharpest tooth, and how she had hidden it so her jaw would no longer ache from her many attempts at conquering it. And all three Baudelaire orphans thought of the hiding place they had chosen.

"Underneath the bed," Violet said.

"Underneath the bed," Klaus agreed.

"Seeka yit," Sunny agreed, and without another word the three children ran down the hallway to Aunt Josephine's room. Normally it is not polite to go into somebody's room without knocking, but you can make an exception if the person is dead, or pretending to be dead, and the Baudelaires went right inside. Aunt Josephine's room was similar to the orphans', with a navy-blue bedspread on the bed and a pile of tin cans in the corner. There was a small window looking out onto the rain-soaked hill, and a pile of new grammar books by the side of the bed that Aunt Josephine had not started reading, and, I'm sad to say, would never read. But the only part of the room that interested the children was underneath the bed, and the three of them knelt down to look there.

Aunt Josephine, apparently, had plenty of things she did not want to look at anymore. Underneath the bed there were pots and pans, which she didn't want to look at because they reminded her of the stove. There were ugly socks somebody had given her as a gift that were too ugly for human eyes. And the

Baudelaires were sad to see a framed photograph of a kind-looking man with a handful of crackers in one hand and his lips pursed as if he were whistling. It was Ike, and the Baudelaires knew that she had placed his photograph there because she was too sad to look at it. But behind one of the biggest pots was a stack of books, and the orphans immediately reached for it.

"*The Tides of Lake Lachrymose,*" Violet said, reading the title of the top book. "That won't help."

"*The Bottom of Lake Lachrymose,*" Klaus said, reading the next one. "That's not useful."

"*Lachrymose Trout,*" Violet read.

"*The History of the Damocles Dock Region,*" Klaus read.

"*Ivan Lachrymose—Lake Explorer,*" Violet read.

"*How Water Is Made,*" Klaus read.

"*A Lachrymose Atlas,*" Violet said.

"Atlas? That's perfect!" Klaus cried. "An atlas is a book of maps!"

There was a flash of lightning outside the window, and it began to rain harder, making a sound on the roof like somebody was dropping marbles on it. Without another word the Baudelaires opened the atlas and began flipping pages. They saw map after map of the lake, but they couldn't find Curdled Cave.

"This book is four hundred seventy-eight pages long," Klaus exclaimed, looking at the last page of the atlas. "It'll take forever to find Curdled Cave."

"We don't have forever," Violet said. "Captain Sham is probably on his way here now. Use the index in the back. Look under 'Curdled.'"

Klaus flipped to the index, which I'm sure you know is an alphabetical list of each thing a book contains and what page it's on. Klaus ran his finger down the list of the C words, muttering out loud to himself. "Carp Cove, Chartreuse Island, Cloudy Cliffs, Condiment Bay, Curdled Cave—here it is! Curdled Cave, page one hundred four." Quickly Klaus flipped to the correct page and looked at the detailed map. "Curdled Cave, Curdled Cave, where is it?"

"There it is!" Violet pointed a finger at the tiny spot on the map marked *Curdled Cave*. "Directly across from Damocles Dock and just west of the Lavender Lighthouse. Let's go."

"Go?" Klaus said. "How will we get across the lake?"

"The Fickle Ferry will take us," Violet said, pointing at a dotted line on the map. "Look, the ferry goes right to the Lavender Lighthouse, and we can walk from there."

"We're going to walk to Damocles Dock, in all this rain?" Klaus asked.

"We don't have any choice," Violet answered. "We have to prove that Aunt Josephine is still alive, or else Captain Sham gets us."

"I just hope she is still—" Klaus started to say, but he stopped himself and pointed out the window. "Look!"

Violet and Sunny looked. The window in

Aunt Josephine's bedroom looked out onto the hill, and the orphans could see one of the spidery metal stilts that kept Aunt Josephine's house from falling into the lake. But they could also see that this stilt had been badly damaged by the howling storm. There was a large black burn mark, undoubtedly from lightning, and the wind had bent the stilt into an uneasy curve. As the storm raged around them, the orphans watched the stilt struggle to stay attached.

"Tafca!" Sunny shrieked, which meant "We have to get out of here *right now*!"

"Sunny's right," Violet said. "Grab the atlas and let's go."

Klaus grabbed *A Lachrymose Atlas*, not wanting to think what would be happening if they were still leafing through the book and had not looked up at the window. As the youngsters stood up, the wind rose to a feverish pitch, a phrase which here means "it shook the house and sent all three orphans toppling to the floor."

Violet fell against one of the bedposts and banged her knee. Klaus fell against the cold radiator and banged his foot. And Sunny fell into the pile of tin cans and banged everything. The whole room seemed to lurch slightly to one side as the orphans staggered back to their feet.

"Come on!" Violet screamed, and grabbed Sunny. The orphans scurried out to the hallway and toward the front door. A piece of the ceiling had come off, and rainwater was steadily pouring onto the carpet, splattering the orphans as they ran underneath it. The house gave another lurch, and the children toppled to the floor again. Aunt Josephine's house was starting to slip off the hill. "Come on!" Violet screamed again, and the orphans stumbled up the tilted hallway to the door, slipping in puddles and on their own frightened feet. Klaus was the first to reach the front door, and yanked it open as the house gave another lurch, followed by a horrible, horrible crunching sound. "Come on!"

Violet screamed again, and the Baudelaires crawled out of the door and onto the hill, huddling together in the freezing rain. They were cold. They were frightened. But they had escaped.

I have seen many amazing things in my long and troubled life history. I have seen a series of corridors built entirely out of human skulls. I have seen a volcano erupt and send a wall of lava crawling toward a small village. I have seen a woman I loved picked up by an enormous eagle and flown to its high mountain nest. But I still cannot imagine what it was like to watch Aunt Josephine's house topple into Lake Lachrymose. My own research tells me that the children watched in mute amazement as the peeling white door slammed shut and began to crumple, as you might crumple a piece of paper into a ball. I have been told that the children hugged each other even more tightly as they heard the rough and earsplitting noise of their home breaking loose from the side of the hill. But I cannot tell you how it felt to watch the whole building fall down, down, down, and hit the dark and stormy waters of the lake below.

The United States Postal Service has a motto. The motto is: "Neither rain nor sleet nor driving snow shall halt the delivery of the mails." All this means is that even when the weather is nasty and your mailperson wants to stay inside and enjoy a cup of cocoa, he or she has to bundle up and go outside and deliver your mail anyway. The United States Postal Service does not think that icy storms should interfere with its duties.

The Baudelaire orphans were distressed to learn that the Fickle Ferry had no such policy. Violet, Klaus, and Sunny had made their way down the hill with much difficulty. The storm was rising, and the children could tell that the wind and the rain wanted nothing more than to grab them and throw them into the raging waters of Lake Lachrymose. Violet and Sunny hadn't had the time to grab their coats as they escaped the house, so all three children took turns wearing Klaus's coat as they stumbled along the flooding road. Once or twice a car drove by, and the Baudelaires had to scurry into the muddy bushes and hide, in case Captain Sham was coming to retrieve them. When they finally reached Damocles Dock, their teeth were chattering and their feet were so cold they could scarcely feel their toes, and the sight of the CLOSED sign in the window of the Fickle Ferry ticket booth was just about more than they could stand.

"It's *closed*," Klaus cried, his voice rising with despair and in order to be heard over Hurricane Herman. "How will we get to Curdled Cave now?"

"We'll have to wait until it opens," Violet replied.

"But it won't open until the storm is past," Klaus pointed out, "and by then Captain Sham will find us and take us far away. We have to get to Aunt Josephine as soon as possible."

"I don't know how we can," Violet said, shivering. "The atlas says that the cave is all the way across the lake, and we can't *swim* all that way in this weather."

"Entro!" Sunny shrieked, which meant something along the lines of "And we don't have enough time to walk around the lake, either."

"There must be other boats on this lake,"

Klaus said, "besides the ferry. Motorboats, or fishing boats, or—" He trailed off, and his eyes met those of his sisters. All three orphans were thinking the same thing.

"Or *sailboats*," Violet finished for him. "Captain Sham's Sailboat Rentals. He said it was right on Damocles Dock."

The Baudelaires stood under the awning of the ticket booth and looked down at the far end of the deserted dock, where they could see a metal gate that was very tall and had glistening spikes on the top of it. Hanging over the metal gate was a sign with some words they couldn't read, and next to the sign there was a small shack, scarcely visible in the rain, with a flickering light in the window. The children looked at it with dread in their hearts. Walking into Captain Sham's Sailboat Rentals in order to find Aunt Josephine would feel like walking into a lion's den in order to escape from a lion.

"We can't go there," Klaus said.

"We have to," Violet said. "We know Captain

Sham isn't there, because he's either on his way to Aunt Josephine's house or still at the Anxious Clown."

"But whoever *is* there," Klaus said, pointing to the flickering light, "won't let us rent a sailboat."

"They won't know we're the Baudelaires," Violet replied. "We'll tell whoever it is that we're the Jones children and that we want to go for a sail."

"In the middle of a hurricane?" Klaus replied. "They won't believe that."

"They'll have to," Violet said resolutely, a word which here means "as if she believed it, even though she wasn't so sure," and she led her siblings toward the shack. Klaus clasped the atlas close to his chest, and Sunny, whose turn it was for Klaus's coat, clutched it around herself, and soon the Baudelaires were shivering underneath the sign that read: CAPTAIN SHAM'S SAILBOAT RENTALS—EVERY BOAT HAS IT'S OWN SAIL. But the tall metal gate was locked up tight, and the Baudelaires paused there, anxious about going inside the shack.

"Let's take a look," Klaus whispered, pointing to a window, but it was too high for him or Sunny to use. Standing on tiptoe, Violet peered into the window of the shack and with one glance she knew there was no way they could rent a sailboat.

The shack was very small, with only room for a small desk and a single lightbulb, which was giving off the flickering light. But at the desk, asleep in a chair, was a person so massive that it looked like an enormous blob was in the shack, snoring away with a bottle of beer in one hand and a ring of keys in the other. As the person snored, the bottle shook, the keys jangled, and the door of the shack creaked open an inch or two, but although those noises were quite spooky, they weren't what frightened Violet. What frightened Violet was that you couldn't tell if this person was a man or a woman. There aren't very many people like that in the world, and Violet knew which one this was. Perhaps you have forgotten about Count Olaf's evil comrades, but the Baudelaires had seen them in the flesh—lots of flesh, in this comrade's case—and remembered all of them in gruesome detail. These people were rude, and they were sneaky, and they did whatever Count Olaf—or in this case, Captain Sham—told them to do, and the orphans never knew when they would turn up. And now, one had turned up right there in the shack, dangerous, treacherous, and snoring.

Violet's face must have shown her disappointment, because as soon as she took a look Klaus asked, "What's wrong? I mean, besides Hurricane Herman, and Aunt Josephine faking her own death, and Captain Sham coming after us and everything."

"One of Count Olaf's comrades is in the shack," Violet said.

"Which one?" Klaus asked.

"The one who looks like neither a man nor a woman," Violet replied.

Klaus shuddered. "That's the scariest one."

"I disagree," Violet said. "I think the bald one is scariest."

"Vass!" Sunny whispered, which probably meant "Let's discuss this at another time."

"Did he or she see you?" Klaus asked.

"No," Violet said. "He or she is asleep. But he or she is holding a ring of keys. We'll need them, I bet, to unlock the gate and get a sail-boat."

"You mean we're going to steal a sailboat?" Klaus asked.

"We have no choice," Violet said. Stealing, of course, is a crime, and a very impolite thing to do. But like most impolite things, it is excusable under certain circumstances. Stealing is not excusable if, for instance, you are in a museum and you decide that a certain painting would look better in your house, and you simply grab the painting and take it there. But if you were very, very hungry, and you had no way of obtaining money, it might be excusable to grab the painting, take it to your house, and eat it. "We have to get to Curdled Cave as quickly as possible," Violet continued, "and the only way we can do it is to steal a sailboat."

"I know that," Klaus said, "but how are we going to get the keys?"

"I don't know," Violet admitted. "The door of the shack is creaky, and I'm afraid if we open it any wider we'll wake him or her up."

"You could crawl through the window," Klaus said, "by standing on my shoulders. Sunny could keep watch."

"Where *is* Sunny?" Violet asked nervously.

Violet and Klaus looked down at the ground and saw Klaus's coat sitting alone in a little heap. They looked down the dock but only saw the Fickle Ferry ticket booth and the foamy waters of the lake, darkening in the gloom of the late afternoon.

"She's gone!" Klaus cried, but Violet put a

finger to her lips and stood on tiptoe to look in the window again. Sunny was crawling through the open door of the shack, flattening her little body enough so as not to open the door any wider.

"She's inside," Violet murmured.

"In the shack?" Klaus said in a horrified gasp. "Oh no. We have to stop her."

"She's crawling very slowly toward that person," Violet said, afraid even to blink.

"We promised our parents we'd take care of her," Klaus said. "We can't let her do this."

"She's reaching toward the key ring," Violet said breathlessly. "She's gently prying it loose from the person's hand."

"Don't tell me any more," Klaus said, as a bolt of lightning streaked across the sky. "No, do tell me. What is happening?"

"She has the keys," Violet said. "She's putting them in her mouth to hold them. She's crawling back toward the door. She's flattening herself and crawling through."

"She's made it," Klaus said in amazement. Sunny came crawling triumphantly toward the orphans, the keys in her mouth. "Violet, she made it," Klaus said, giving Sunny a hug as a huge *boom!* of thunder echoed across the sky.

Violet smiled down at Sunny, but stopped smiling when she looked back into the shack. The thunder had awoken Count Olaf's comrade, and Violet watched in dismay as the person looked at its empty hand where the key ring had been, and then down on the floor where Sunny had left little crawl-prints of rainwater, and then up to the window and right into Violet's eyes.

"She's awake!" Violet shrieked. "He's awake! It's awake! Hurry, Klaus, open the gate and I'll try to distract it."

Without another word, Klaus took the key ring from Sunny's mouth and hurried to the tall metal gate. There were three keys on the ring—a skinny one, a thick one, and one with teeth as jagged as the glistening spikes hanging over the children. He put the atlas down on the ground and began to try the skinny key in the lock, just as Count Olaf's comrade came lumbering out of the shack.

Her heart in her throat, Violet stood in front of the creature and gave it a fake smile. "Good afternoon," she said, not knowing whether to add "sir" or "madam." "I seem to have gotten lost on this dock. Could you tell me the way to the Fickle Ferry?"

Count Olaf's comrade did not answer, but kept shuffling toward the orphans. The skinny key fit into the lock but didn't budge, and Klaus tried the thick one.

"I'm sorry," Violet said, "I didn't hear you. Could you tell me—"

Without a word the mountainous person grabbed Violet by the hair, and with one swing of its arm lifted her up over its smelly shoulder the way you might carry a backpack. Klaus couldn't get the thick key to fit in the lock and tried the jagged one, just as the person scooped up Sunny with its other hand and held her up, the way you might hold an ice cream cone.

"*Klaus!*" Violet screamed. "*Klaus!*"

The jagged key wouldn't fit in the lock, either. Klaus, in frustration, shook and shook the metal gate. Violet was kicking the creature from behind, and Sunny was biting its wrist, but the person was so Brobdingnagian—a word which here means "unbelievably husky"—that the children were causing it minimal pain, a phrase which here means "no pain at all." Count Olaf's comrade lumbered toward Klaus, holding the other two orphans in its grasp. In desperation, Klaus tried the skinny key again in the lock, and to his surprise and relief it turned and the tall metal gate swung open. Just a few feet away were six sailboats tied to the end of the dock with thick rope—sailboats that could take them to Aunt Josephine. But Klaus was too late. He felt something grab the back of his shirt, and he was lifted up in the air. Something slimy began running down his back, and Klaus realized with horror that the person was holding him in his or her mouth.

"Put me down!" Klaus screamed. "Put me down!"

"Put me down!" Violet yelled. "Put me down!"

"Poda rish!" Sunny shrieked. "Poda rish!"

But the lumbering creature had no concern for the wishes of the Baudelaire orphans. With great sloppy steps it turned itself around and began to carry the youngsters back toward the shack. The children heard the gloppy sound of its chubby feet sloshing through the rain, *gumsh, gumsh, gumsh, gumsh*. But then, instead of a *gumsh*, there was a *skittle-wat* as the person stepped on Aunt Josephine's atlas, which slipped from under its feet. Count Olaf's comrade waved its arms to keep its balance, dropping Violet and Sunny, and then fell to the ground, opening its mouth in surprise and dropping Klaus. The orphans, being in reasonably good physical shape, got to their feet much more quickly than this despicable creature, and ran through the open gate to the nearest sailboat. The creature struggled to right itself and chase them, but Sunny had already bitten the rope that tied the boat to the dock. By the time the creature reached the spiky metal gate, the orphans were already on the stormy waters of Lake Lachrymose. In the dim light of the late afternoon, Klaus wiped the grime of the creature's foot off the cover of the atlas, and began to read it. Aunt Josephine's book of maps had saved them once, in showing them the location of Curdled Cave, and now it had saved them again.

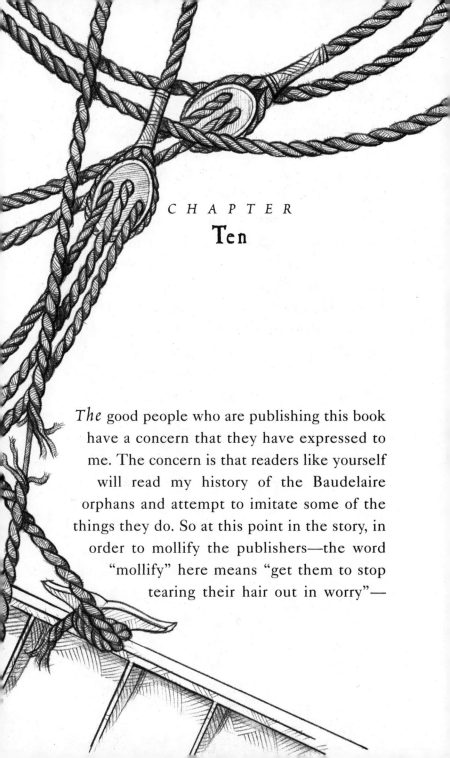

The good people who are publishing this book
have a concern that they have expressed to
me. The concern is that readers like yourself
will read my history of the Baudelaire
orphans and attempt to imitate some of the
things they do. So at this point in the story, in
order to mollify the publishers—the word
"mollify" here means "get them to stop
tearing their hair out in worry"—

please allow me to give you a piece of advice, even though I don't know anything about you. The piece of advice is as follows: If you ever need to get to Curdled Cave in a hurry, do not, under any circumstances, steal a boat and attempt to sail across Lake Lachrymose during a hurricane, because it is very dangerous and the chances of your survival are practically zero. You should especially not do this if, like the Baudelaire orphans, you have only a vague idea of how to work a sailboat.

Count Olaf's comrade, standing at the dock and waving a chubby fist in the air, grew smaller and smaller as the wind carried the sailboat away from Damocles Dock. As Hurricane Herman raged over them, Violet, Klaus, and Sunny examined the sailboat they had just stolen. It was fairly small, with wooden seats and bright orange life jackets for five people. On top of the mast, which is a word meaning "the tall wooden post found in the middle of boats," was a grimy white sail controlled by a series of ropes, and on the floor was a pair of wooden oars in case there was no wind. In the back, there was a sort of wooden lever with a handle for moving it this way and that, and under one of the seats was a shiny metal bucket for bailing out any water in case of a leak. There was also a long pole with a fishing net at the end of it, a small fishing rod with a sharp hook and a rusty spying glass, which is a sort of telescope used for navigating. The three siblings struggled into their life vests as the stormy waves of Lake Lachrymose took them farther and farther away from the shore.

"I read a book about working a sailboat," Klaus shouted over the noise of the hurricane. "We have to use the sail to catch the wind. Then it will push us where we want to go."

"And this lever is called a tiller," Violet shouted. "I remember it from studying some naval blueprints. The tiller controls the rudder, which is below the water, steering the ship. Sunny, sit in back and work the tiller. Klaus, hold the atlas so we can tell where we're going, and I'll try to work the sail. I think if I pull on *this* rope, I can control the sail."

Klaus turned the damp pages of the atlas to page 104. "*That* way," he called, pointing to the right. "The sun is setting over there, so that must be west."

Sunny scurried to the back of the sailboat and put her tiny hands on the tiller just as a wave hit the boat and sprayed her with foam. "Karg tem!" she called, which meant something along the lines of "I'm going to move the tiller *this* way, in order to steer the boat according to Klaus's recommendation."

The rain whipped around them, and the wind howled, and a small wave splashed over the side, but to the orphans' amazement, the sailboat moved in the exact direction they wanted it to go. If you had come across the three Baudelaires at this moment, you would have thought their lives were filled with joy and happiness, because even though they were exhausted, damp, and in very great danger, they began to laugh in their triumph. They were so relieved that something had finally gone right that they laughed as if they were at the circus instead of in the middle of a lake, in the middle of a hurricane, in the middle of trouble.

As the storm wore itself out splashing waves over the sailboat and flashing lightning over their heads, the Baudelaires sailed the tiny boat across the vast and dark lake. Violet pulled ropes this way and that to catch the wind, which kept changing direction as wind tends to do. Klaus kept a close eye on the atlas and made sure they weren't heading off course to the Wicked Whirlpool or the Rancorous Rocks. And Sunny kept the boat level by turning the tiller whenever Violet signaled. And just when the evening turned to night, and it was too dark to read the atlas, the Baudelaires saw a blinking light of pale purple. The orphans had always thought lavender was a rather sickly color, but for the first time in their lives they were glad to see it. It meant that the sailboat was approaching the

Lavender Lighthouse, and soon they'd be at Curdled Cave. The storm finally broke—the word "broke" here means "ended," rather than "shattered" or "lost all its money"—and the clouds parted to reveal an almost-full moon. The children shivered in their soaking clothes and stared out at the calming waves of the lake, watching the swirls of its inky depths.

"Lake Lachrymose is actually very pretty," Klaus said thoughtfully. "I never noticed it before."

"Cind," Sunny agreed, adjusting the tiller slightly.

"I guess we never noticed it because of Aunt Josephine," Violet said. "We got used to looking at the lake through her eyes." She picked up the spying glass and squinted into it, and she was just able to see the shore. "I think I can see the lighthouse over there. There's a dark hole in the cliff right next to it. It must be the mouth of Curdled Cave."

Sure enough, as the sailboat drew closer

and closer, the children could just make out the Lavender Lighthouse and the mouth of the nearby cave, but when they looked into its depths, they could see no sign of Aunt Josephine, or of anything else for that matter. Rocks began to scrape the bottom of the boat, which meant they were in very shallow water, and Violet jumped out to drag the sailboat onto the craggy shore. Klaus and Sunny stepped out of the boat and took off their life jackets. Then they stood at the mouth of Curdled Cave and paused nervously. In front of the cave there was a sign saying it was for sale, and the orphans could not imagine who would want to buy such a phantasmagorical—the word "phantasmagorical" here means "all the creepy, scary words you can think of put together"—place. The mouth of the cave had jagged rocks all over it like teeth in the mouth of a shark. Just beyond the entrance the youngsters could see strange white rock formations, all melted and twisted together so they looked like moldy milk. The floor of the cave was as pale and dusty as if it were made of chalk. But it was not these sights that made the children pause. It was the sound coming out of the cave. It was a high-pitched, wavering wail, a hopeless and lost sound, as strange and as eerie as Curdled Cave itself.

"What is that sound?" Violet asked nervously.

"Just the wind, probably," Klaus replied. "I read somewhere that when wind passes through small spaces, like caves, it can make weird noises. It's nothing to be afraid of."

The orphans did not move. The sound did not stop.

"I'm afraid of it, anyway," Violet said.

"Me too," Klaus said.

"Geni," Sunny said, and began to crawl into the mouth of the cave. She probably meant something along the lines of "We didn't sail a stolen sailboat across Lake Lachrymose in the middle of Hurricane Herman just to stand nervously at the mouth of a cave," and her siblings had to agree with her and follow her inside. The wailing was louder as it echoed off the walls and rock formations, and the Baudelaires could tell it wasn't the wind. It was Aunt Josephine, sitting in a corner of the cave and sobbing with her head in her hands. She was crying so hard that she hadn't even noticed the Baudelaires come into the cave.

"Aunt Josephine," Klaus said hesitantly, "we're here."

Aunt Josephine looked up, and the children could see that her face was wet from tears and chalky from the cave. "You figured it out," she said, wiping her eyes and standing up. "I knew you could figure it out," she said, and took each of the Baudelaires in her arms. She looked at Violet, and then at Klaus, and then at Sunny, and the orphans looked at her and found themselves with tears in their own eyes as they greeted their guardian. It was as if they had not quite believed that Aunt Josephine's death was fake until they had seen her alive with their own eyes.

"I knew you were clever children," Aunt Josephine said. "I knew you would read my message."

"Klaus really did it," Violet said.

"But Violet knew how to work the sailboat," Klaus said. "Without Violet we never would have arrived here."

"And Sunny stole the keys," Violet said, "and worked the tiller."

"Well, I'm glad you all made it here," Aunt Josephine said. "Let me just catch my breath and I'll help you bring in your things."

The children looked at one another. "What things?" Violet asked.

"Why, your luggage of course," Aunt Josephine replied. "And I hope you brought some food, because the supplies I brought are almost gone."

"We didn't bring any food," Klaus said.

"No food?" Aunt Josephine said. "How in the world are you going to live with me in this cave if you didn't bring any food?"

"We didn't come here to live with you," Violet said.

Aunt Josephine's hands flew to her head and she rearranged her bun nervously. "Then why are you here?" she asked.

"Stim!" Sunny shrieked, which meant "Because we were worried about you!"

"'Stim' is not a sentence, Sunny," Aunt Josephine said sternly. "Perhaps one of your older siblings could explain in correct English why you're here."

"Because Captain Sham almost had us in his clutches!" Violet cried. "Everyone thought you were dead, and you wrote in your will and testament that we should be placed in the care of Captain Sham."

"But he forced me to do that," Aunt Josephine whined. "That night, when he called me on the phone, he told me he was really Count Olaf. He said I had to write out a will saying you children would be left in his care. He said if I didn't write what he said, he would drown me in the lake. I was so frightened that I agreed immediately."

"Why didn't you call the police?" Violet asked. "Why didn't you call Mr. Poe? Why didn't you call somebody who could have helped?"

"You know why," Aunt Josephine said crossly. "I'm afraid of using the phone. Why, I was just getting used to answering it. I'm nowhere near ready to use the numbered buttons. But in any case, I didn't need to call anybody. I threw a footstool through the window and then sneaked out of the house. I left you the note so that you would know I wasn't really dead, but I hid my message so that Captain Sham wouldn't know I had escaped from him."

"Why didn't you take us with you? Why did you leave us all alone by ourselves? Why didn't you protect us from Captain Sham?" Klaus asked.

"It is not grammatically correct," Aunt Josephine said, "to say 'leave us all alone by ourselves.' You can say 'leave us all alone,' or 'leave us by ourselves,' but not both. Do you understand?"

The Baudelaires looked at one another in sadness and anger. They understood. They understood that Aunt Josephine was more concerned with grammatical mistakes than with saving the lives of the three children. They understood that she was so wrapped up in her own fears that she had not given a thought to what might have happened to them. They understood that Aunt Josephine had been a terrible guardian, in leaving the children all by themselves in great danger. They understood and they wished more than ever that their parents, who never would have run away and left them alone, had not been killed in that terrible fire which had begun all the misfortune in the Baudelaire lives.

"Well, enough grammar lessons for today," Aunt Josephine said. "I'm happy to see you, and you are welcome to share this cave with me.

I don't think Captain Sham will ever find us here."

"We're not *staying here*," Violet said impatiently. "We're sailing back to town, and we're taking you with us."

"No way, José," Aunt Josephine said, using an expression which means "No way" and has nothing to do with José, whoever he is. "I'm too frightened of Captain Sham to face him. After all he's done to you I would think that you would be frightened of him, too."

"We *are* frightened of him," Klaus said, "but if we prove that he's really Count Olaf he will go to jail. You are the proof. If you tell Mr. Poe what happened, then Count Olaf will be locked away and we will be safe."

"You can tell him, if you want to," Aunt Josephine said. "I'm staying here."

"He won't believe us unless you come with us and prove that you're alive," Violet said.

"No, no, no," Aunt Josephine said. "I'm too afraid."

Violet took a deep breath and faced her frightened guardian. "We're *all* afraid," she said firmly. "We were afraid when we met Captain Sham in the grocery store. We were afraid when we thought that you had jumped out the window. We were afraid to give ourselves allergic reactions, and we were afraid to steal a sailboat and we were afraid to make our way across this lake in the middle of a hurricane. But that didn't stop us."

Aunt Josephine's eyes filled up with tears. "I can't help it that you're braver than I," she said. "I'm not sailing across that lake. I'm not making any phone calls. I'm going to stay right here for the rest of my life, and nothing you can say will change my mind."

Klaus stepped forward and played his trump card, a phrase which means "said something very convincing, which he had saved for the end of the argument." "Curdled Cave," he said, "is for sale."

"So what?" Aunt Josephine said.

"That means," Klaus said, "that before long certain people will come to look at it. And some of those people"—he paused here dramatically—"will be realtors."

Aunt Josephine's mouth hung open, and the orphans watched her pale throat swallow in fear. "Okay," she said finally, looking around the cave anxiously as if a realtor were already hiding in the shadows. "I'll go."

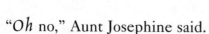

"*Oh* no," Aunt Josephine said.

The children paid no attention. The worst of Hurricane Herman was over, and as the Baudelaires sailed across the dark lake there seemed to be very little danger. Violet moved the sail around with ease now that the wind was calm. Klaus looked back at the lavender light of the lighthouse and confidently guided the way back to Damocles Dock. And Sunny moved the tiller as if she had been a tiller-mover all her life. Only Aunt Josephine was scared. She was wearing two life jackets instead of one, and every few seconds she cried "Oh no," even though nothing frightening was happening.

"Oh no," Aunt Josephine said, "and I mean it this time."

"What's wrong, Aunt Josephine?" Violet said tiredly. The sailboat had reached the approximate middle of the lake. The water was still fairly calm, and the lighthouse still glowed, a pinpoint of pale purple light. There seemed to be no cause for alarm.

"We're about to enter the territory of the Lachrymose Leeches," Aunt Josephine said.

"I'm sure we'll pass through safely," Klaus said, peering through the spying glass to see if Damocles Dock was visible yet. "You told us that the leeches were harmless and only preyed on small fish."

"Unless you've eaten recently," Aunt Josephine said.

"But it's been hours since we've eaten," Violet said soothingly. "The last thing we ate were peppermints at the Anxious Clown. That was in the afternoon, and now it's the middle of the night."

Aunt Josephine looked down, and moved away from the side of the boat. "But I ate a banana," she whispered, "just before you arrived."

"Oh no," Violet said. Sunny stopped moving the tiller and looked worriedly into the water.

"I'm sure there's nothing to worry about," Klaus said. "Leeches are very small animals. If we were in the water, we might have reason to fear, but I don't think they'd attack a sail-boat. Plus, Hurricane Herman may have fright-ened them away from their territory. I bet the Lachrymose Leeches won't even show up."

Klaus thought he was done speaking for the moment, but in the moment that followed he added one more sentence. The sentence was "Speak of the Devil," and it is an expression that you use when you are talking about some-thing only to have it occur. For instance, if you were at a picnic and said, "I hope it doesn't snow," and at that very minute a blizzard began, you could say, "Speak of the Devil" before gathering up your blanket and potato salad and driving away to a good restaurant. But in the case of the Baudelaire orphans, I'm sure you can guess what happened to prompt Klaus to use this expression.

"Speak of the Devil," Klaus said, looking into the waters of the lake. Out of the swirling blackness came skinny, rising shapes, barely visible in the moonlight. The shapes were scarcely longer than a finger, and at first it looked as if someone were swimming in the lake and drumming their fingers on the surface of the water. But most people have only ten fingers, and in the few minutes that followed there were hundreds of these tiny shapes, wriggling hungrily from all sides toward the sailboat. The Lachrymose Leeches made a quiet, whispering sound on the water as they swam, as if the Baudelaire orphans were surrounded by people murmuring terrible secrets. The children watched in silence as the swarm approached the boat, each leech knocking lightly against the wood. Their tiny leech-mouths puckered in disappointment as they tried to taste the sailboat. Leeches are blind, but they aren't stupid, and the Lachrymose Leeches knew that they were not eating a banana.

"You see?" Klaus said nervously, as the tapping of leech-mouths continued. "We're perfectly safe."

"Yes," Violet said. She wasn't sure they were perfectly safe, not at all, but it seemed best to tell Aunt Josephine they were perfectly safe. "We're perfectly safe," she said.

The tapping sound continued, getting a little rougher and louder. Frustration is an interesting emotional state, because it tends to bring out the worst in whoever is frustrated. Frustrated babies tend to throw food and make a mess. Frustrated citizens tend to execute kings and queens and make a democracy. And frustrated moths tend to bang up against lightbulbs and make light fixtures all dusty. But unlike babies, citizens, and moths, leeches are quite unpleasant to begin with. Now that the Lachrymose Leeches were getting frustrated, everyone on board the sailboat was quite anxious to see what would happen when frustration brought out the worst in leeches. For a while, the small creatures tried and tried to eat the wood, but their tiny teeth didn't really do anything but make an unpleasant knocking sound. But then, all at once, the leeches knocked off, and the Baudelaires watched them wriggle away from the sailboat.

"They're leaving," Klaus said hopefully, but they weren't leaving. When the leeches had reached a considerable distance, they suddenly swiveled their tiny bodies around and came rushing back to the boat. With a loud *thwack!* the leeches all hit the boat more or less at once, and the sailboat rocked precariously, a word which here means "in a way which almost threw Aunt

Josephine and the Baudelaire youngsters to their doom." The four passengers were rocked to and fro and almost fell into the waters of the lake, where the leeches were wriggling away again to prepare for another attack.

"Yadec!" Sunny shrieked and pointed at the side of the boat. Yadec, of course, is not grammatically correct English, but even Aunt Josephine understood that the youngest Baudelaire meant "Look at the crack in the boat that the leeches have made!" The crack was a tiny one, about as long as a pencil and about as wide as a human hair, and it was curved downward so it looked as if the sailboat were frowning at them. If the leeches kept hitting the side of the boat, the frown would only get wider.

"We have to sail much faster," Klaus said, "or this boat will be in pieces in no time."

"But sailing relies on the wind," Violet pointed out. "We can't make the wind go faster."

"I'm frightened!" Aunt Josephine cried. "Please don't throw me overboard!"

"Nobody's going to throw you overboard," Violet said impatiently, although I'm sorry to tell you that Violet was wrong about that. "Take an oar, Aunt Josephine. Klaus, take the other one. If we use the sail, the tiller, *and* the oars we should move more quickly."

Thwack! The Lachrymose Leeches hit the side of the boat, widening the crack in the side and rocking the boat again. One of the leeches was thrown over the side in the impact, and twisted this way and that on the floor of the boat, gnashing its tiny teeth as it looked for food. Grimacing, Klaus walked cautiously over to it and tried to kick the leech overboard, but it clung onto his shoe and began gnawing through the leather. With a cry of disgust, Klaus shook his leg, and the leech fell to the floor of the sailboat again, stretching its tiny neck and opening and shutting its mouth. Violet grabbed the long pole with the net at the end of it, scooped up the leech, and tossed it overboard.

Thwack! The crack widened enough that a bit

of water began to dribble through, making a small puddle on the sailboat's floor. "Sunny," Violet said, "keep an eye on that puddle. When it gets bigger, use the bucket to throw it back in the lake."

"Mofee!" Sunny shrieked, which meant "I certainly will." There was the whispering sound as the leeches swam away to ram the boat again. Klaus and Aunt Josephine began rowing as hard as they could, while Violet adjusted the sail and kept the net in her hand for any more leeches who got on board.

Thwack! Thwack! There were two loud noises now, one on the side of the boat and one on the bottom, which cracked immediately. The leeches had divided up into two teams, which is good news for playing kickball but bad news if you are being attacked. Aunt Josephine gave a shriek of terror. Water was now leaking into the sailboat in two spots, and Sunny abandoned the tiller to bail the water back out. Klaus stopped rowing, and held the oar up without a word. It had several small bite marks in it—the work of the Lachrymose Leeches.

"Rowing isn't going to work," he reported to Violet solemnly. "If we row any more these oars will be completely eaten."

Violet watched Sunny crawl around with the bucket full of water. "Rowing won't help us, anyway," she said. "This boat is sinking. We need help."

Klaus looked around at the dark and still waters, empty except for the sailboat and swarms of leeches. "Where can we get help in the middle of a lake?" he asked.

"We're going to have to signal for help," Violet said, and reached into her pocket and took out a ribbon. Handing Klaus the fishing net, she used the ribbon to tie her hair up, keeping it out of her eyes. Klaus and Sunny watched her, knowing that she only tied her hair up this way when she was thinking of an invention, and right now they needed an invention quite desperately.

"That's right," Aunt Josephine said to Violet, "close your eyes. That's what I do when I'm afraid, and it always makes me feel better to block out the fear."

"She's not blocking out anything," Klaus said crossly. "She's concentrating."

Klaus was right. Violet concentrated as hard as she could, racking her brain for a good way to signal for help. She thought of fire alarms. With flashing lights and loud sirens, fire alarms were an excellent way to signal for assistance. Although the Baudelaire orphans, of course, sadly knew that sometimes the fire engines arrived too late to save people's lives, a fire alarm was still a good invention, and Violet tried to think of a way she could imitate it using the materials around her. She needed to make a loud sound, to get somebody's attention. And she needed to make a bright light, so that person would know where they were.

Thwack! Thwack! The two teams of leeches hit the boat again, and there was a splash as more water came pouring into the sailboat. Sunny started to fill the bucket with water, but Violet reached forward and took it from Sunny's hands. "Bero?" Sunny shrieked, which meant "Are you crazy?" but Violet had no time to answer "No, as a matter of fact I'm not." So she merely said "No," and, holding the bucket in one hand, began to climb up the mast. It is difficult enough to climb up the mast of a boat, but it is triple the difficulty if the boat is being rocked by a bunch of hungry leeches, so allow me to advise you that this is another thing that you should under no circumstances try to do. But Violet Baudelaire was a wunderkind, a German word which here means "someone who is able to quickly climb masts on boats being attacked by leeches," and soon she was on the top of the swaying mast of the boat. She took the bucket and hung it by its handle on the tip of the mast so it swung this way and that, the way a bell might do in a bell tower.

"I don't mean to interrupt you," Klaus called, scooping up a furious leech in the net and tossing it as far as he could, "but this boat is really sinking. Please hurry."

Violet hurried. Hurriedly, she grabbed ahold of a corner of the sail and, taking a deep breath to prepare herself, jumped back down to the floor of the boat. Just as she had hoped, the sail ripped as she hurtled to the ground, slowing her down and leaving her with a large piece of torn cloth. By now the sailboat had quite a lot of water in it, and Violet splashed over to Aunt Josephine, avoiding the many leeches that Klaus was tossing out of the boat as quickly as he could.

"I need your oar," Violet said, wadding the piece of sail up into a ball, "and your hairnet."

"You can have the oar," Aunt Josephine said, handing it over. "But I need my hairnet. It keeps my bun in place."

"Give her the hairnet!" Klaus cried, hopping up on one of the seats as a leech tried to bite his knee.

"But I'm scared of having hair in my face," Aunt Josephine whined, just as another pair of *thwack!*s hit the boat.

"I don't have time to argue with you!" Violet cried. "I'm trying to save each of our lives! Give me your hairnet right now!"

"The expression," Aunt Josephine said, "is saving *all of our lives*, not *each of our lives*," but Violet had heard enough. Splashing forward and avoiding a pair of wriggling leeches, the eldest Baudelaire reached forward and grabbed Aunt Josephine's hairnet off of her head. She wrapped the crumpled part of the sail in the hairnet, and then grabbed the fishing pole and attached the messy ball of cloth to the fishhook. It looked like she was about to go fishing for some kind of fish that liked sailboats and hair accessories for food.

Thwack! Thwack! The sailboat tilted to one side and then to the other. The leeches had almost smashed their way through the side. Violet took the oar and began to rub it up and down the side of the boat as fast and as hard as she could.

"What are you doing?" Klaus asked, catching three leeches in one swoop of his net.

"I'm trying to create friction," Violet said. "If I rub two pieces of wood enough, I'll create friction. Friction creates sparks. When I get a spark, I'll set the cloth and hairnet on fire and use it as a signal."

"You want to set a fire?" Klaus cried. "But a fire will mean more danger."

"Not if I wave the fire over my head, using the fishing pole," Violet said. "I'll do that, and hit the bucket like a bell, and that should create enough of a signal to fetch us some help." She rubbed and rubbed the oar against the side of the boat, but no sparks appeared. The sad truth was that the wood was too wet from Hurricane Herman and from Lake Lachrymose to create enough friction to start a fire. It was a good idea, but Violet realized, as she rubbed and rubbed without any result, that it was the wrong idea.

Thwack! Thwack! Violet looked around at Aunt Josephine and her terrified siblings and felt hope leak out of her heart as quickly as water was leaking into the boat. "It's not working," Violet said miserably, and felt tears fall down her cheeks. She thought of the promise she made to her parents, shortly before they were killed, that she would always take care of her younger siblings. The leeches swarmed around the sinking boat, and Violet feared that she had not lived up to her promise. "It's not working," she said again, and dropped the oar in despair. "We need a fire, but I can't invent one."

"It's okay," Klaus said, even though of course it was not. "We'll think of something."

"Tintet," Sunny said, which meant something along the lines of "Don't cry. You tried your best," but Violet cried anyway. It is very easy to say that the important thing is to try your best, but if you are in real trouble the most important thing is not trying your best, but getting to safety. The boat rocked back and forth, and water poured through the cracks, and Violet cried because it looked like they would never get to safety. Her shoulders shaking with sobs, she held the spying glass up to her eye to see if, by any chance, there was a boat nearby, or if the tide had happened to carry the sailboat to shore, but all she could see was the moonlight reflecting on the rippling waters of the lake. And this was a lucky thing. Because as soon as Violet saw the flickering reflection, she remembered the scientific principles of the convergence and refraction of light.

The scientific principles of the convergence and refraction of light are very confusing, and quite frankly I can't make head or tail of them, even when my friend Dr. Lorenz explains them to me. But they made perfect sense to Violet. Instantly, she thought of a story her father had told her, long ago, when she was just beginning to be interested in science. When her father was a boy, he'd had a dreadful cousin who liked to burn ants, starting a fire by focusing the light of the sun with her magnifying glass. Burning ants, of course, is an abhorrent hobby—the word "abhorrent" here means "what Count Olaf used to do when he was about your age"—but remembering the story made Violet see that she could use the lens of the spying glass to focus the light of the moon and make a fire. Without wasting another moment, she grabbed the spying glass and removed the lens, and then, looking up at the moon, tilted the lens at an angle she hastily computed in her head.

The moonlight passed through the lens and was concentrated into a long, thin band of light, like a glowing thread leading right to the piece of sail, held in a ball by Aunt Josephine's hairnet. In a moment the thread had become a small flame.

"It's miraculous!" Klaus cried, as the flame took hold.

"It's unbelievable!" Aunt Josephine cried.

"Fonti!" Sunny shrieked.

"It's the scientific principles of the convergence and refraction of light!" Violet cried, wiping her eyes. Stepping carefully to avoid onboard leeches and so as not to put out the fire, she moved to the front of the boat. With one hand, she took the oar and rang the bucket, making a loud sound to get somebody's attention. With the other hand, she held the fishing rod up high, making a bright light so the person would know where they were. Violet looked up at her homemade signaling device that had finally caught fire, all because of a silly story her father had told her. Her father's ant-burning cousin sounded like a dreadful person, but if she had suddenly appeared on the sailboat Violet would have given her a big grateful hug.

As it turned out, however, this signal was a mixed blessing, a phrase which means "something half good and half bad." Somebody saw the signal almost immediately, somebody who was already sailing in the lake, and who headed toward the Baudelaires in an instant. Violet, Klaus, Sunny, and even Aunt Josephine all grinned as they saw another boat sail into view. They were being rescued, and that was the good half. But their smiles began to fade as the boat drew closer and they saw who was sailing it. Aunt Josephine and the orphans saw the wooden peg leg, and the navy-blue sailor cap, and the eye patch, and they knew who was coming to their aid. It was Captain Sham, of course, and he was probably the worst half in the world.

"*Welcome* aboard," Captain Sham said, with a wicked grin that showed his filthy teeth. "I'm happy to see you all. I thought you had been killed when the old lady's house fell off the hill, but luckily my associate told me you had stolen a boat and run away. And you, Josephine—I thought you'd done the sensible thing and jumped out the window."

"I tried to do the sensible

thing," Aunt Josephine said sourly. "But these children came and got me."

Captain Sham smiled. He had expertly steered his sailboat so it was alongside the one the Baudelaires had stolen, and Aunt Josephine and the children had stepped over the swarming leeches to come aboard. With a gurgly *whoosh!* their own sailboat was overwhelmed with water and quickly sank into the depths of the lake. The Lachrymose Leeches swarmed around the sinking sailboat, gnashing their tiny teeth. "Aren't you going to say thank you, orphans?" Captain Sham asked, pointing to the swirling place in the lake where their sailboat had been. "If it weren't for me, all of you would be divided up into the stomachs of those leeches."

"If it weren't for you," Violet said fiercely, "we wouldn't be in Lake Lachrymose to begin with."

"You can blame *that* on the old woman," he said, pointing to Aunt Josephine. "Faking your own death was pretty clever, but not clever enough. The Baudelaire fortune—and, unfortunately, the brats who come with it—now belong to me."

"Don't be ridiculous," Klaus said. "We don't belong to you and we never will. Once we tell Mr. Poe what happened he will send you to jail."

"Is that so?" Captain Sham said, turning the sailboat around and sailing toward Damocles Dock. His one visible eye was shining brightly as if he were telling a joke. "Mr. Poe will send me to jail, eh? Why, Mr. Poe is putting finishing touches on your adoption papers this very moment. In a few hours, you orphans will be Violet, Klaus, and Sunny Sham."

"Neihab!" Sunny shrieked, which meant "I'm Sunny Baudelaire, and I will always be Sunny Baudelaire unless I decide for myself to legally change my name!"

"When we explain that you forced Aunt Josephine to write that note," Violet said,

"Mr. Poe will rip up those adoption papers into a thousand pieces."

"Mr. Poe won't believe you," Captain Sham said, chuckling. "Why should he believe three runaway pipsqueaks who go around stealing boats?"

"Because we're telling the truth!" Klaus cried.

"Truth, schmuth," Captain Sham said. If you don't care about something, one way to demonstrate your feelings is to say the word and then repeat the word with the letters S-C-H-M replacing the real first letters. Somebody who didn't care about dentists, for instance, could say "Dentists, schmentists." But only a despicable person like Captain Sham wouldn't care about the truth. "Truth, schmuth," he said again. "I think Mr. Poe is more likely to believe the owner of a respectable sailboat rental place, who went out in the middle of a hurricane to rescue three ungrateful boat thieves."

"We only stole the boat," Violet said, "to

retrieve Aunt Josephine from her hiding place so she could tell everyone about your terrible plan."

"But nobody will believe the old woman, either," Captain Sham said impatiently. "Nobody believes a dead woman."

"Are you blind in *both* eyes?" Klaus asked. "Aunt Josephine isn't dead!"

Captain Sham smiled again, and looked out at the lake. Just a few yards away the water was rippling as the Lachrymose Leeches swam toward Captain Sham's sailboat. After searching every inch of the Baudelaires' boat and failing to find any food, the leeches had realized they had been tricked and were once again following the scent of banana still lingering on Aunt Josephine. "She's not dead *yet*," Captain Sham said, in a terrible voice, and took a step toward her.

"Oh no," she said. Her eyes were wide with fear. "Don't throw me overboard," she pleaded. *"Please!"*

"You're not going to reveal my plan to Mr. Poe," Captain Sham said, taking another step toward the terrified woman, "because you will be joining your beloved Ike at the bottom of the lake."

"No she won't," Violet said, grabbing a rope. "I will steer us to shore before you can do anything about it."

"I'll help," Klaus said, running to the back and grabbing the tiller.

"Igal!" Sunny shrieked, which meant something along the lines of "And I'll guard Aunt Josephine." She crawled in front of the Baudelaires' guardian and bared her teeth at Captain Sham.

"I promise not to say anything to Mr. Poe!" Aunt Josephine said desperately. "I'll go someplace and hide away, and never show my face! You can tell him I'm dead! You can have the fortune! You can have the children! Just don't throw me to the leeches!"

The Baudelaires looked at their guardian in

horror. "You're supposed to be caring for us," Violet told Aunt Josephine in astonishment, "not putting us up for grabs!"

Captain Sham paused, and seemed to consider Aunt Josephine's offer. "You have a point," he said. "I don't necessarily have to kill you. People just have to *think* that you're dead."

"I'll change my name!" Aunt Josephine said. "I'll dye my hair! I'll wear colored contact lenses! And I'll go very, very far away! Nobody will ever hear from me!"

"But what about us, Aunt Josephine?" Klaus asked in horror. "What about *us?*"

"Be quiet, orphan," Captain Sham snapped. The Lachrymose Leeches reached the sailboat and began tapping on the wooden side. "The adults are talking. Now, old woman, I wish I could believe you. But you hadn't been a very trustworthy person."

"*Haven't* been," Aunt Josephine corrected, wiping a tear from her eye.

"What?" Captain Sham asked.

"You made a grammatical error," Aunt Josephine said. "You said 'But you hadn't been a very trustworthy person,' but you should have said, 'you *haven't* been a very trustworthy person.'"

Captain Sham's one shiny eye blinked, and his mouth curled up in a terrible smile. "Thank you for pointing that out," he said, and took one last step toward Aunt Josephine. Sunny growled at him, and he looked down and in one swift gesture moved his peg leg and knocked Sunny to the other end of his boat. "Let me make sure I completely understand the grammatical lesson," he said to the Baudelaires' trembling guardian, as if nothing had happened. "You wouldn't say 'Josephine Anwhistle *had* been thrown overboard to the leeches,' because that would be incorrect. But if you said 'Josephine Anwhistle *has* been thrown overboard to the leeches,' that would be all right with you."

"Yes," Aunt Josephine said. "I mean *no*. I mean—"

But Aunt Josephine never got to say what she meant. Captain Sham faced her and, using both hands, pushed her over the side of the boat. With a little gasp and a big splash she fell into the waters of Lake Lachrymose.

"*Aunt Josephine!*" Violet cried. "*Aunt Josephine!*"

Klaus leaned over the side of the boat and stretched his hand out as far as he could. Thanks to her two life jackets, Aunt Josephine was floating on top of the water, waving her hands in the air as the leeches swam toward her. But Captain Sham was already pulling at the ropes of the sail, and Klaus couldn't reach her. "You *fiend*!" he shouted at Captain Sham. "You evil fiend!"

"That's no way to talk to your father," Captain Sham said calmly.

Violet tried to tug a rope out of Captain Sham's hand. "Move the sailboat back!" she shouted. "Turn the boat around!"

"Not a chance," he replied smoothly. "Wave

good-bye to the old woman, orphans. You'll never see her again."

Klaus leaned over as far as he could. "Don't worry, Aunt Josephine!" he called, but his voice revealed that he was very worried himself. The boat was already quite a ways from Aunt Josephine, and the orphans could only see the white of her hands as she waved them over the dark water.

"She has a chance," Violet said quietly to Klaus as they sailed toward the dock. "She has those life jackets, and she's a strong swimmer."

"That's true," Klaus said, his voice shaky and sad. "She's lived by the lake her whole life. Maybe she knows of an escape route."

"Legru," Sunny said quietly, which meant "All we can do is hope."

The three orphans huddled together, shivering in cold and fear, as Captain Sham sailed the boat by himself. They didn't dare do anything but hope. Their feelings for Aunt Josephine were all a tumble in their minds. The

Baudelaires had not really enjoyed most of their time with her—not because she cooked horrible cold meals, or chose presents for them that they didn't like, or always corrected the children's grammar, but because she was so afraid of everything that she made it impossible to really enjoy anything at all. And the worst of it was, Aunt Josephine's fear had made her a bad guardian. A guardian is supposed to stay with children and keep them safe, but Aunt Josephine had run away at the first sign of danger. A guardian is supposed to help children in times of trouble, but Aunt Josephine practically had to be dragged out of the Curdled Cave when they needed her. And a guardian is supposed to protect children from danger, but Aunt Josephine had offered the orphans to Captain Sham in exchange for her own safety.

But despite all of Aunt Josephine's faults, the orphans still cared about her. She had taught them many things, even if most of them were boring. She had provided a home, even if it was cold and unable to withstand hurricanes. And the children knew that Aunt Josephine, like the Baudelaires themselves, had experienced some terrible things in her life. So as their guardian faded from view and the lights of Damocles Dock approached closer and closer, Violet, Klaus, and Sunny did not think "Josephine, schmosephine." They thought "We hope Aunt Josephine is safe."

Captain Sham sailed the boat right up to the shore and tied it expertly to the dock. "Come along, little idiots," he said, and led the Baudelaires to the tall metal gate with the glistening spikes on top, where Mr. Poe was waiting with his handkerchief in his hand and a look of relief on his face. Next to Mr. Poe was the Brobdingnagian creature, who gazed at them with a triumphant expression on his or her face.

"You're safe!" Mr. Poe said. "Thank goodness! We were so worried about you! When Captain Sham and I reached the Anwhistle home and saw that it had fallen into the sea, we thought you were done for!"

"It is lucky my associate told me that they had stolen a sailboat," Captain Sham told Mr. Poe. "The boat was nearly destroyed by Hurricane Herman, and by a swarm of leeches. I rescued them just in time."

"He did not!" Violet shouted. "He threw Aunt Josephine into the lake! We have to go and rescue her!"

"The children are upset and confused," Captain Sham said, his eye shining. "As their father, I think they need a good night's sleep."

"He's not our father!" Klaus shouted. "He's Count Olaf, and he's a murderer! Please, Mr. Poe, alert the police! We have to save Aunt Josephine!"

"Oh, dear," Mr. Poe said, coughing into his handkerchief. "You certainly *are* confused, Klaus. Aunt Josephine is dead, remember? She threw herself out the window."

"No, no," Violet said. "Her suicide note had a secret message in it. Klaus decoded the note and it said 'Curdled Cave.' Actually, it said 'apostrophe Curdled Cave,' but the apostrophe was just to get our attention."

"You're not making any sense," Mr. Poe said. "What cave? What apostrophe?"

"Klaus," Violet said, "show Mr. Poe the note."

"You can show it to him in the morning," Captain Sham said, in a falsely soothing tone. "You need a good night's sleep. My associate will take you to my apartment while I stay here and finish the adoption paperwork with Mr. Poe."

"But—" Klaus said.

"But nothing," Captain Sham said. "You're very distraught, which means 'upset.'"

"I *know* what it means," Klaus said.

"*Please* listen to us," Violet begged Mr. Poe. "It's a matter of life or death. *Please* just take a look at the note."

"You can show it to him," Captain Sham said, his voice rising in anger, "*in the morning*. Now please follow my associate to my minivan and go straight to bed."

"Hold on a minute, Captain Sham," Mr. Poe said. "If it upsets the children so much, I'll take a look at the note. It will only take a moment."

"Thank you," Klaus said in relief, and reached into his pocket for the note. But as soon as he reached inside his face fell in disappointment, and I'm sure you can guess why. If you place a piece of paper in your pocket, and then soak yourself in a hurricane, the piece of paper, no matter how important it is, will turn into a soggy mess. Klaus pulled a damp lump out of his pocket, and the orphans looked at the remains of Aunt Josephine's note. You could scarcely tell that it had been a piece of paper, let alone read the note or the secret it contained.

"This *was* the note," Klaus said, holding it out to Mr. Poe. "You'll just have to take our word for it that Aunt Josephine was still alive."

"And she might *still* be alive!" Violet cried. "*Please*, Mr. Poe, send someone to rescue her!"

"Oh my, children," Mr. Poe said. "You're so sad and worried. But you don't have to worry anymore. I have always promised to provide for you, and I think Captain Sham will do an excellent job of raising you. He has a steady business and doesn't seem likely to throw himself out of a window. And it's obvious he cares for you very much—why, he went out alone, in the middle of a hurricane, to search for you."

"The only thing he cares about," Klaus said bitterly, "is our fortune."

"Why, that's not true," Captain Sham said. "I don't want a penny of your fortune. Except, of course, to pay for the sailboat you stole and wrecked."

Mr. Poe frowned, and coughed into his handkerchief. "Well, that's a surprising request," he said, "but I suppose that can be arranged. Now, children, please go to your new home while I make the final arrangements with Captain Sham. Perhaps we'll have time for breakfast tomorrow before I head back to the city."

"*Please,*" Violet cried. "*Please,* won't you listen to us?"

"*Please,*" Klaus cried. "*Please,* won't you believe us?"

Sunny did not say anything. Sunny had not said anything for a long time, and if her siblings hadn't been so busy trying to reason with Mr. Poe, they would have noticed that she wasn't even looking up to watch everyone talking. During this whole conversation, Sunny was looking straight ahead, and if you are a baby this means looking at people's legs. The leg she was looking at was Captain Sham's. She wasn't looking at his right leg, which was perfectly normal, but at his peg leg. She was looking at the stump of dark polished wood, attached to his left knee with a curved metal hinge, and concentrating very hard.

It may surprise you to learn that at this moment, Sunny resembled the famous Greek conqueror Alexander the Great. Alexander the Great lived more than two thousand years ago, and his last name was not actually "The Great." "The Great" was something that he forced people to call him, by bringing a bunch of soldiers into their land and proclaiming himself king. Besides invading other people's countries and forcing them to do whatever he said, Alexander the Great was famous for something called the Gordian Knot. The Gordian Knot was a fancy knot tied in a piece of rope by a king named Gordius. Gordius said that if Alexander could untie it, he could rule the whole kingdom. But Alexander, who was too busy conquering places to learn how to untie knots, simply drew his sword and cut the Gordian Knot in two. This was cheating, of course, but Alexander had too many soldiers for Gordius to argue, and soon everybody in Gordium had to bow down to You-Know-Who the Great. Ever since then, a difficult problem can be called a Gordian Knot, and if you solve the problem in a simple way— even if the way is rude—you are cutting the Gordian Knot.

The problem the Baudelaire orphans were experiencing could certainly be called a Gordian Knot, because it looked impossible to solve. The problem, of course, was that Captain Sham's despicable plan was about to succeed, and the way to solve it was to convince Mr. Poe of what was really going on. But with Aunt Josephine thrown in the lake, and her note a ruined lump of wet paper, Violet and Klaus were unable to convince Mr. Poe of anything. Sunny, however, stared at Captain Sham's peg leg and thought of a simple, if rude, way of solving the problem.

As all the taller people argued and paid no attention to Sunny, the littlest Baudelaire crawled as close as she could to the peg leg, opened her mouth and bit down as hard as she could. Luckily for the Baudelaires, Sunny's teeth were as sharp as the sword of Alexander the Great, and Captain Sham's peg leg split right in half with a *crack!* that made everybody look down.

As I'm sure you've guessed, the peg leg was fake, and it split open to reveal Captain Sham's real leg, pale and sweaty from knee to toes. But it was neither the knee nor the toes that interested everyone. It was the ankle. For there on the pale and sweaty skin of Captain Sham was the solution to their problem. By biting the peg leg, Sunny had cut the Gordian Knot, for as the wooden pieces of fake peg leg fell to the floor of Damocles Dock, everyone could see a tattoo of an eye.

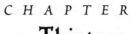

Thirteen

Mr. Poe looked astonished. Violet looked
relieved. Klaus looked assuaged, which
is a fancy word for "relieved" that he
had learned by reading a magazine
article. Sunny looked triumphant. The
person who looked like neither a man
nor a woman looked disappointed.
And Count Olaf—it is such a relief
to call him by his true name—at
first looked afraid, but
in a blink

of his one shiny eye, he twisted his face to make it look as astonished as Mr. Poe's.

"My leg!" Count Olaf cried, in a voice of false joy. "My leg has grown back! It's amazing! It's wonderful! It's a medical miracle!"

"Oh come now," Mr. Poe said, folding his arms. "That won't work. Even a child can see that your peg leg was false."

"A child *did* see it," Violet whispered to Klaus. "*Three* children, in fact."

"Well, maybe the peg leg was false," Count Olaf admitted, and took a step backward. "But I've never seen this tattoo in my life."

"Oh come now," Mr. Poe said again. "That won't work, either. You tried to hide the tattoo with the peg leg, but now we can see that you are really Count Olaf."

"Well, maybe the tattoo is mine," Count Olaf admitted, and took another step backward. "But I'm not this Count Olaf person. I'm Captain Sham. See, I have a business card here that says so."

"Oh come now," Mr. Poe said yet again. "That won't work. Anyone can go to a print shop and have cards made that say anything they like."

"Well, maybe I'm not Captain Sham," Count Olaf admitted, "but the children still belong to me. Josephine said that they did."

"Oh come now," Mr. Poe said for the fourth and final time. "That won't work. Aunt Josephine left the children to Captain Sham, not to Count Olaf. And you are Count Olaf, not Captain Sham. So it is once again up to me to decide who will care for the Baudelaires. I will send these three youngsters somewhere else, and I will send you to jail. You have performed your evil deeds for the last time, Olaf. You tried to steal the Baudelaire fortune by marrying Violet. You tried to steal the Baudelaire fortune by murdering Uncle Monty."

"And this," Count Olaf growled, "was my greatest plan yet." He reached up and tore off his eyepatch—which was fake, of course, like his peg leg—and stared at the Baudelaires with both of his shiny eyes. "I don't like to brag—actually, why should I lie to you fools anymore?—I *love* to brag, and forcing that stupid old woman to write that note was really something to brag about. What a ninny Josephine was!"

"She was not a ninny!" Klaus cried. "She was kind and sweet!"

"*Sweet?*" Count Olaf repeated, with a horrible smile. "Well, at this very moment the Lachrymose Leeches are probably finding her very sweet indeed. She might be the sweetest breakfast they ever ate."

Mr. Poe frowned, and coughed into his white handkerchief. "That's enough of your revolting talk, Olaf," he said sternly. "We've caught you now, and there's no way you'll be getting away. The Lake Lachrymose Police Department will be happy to capture a known criminal wanted for fraud, murder, and the endangerment of children."

"And arson," Count Olaf piped up.

"*I said that's enough,*" Mr. Poe growled. Count Olaf, the Baudelaire orphans, and even the massive creature looked surprised that Mr. Poe had spoken so sternly. "You have preyed upon these children for the last time, and I am making absolutely sure that you are handed over to the proper authorities. Disguising yourself won't work. Telling lies won't work. In fact there's nothing at all you can do about your situation."

"Really?" Count Olaf said, and his filthy lips curved up in a smile. "I can think of something that I can do."

"And what," said Mr. Poe, "is that?"

Count Olaf looked at each one of the Baudelaire orphans, giving each one a smile as if the children were tiny chocolates he was saving to eat for later. Then he smiled at the massive creature, and then, slowly, he smiled at Mr. Poe. "I can run," he said, and ran. Count Olaf ran, with the massive creature lumbering behind him, in the direction of the heavy metal gate.

"Get back here!" Mr. Poe shouted. "Get back here in the name of the law! Get back here in the name of justice and righteousness! Get back here in the name of Mulctuary Money Management!"

"We can't just shout at them!" Violet shouted. "Come on! We have to chase them!"

"I'm not going to allow children to chase after a man like that," Mr. Poe said, and called out again, "Stop, I say! Stop right there!"

"We can't let them escape!" Klaus cried. "Come on, Violet! Come on, Sunny!"

"No, no, this is no job for children," Mr. Poe said. "Wait here with your sisters, Klaus. I'll retrieve them. They won't get away from Mr. Poe. *You, there! Stop!*"

"But we can't wait here!" Violet cried. "We have to get into a sailboat and look for Aunt Josephine! She may still be alive!"

"You Baudelaire children are under my care," Mr. Poe said firmly. "I'm not going to let small children sail around unaccompanied."

"But if we hadn't sailed unaccompanied," Klaus pointed out, "we'd be in Count Olaf's clutches by now!"

"That's not the point," Mr. Poe said, and began to walk quickly toward Count Olaf and the creature. "The point is—"

But the children didn't hear the point over the loud *slam!* of the tall metal gate. The creature had slammed it shut just as Mr. Poe had reached it.

"Stop immediately!" Mr. Poe ordered, calling through the gate. "Come back here, you unpleasant person!" He tried to open the tall gate and found it locked. "It's locked!" he cried to the children. "Where is the key? We must find the key!"

The Baudelaires rushed to the gate but stopped as they heard a jingling sound. "I have the key," said Count Olaf's voice, from the other side of the gate. "But don't worry. I'll see you soon, orphans. *Very soon.*"

"Open this gate immediately!" Mr. Poe

shouted, but of course nobody opened the gate. He shook it and shook it, but the spiky metal gate never opened. Mr. Poe hurried to a phone booth and called the police, but the children knew that by the time help arrived Count Olaf would be long gone. Utterly exhausted and more than utterly miserable, the Baudelaire orphans sank to the ground, sitting glumly in the very same spot where we found them at the beginning of this story.

In the first chapter, you will remember, the Baudelaires were sitting on their suitcases, hoping that their lives were about to get a little bit better, and I wish I could tell you, here at the end of the story, that it was so. I wish I could write that Count Olaf was captured as he tried to flee, or that Aunt Josephine came swimming up to Damocles Dock, having miraculously escaped from the Lachrymose Leeches. But it was not so. As the children sat on the damp ground, Count Olaf was already halfway across the lake and would soon be on board a train, disguised as a rabbi to fool the police, and I'm sorry to tell you that he was already concocting another scheme to steal the Baudelaire fortune. And we can never know exactly what was happening to Aunt Josephine as the children sat on the dock, unable to help her, but I will say that eventually—about the time when the Baudelaire orphans were forced to attend a miserable boarding school—two fishermen found both of Aunt Josephine's life jackets, all in tatters and floating alone in the murky waters of Lake Lachrymose.

In most stories, as you know, the villain would be defeated, there would be a happy ending, and everybody would go home knowing the moral of the story. But in the case of the Baudelaires everything was wrong. Count Olaf, the villain, had not succeeded with his evil plan, but he certainly hadn't been defeated, either. You certainly couldn't say that there was a happy ending. And the Baudelaires could not go home knowing the moral of the story, for the simple reason that they could not go home at all. Not only had Aunt Josephine's house fallen into the lake, but the Baudelaires' real home—the house where they had lived with their parents—was just a pile of ashes in a vacant lot, and they couldn't go back there no matter how much they wanted to.

But even if they could go home it would be difficult for me to tell you what the moral of the story is. In some stories, it's easy. The moral of "The Three Bears," for instance, is "Never break into someone else's house." The moral of "Snow White" is "Never eat apples." The moral of World War One is "Never assassinate Archduke Ferdinand." But Violet, Klaus, and Sunny sat on the dock and watched the sun come up over Lake Lachrymose and wondered exactly what the moral was of their time with Aunt Josephine.

The expression "It dawned on them," which I am about to use, does not have anything to do with the sunlight spreading out over Damocles

Dock. "It dawned on them" simply means "They figured something out," and as the Baudelaire orphans sat and watched the dock fill with people as the business of the day began, they figured out something that was very important to them. It dawned on them that unlike Aunt Josephine, who had lived up in that house, sad and alone, the three children had one another for comfort and support over the course of their miserable lives. And while this did not make them feel entirely safe, or entirely happy, it made them feel appreciative.

"Thank you, Klaus," Violet said appreciatively, "for figuring out that note. And thank you, Sunny, for stealing the keys to the sailboat. If it weren't for the two of you we would now be in Count Olaf's clutches."

"Thank you, Violet," Klaus said appreciatively, "for thinking of the peppermints to gain us some time. And thank you, Sunny, for biting the peg leg just at the right moment. If it weren't for the two of you, we would now be doomed."

"Pilums," Sunny said appreciatively, and her siblings understood at once that she was thanking Violet for inventing the signaling device, and thanking Klaus for reading the atlas and guiding them to Curdled Cave.

They leaned up against one another appreciatively, and small smiles appeared on their damp and anxious faces. They had each other. I'm not sure that "The Baudelaires had each other" is the moral of this story, but to the three siblings it was enough. To have each other in the midst of their unfortunate lives felt like having a sailboat in the middle of a hurricane, and to the Baudelaire orphans this felt very fortunate indeed.

To My Kind Editor,

I am writing to you from the Paltryville
Town Hall, where I have convinced the mayor
to allow me inside the eye-shaped office of
Dr. Orwell in order to further investigate
what happened to the Baudelaire orphans
while they were living in the area.

Next Friday, a black jeep will be in
the northwest corner of the parking lot
of the Orion Observatory. Break into it.
In the glove compartment, you should find
my description of this frightening chapter
in the Baudelaires' lives, entitled THE
MISERABLE MILL, as well as some information
on hypnosis, a surgical mask, and sixty-
eight sticks of gum. I have also included
the blueprint of the pincher machine, which
I believe Mr. Helquist will find useful for
his illustrations.

Remember, you are my last hope that
the tales of the Baudelaire orphans can
finally be told to the general public.

With all due respect,

Lemony Snicket

Lemony Snicket

© Meredith Heuer

LEMONY SNICKET was born before you were and is likely to die before you as well. A studied expert in rhetorical analysis, Mr. Snicket has spent the last several eras researching the travails of the Baudelaire orphans. His findings are being published serially by Harper-Collins.

Visit him on the Web at www.lemonysnicket.com

BRETT HELQUIST was born in Ganado, Arizona, grew up in Orem, Utah, and now lives in New York City. He earned a bachelor's degree in fine arts from Brigham Young University and has been illustrating ever since. His art has appeared in many publications, including *Cricket* magazine and *The New York Times*.